BOOK # 22
Roxy
C
S

THE CALICO TRAIL

PATCHWORK MYSTERIES

THE CALICO TRAIL

KRISTIN ECKHARDT

Guideposts
New York

Guideposts.org
(800) 932-2145
Guideposts Books & Inspirational Media

Cover design by Wendy Bass
Cover illustration by Joyce Patti
Interior design by Lorie Pagnozzi
Typeset by Aptara

Printed and bound in the United States of America
10 9 8 7 6 5 4 3

PATCHWORK MYSTERIES

 CHAPTER ONE

S arah Hart couldn't stop gazing at the beautiful photograph of her new granddaughter, Leah Nicole. She had flown down to Texas as soon as her daughter Jenna had called with the news that she was in labor. Sarah had arrived in Texas shortly after the newest member of their family had made her entrance into the world. Little Leah Nicole had stolen Sarah's heart the moment she had seen her in Jenna's arms.

After so many months of waiting, God had answered Sarah's prayers for a safe birth and a healthy grandchild. The last few weeks had been the most difficult, especially for Jenna. They had burned up the phone lines between Massachusetts and Texas, both of them impatient for the baby's arrival.

Now the waiting was over, and Sarah had returned from Texas the night before after spending a glorious week helping Jenna with the new baby. She had spent plenty of grandma-time with her two grandsons, Thomas and

1

Jonathan, and did her best to keep the household running smoothly so Jenna and her husband David could get to know their new daughter.

Sarah breathed a happy sigh as she picked up the quilted picture frame that held Leah's photo. She had created the frame from the fabric remnants of the baby quilt she had made for her granddaughter. "Dear Lord, thank you for my beautiful grandchildren," she prayed softly, "for Amy and Audrey and Thomas and Jonathan. And thank you for the newest blessing in my life, little Leah Nicole. Give me the wisdom and guidance to be a blessing in all of their lives, Lord, and to be the best grandma I can be. Amen."

With a happy sigh, Sarah placed the picture frame back on her desk, next to the photos of her other grandchildren. Then she rose out of her chair, ready to do some spring cleaning now that May had finally arrived. And she knew just where to start.

Sarah walked over to the closet where she kept all of her fabric remnants, some piled almost as high as the ceiling. This time she was going to do it. She was going to go through her fabric stash and decide which fabrics to keep and which to clear out of her closet.

Like most quilters, Sarah found it difficult to give up any fabric in her stash. She wouldn't call herself a fabric hoarder, but there were some fabric remnants she would probably never use. Sometimes certain fabrics that had seemed perfect in the planning stage just didn't look quite right when it was time to add them to a quilt.

She placed several fabric remnants on her quilting table, wanting to see them side by side before she made any final decisions. Each remnant was wrapped around a nine-by-twelve-inch piece of cardboard she had cut from old cardboard boxes, the fabric end pinned down to keep it nice and neat. This made it easy to stack her remnants on the closet shelves and see what she had in stock with a quick glance.

Now she spread them out on the table, wanting to see them in the sunlight streaming in from the window. She arranged them according to color and soon had a rainbow of fabrics filling the large table.

Then she stood at the table for the next five minutes, trying to decide which fabric remnants she could live without.

"Just pick one," Sarah told herself.

But as she reached for a green cotton print with tiny horses on it, the telephone rang.

Grateful for the reprieve, Sarah walked into the kitchen and picked up the phone. "Hello?"

"Hi, Sarah, it's Maggie. How was your trip?"

"It was perfect." Sarah settled into a kitchen chair, in the mood for a long chat with her daughter-in-law. "Leah is so sweet, and I had so much fun with Thomas and Jonathan."

"We can't wait to meet her," Maggie said. "The girls loved the pictures Jenna posted on her Facebook page. It's so much fun to have a baby in the family again!"

"I know. I miss her already, but Jenna promised to keep sending pictures. And you should see the boys—they are such proud big brothers and so protective of her."

"Oh, I can just imagine," Maggie said, chuckling. "Jason and I are trying to figure out a good time to make a visit. The girls would leave tomorrow if we'd let them, but I told them we can't go anywhere while school is still in session. Only a few more weeks to go."

Sarah smiled, looking forward to spending extra time with her granddaughters this summer.

"Sarah, I was wondering…," Maggie began, her voice jumping a little, "I was wondering if you could come over to the house. Sooner rather than later."

Alarmed, Sarah sat up in the chair. "Is something wrong?"

"No, not at all," Maggie assured her. "I'm just so excited. My mom just sent me a whole bunch of wonderful antiques, including a nineteenth-century quilt that I'd love for you to see. Can you make it?"

"I'll be there in five minutes."

"Great," Maggie replied. "See you soon."

Sarah grabbed her purse. She felt a familiar thrill of excitement coursing through her as she made her way out the back door. There was nothing she liked better than examining an antique quilt and learning the history behind it. Sometimes it was easy to do and other times it took all her ingenuity to ferret out the secrets sewn into the vintage quilt blocks.

When she arrived at Maggie's house, the twins greeted her at the door, chattering with excitement.

"Hey, Grandma! How's Leah," Amy said, swinging the front door wide open. "Are her eyes really that blue?"

Sarah reached out to give both girls a hug. "They are blue, but most babies have blue eyes when they're born. They'll either stay blue or slowly change to a different color."

"Cool," Audrey said. "I wonder what color they'll be."

"I think I saw a little bit of green in them," Sarah said. "But we'll have to wait and see."

"We each got to buy her a present," Audrey told Sarah. "We just sent them yesterday. I got her a pink dress and bonnet."

"And I got her a stuffed, purple octopus. Each one of the eight arms has a rattle in it," Amy added. "It's so cute."

Sarah relished the twins' excitement about Leah and realized how much she had missed them in the week she had been gone.

"And guess what else?" Amy said. "Grammy sent us a whole bunch of cool stuff!"

"I got a new MP3 player." Audrey danced around the front hallway, pulling a pair of hot pink earbuds out of her pocket. "It holds over four thousand songs."

"You already have one that holds a thousand songs," Amy told her sister. "The camera she sent me is wicked cool." She dug a small blue camera, the size of a deck of cards, out of her pocket. "It will even do video-recording. I can't wait to record Leah on it."

Sarah could see a trail of boxes and packing paper leading from the front hall into the parlor. Patty's generosity was one of the things she liked best about Maggie's mother. Patty had other traits that sometimes rubbed Sarah the wrong way, but she tried not to let them bother her. Last Christmas, Patty had hatched a plan to entice Maggie and Jason to move back to California. Some of Patty's antics over the holiday had caused tension in the family, but it had been smoothed over by the time she and her husband Larry had headed home after the holidays.

"Hey, Amy, record me," Audrey said to her sister, putting her earbuds in and bopping to a beat that only she could hear. "I want to see what I look like when I dance."

"I don't think you do," Amy teased as she held the camera in front of Audrey.

Sarah ducked out of the view of the camera and followed the packing paper trail into the parlor. Maggie sat on the floor wearing a royal blue and white Hawthorne Middle School sweatshirt and a pair of blue jeans. Her auburn hair was pulled back in a messy ponytail.

"What's all this?" Sarah asked.

Maggie rose off the floor when she saw her. "My mom told me she had a surprise for me, but I never expected anything like this. There was a freight truck parked in our driveway when I got home from the shop and the driver kept unloading boxes until I thought we were going to run out of room. The big stuff is in the garage."

Sarah moved into the room, spotting some treasures among the packing materials strewn across the floor. She saw an antique butter crock, a copper teakettle, a vintage mantel clock, a crank-style phonograph, and other various collectibles. "Where did all of this come from?"

"My great-aunt Myrna. She passed away last week at the grand old age of ninety-eight." Maggie cleared off the sofa so they could sit down. "Do you remember her from our wedding?"

"I think so." Sarah thought about an older woman at the reception who had sought her out and told her how proud they were to add Jason to their family. "Did your great-aunt walk with an ebony cane?"

Maggie nodded as she plopped down on the sofa. "That was her. Aunt Myrna was an amazing woman and the self-proclaimed matriarch of my mom's side of the family. The Hollanders have a long and rich heritage, carefully chronicled by Aunt Myrna. She was in charge of the Hollander family reunion, which was held every year. Family members would come from all over the country."

Sarah reached out to squeeze Maggie's hand. "It sounds like you're going to miss her."

Maggie nodded, tears shining in her green eyes. "I am. Her memorial service is scheduled for the end of the month in Willow Creek, Pennsylvania. That was the original settlement of the Hollanders before they migrated west. She's giving us all one more family reunion as her farewell gift."

"What a perfect way to honor her memory," Sarah said softly.

Maggie wiped a tear off her cheek. "She meant a lot to me." Then she looked out over the bounty on the parlor floor. "And she liked to collect antiques, as you can see. The family heirlooms were all divided between her nieces and nephews, but this is just some of what was left in her house." She picked up a small card from the end table. "Here's the note Mom included in one of the boxes."

Sarah took the card from her as she sat down on the sofa and began to read it to herself.

My dear Maggie,

As you know, your great-aunt Myrna was thrilled when she heard you had opened an antique store in Maple Hill. She wanted you to have the items that didn't have a Hollander family connection, so I'm fulfilling one of her last wishes. There is one item, however, that she specifically left to you in her will. It's the pioneer quilt that was made by the Hollander family as they made their way along the Oregon Trail in 1849. It has a few imperfections, but I know that Sarah likes to dabble in quilts so perhaps she can help you fix them. I think it would make a nice display piece in your shop and be a wonderful way to showcase the Hollander family history.

Love and kisses,
Mom

Sarah set the card back on the table, trying to ignore the jibe about *dabbling* in quilts. "Have you opened the box with the quilt yet?"

"I have," Maggie said, rising off the sofa. "It's in the dining room."

Sarah followed Maggie to the dining room, her curiosity putting a spring in her step. She had seen a few pioneer quilts before, mostly in magazines and at quilt shows, but they were all so unique that she didn't know what to expect.

Maggie stood in the doorway of the dining room and pointed to the table. "There it is."

Sarah approached it with a sense of awe, seeing such a smorgasbord of history spread out before her. She gently touched a corner edge of the quilt as her gaze took in each individual block. "Oh, Maggie, this is amazing."

"I've only seen it once before," Maggie said, "when I was a little girl. Aunt Myrna always kept it carefully packed away. I couldn't wait for you to see it."

Sarah could see the quilt was in good condition for its age. There were a few loose threads, some fraying and light stains, but nothing that couldn't be repaired. "Maggie, do you know what this quilt is telling us?"

Maggie met her gaze. "Well, some of the blocks have names embroidered on them, like the one that says *Fort Kearney*, but the others just look like pretty designs to me."

The twins walked into the dining room as Sarah moved to the other end of the table and pointed out the block in the top left corner of the quilt. "This is an appliqué of a mountain laurel tree," Sarah said, running her fingers lightly over the dark green leaves on the ivory background. "Which happens to be the state tree of Pennsylvania."

"Look at that workmanship." Maggie moved beside her and leaned down to inspect it more closely. "All the branches are curved and each leaf is quilted individually."

Sarah nodded. "And the block on the other end, on the bottom right side is called Cross and Crowns." She admired the triple border in deep russet, brown, and green. "I believe these quilt blocks chronicle your ancestors' journey west from Pennsylvania to Oregon. The Cross and Crowns block has the words Willow Bend, Oregon, embroidered in the corner."

Audrey walked up to the table. "You mean it's like a picture book?"

"That's a great way to describe it," Sarah said, studying the different blocks. There were sixteen in all and she recognized a few of them, although they each had at least one deviation to the pattern. "It's a variation of an album quilt, which was quite popular in the mid-nineteenth century. Album quilts were usually appliquéd and sometimes they were called signature quilts. For instance, if a girl was graduating from school, she might make a quilt and have all of her classmates sign it as a keepsake."

"Like a yearbook," Audrey chimed in.

"That's right." Sarah looked over the quilt. "This has a combination of appliqué blocks and pieced blocks. As you can see, some of the appliqué blocks have place names written on them, but I think the pieced blocks are conveying a message about the journey too."

"So if we know the meaning of each one of these quilt blocks," Maggie said, "we could find out more about the Hollander family's trip west?"

"I think you could," Sarah replied. "Look at this one," she pointed to the center of the quilt. "It's another appliqué block, but this one is a gravestone, which may represent a death on the journey."

"This is fascinating," Maggie breathed as she slowly walked around the table and studied the quilt.

"I've heard of pioneer quilts like this," Sarah said, "but I've never actually seen one before. Many people don't even realize they have one and just assume the quilt is made up of several different patterns."

"I wonder if Aunt Myrna knew," Maggie said. "If she did, I never heard about it. And I'm sure my mother would have said something—she's very proud of her heritage."

The girls moved closer to the table and Amy held up her new camera and began to snap some pictures.

"Speaking of heritage," Maggie continued, looking at the girls. "Don't you two have a genealogy project coming up in your history class?"

Amy lowered the camera. "Yeah, we have to turn in our project idea by Friday. Most of the kids are doing a family tree and a report on one of their ancestors."

Audrey turned to her sister. "Maybe we could do a report on the quilt. Then we could talk about our ancestors traveling on the Oregon Trail."

"That does sound kind of cool," Amy admitted. "Definitely cooler than a family tree." She turned to her mother. "Could we take the quilt to class during our presentation?"

Maggie hesitated, exchanging a look with Sarah. "I could *bring* the quilt to your classroom so your teacher and classmates could see it, but it's too valuable to let you haul it around the school all day."

Audrey looked up at Sarah. "Can you tell us what the rest of the blocks mean, Gram?"

Before Sarah could answer, Audrey turned to her sister. "It would be cool to have a big map that shows the trip they took. We'd get extra credit for two visual aids with a map *and* the quilt."

Amy's eyes widened in excitement. "We could even make cutouts of a covered wagon and people and horses and show them all moving along the trail as we talk about their trip."

Maggie looked over at Sarah. "Looks like they've selected a project."

Audrey walked over to Sarah. "Will you help us?"

Sarah smiled at her. "I'll be happy to help you, but I won't do your work for you. It's going to take some time to figure out all of these quilt blocks. Are you girls up to the job?"

Audrey nodded. "I think it sounds like fun."

"Me too," Amy added. "When can we start?"

"Well, the first thing you can do," Sarah told Amy, "is to take a picture of each quilt block, as close and clear as you can get. That's a good first step when you're trying to document a quilt. Then take a picture of the front of the quilt and another of the back of the quilt."

Audrey snatched at the camera. "I want to take some of the pictures."

"It's my camera!"

Maggie clapped her hands together. "Girls, that's enough. We need to set some ground rules. First, there will be no fighting in this room. I don't want you two to accidentally damage the quilt. The second rule is no food or drink in here until we've found another place for it."

"Good rule," Sarah agreed.

Audrey grinned. "When Dad comes home tonight, I'm going to tell him that he's not allowed to eat in the dining room anymore."

"The third rule," Maggie said, ignoring the comment, "is that you have to do what your grandmother tells you. She knows more about quilts than the three of us put together and then some. Are we clear?"

Amy and Audrey spoke in unison, "Clear."

Maggie turned to Sarah with a twinkle of amusement in her green eyes. "They're all yours."

Maggie stood back and watched as Sarah corralled her granddaughters.

"All right, girls, you've got two homework assignments for tonight," Sarah told them. "The first is to take the pictures of the quilt."

When she saw Audrey eyeing Amy's camera, Sarah said, "Why don't you each take half of the pictures? That means, Amy, you take photos of the top two rows of blocks and the front of the quilt." She looked over at Audrey. "And you take photographs of the bottom two rows of blocks and the back of the quilt."

"I guess that's fair," Amy said grudgingly.

"Just make sure that all the pictures are in focus," Sarah said, "and close enough to see all the details in the quilt pattern."

Audrey looked at Sarah. "So what's our second assignment, Gram?"

"I want you two to research the Oregon Trail. It will be easier to identify these quilt blocks if we have some idea of the route they might have traveled."

A frown crinkled the center of Audrey's forehead. "This is starting to sound like a lot more work than I thought it would be."

"Who cares?" Amy said. "We'll have the coolest project of the whole class."

"You're right," Audrey replied, her forehead clearing. "I can't wait to get started. Now give me your camera."

 CHAPTER TWO

O n Wednesday morning, Sarah carried her coffee cup into the sewing room and set it on her desk. Then she walked over to the table where her fabric remnants were still lined up in rows that stretched from one end of the table to the other.

She closed her eyes, dropped her hand on the table and grabbed a remnant. Then she opened her eyes to see an ethereal orange taffeta that she had bought on a whim at Wild Goose Chase more than two years ago. So far, she hadn't found a use for it, but as she caressed the shiny fabric, Sarah knew she couldn't give it up. It might make a cute headband for Leah.

"This is going to be harder than I thought," she murmured, setting the remnant back on the table, then moving to the desk to pick up her coffee cup. She glanced out the window, thrilled to see the sun finally peeking out from behind a cloud. She couldn't wait until the soil was warm enough to add more vegetable plants to her garden.

Her mouth watered at the thought of fresh tomatoes and cucumbers.

She walked back over to the table, taking a sip from her cup and asking herself if she really needed to get rid of any fabric remnants.

"Yoo-hoo," called out a familiar voice.

"Martha?" Sarah walked out of the sewing room to see her best friend standing at the back door. "Come on in. You're just the person I wanted to see."

"I wish more people felt that way." Martha grinned as she walked into the kitchen and set her crochet bag down on the table. "How's that new grandbaby? Do you have pictures?"

"I sure do," Sarah said, leading her into the sewing room. She picked up the quilted frame and handed it to her. "Meet Leah Nicole. Seven pounds, six ounces, and twenty inches long."

"Oh, Sarah," Martha breathed, admiring the photo. "She is absolutely gorgeous."

"I know," Sarah agreed, too proud to be modest. "And don't you love the silk flower headband she's wearing? Jenna got it as a gift and I promised her that I'd make some more just like it and mail them. Leah doesn't have much hair, but no one will mistake her for a boy with these flowery headbands."

"They sure won't." Martha laughed. "That flower is almost as big as her head! She is so precious." She handed the frame back to Sarah. "And how is Jenna doing?"

"Wonderful." Sarah set the frame on the desk. "The birth went well and she's always taken such good care of herself, so she should have a quick recovery. David and the boys help out a lot too."

Martha breathed a happy sigh. "Well, I can't wait to meet your new granddaughter. I hope they can make a visit to Maple Hill sometime soon."

"So do I," Sarah said, eager to show off Leah and her grandsons around town. But that would have to wait until Leah was a little older. "Now, how about some coffee? And then I want to get your opinion on something."

"Coffee sounds great." Martha grinned. "And I have opinions on just about everything under the sun, but I think you've heard most of them."

"I'm sure I have." Sarah smiled as she headed for the kitchen. "Wait right here, I'll be back." A few moments later, she returned to the sewing room to see Martha perusing the fabric remnants on her table.

"It looks like you've been busy," Martha said.

"Looks can be deceiving, I'm afraid," Sarah said, handing her friend a steaming coffee mug. "I'm trying to clear out some of my fabric clutter, but I can't seem to make a decision." She picked up the green fabric with the tiny horses. "I had this in my giveaway bag, then I got up in the middle of the night and put it back on the table."

Martha started to laugh. "Oh my. I'm the last person you want to turn to for advice. Have you seen my yarn stash lately?" Martha loved to crochet and a day rarely passed when she didn't have a crochet hook in her hand.

"Maybe we can help each other," Sarah suggested. "I'll help you clear out your yarn stash if you help me decide which fabrics I can live without."

Martha took a sip of her coffee, a twinkle in her hazel eyes. "Ernie did mention that he doesn't want to see any more yarn come into the house until I have room for it in my bedroom closet." She chuckled. "Lately, every time I open my closet door, another ball of yarn rolls off the top shelf. The last one landed on his head."

Sarah smiled at the image. "Good thing that yarn can't do any damage, but I imagine he wasn't too happy about it."

"You've got that right." Martha took another sip of coffee. "I could donate some of my yarn to the 4-H kids. They've invited me to give a crochet lesson at their next meeting."

"That sounds like a worthwhile project."

She nodded. "I think so. Maybe I could bring a ball of yarn for each member. That should leave me plenty of room on the shelf for new yarn."

"I want new fabric remnants," Sarah said. "There will probably be some for sale at the quilt show in Albany."

Martha's eyes widened. "You're going to Albany?"

Sarah nodded. "Yes, there's a one-day quilt show at the Desmond Hotel there in about a week. I thought I already mentioned it to you."

"You probably did," Martha said, looking thoughtful. "But that was before I decided to clear out some yarn.

There's an amazing yarn shop in Albany. They spin and dye much of their own yarn."

Sarah arched a brow. "Does this mean you want to ride along?"

"I'll not only ride along, I'll drive." Martha grinned.

"Great! I'd love the company." Sarah turned back to the table. "Now, which remnants should I get rid of?"

Martha didn't hesitate. She set down her coffee cup, then plucked ten fabric remnants off the table and stuffed them in the canvas bag on the chair. "There. Done."

"Just like that," Sarah said, wincing a little.

"It's like a bandage," Martha said. "The faster you rip it off, the sooner the pain is over." Then she picked up the bag and slung it over her shoulder. "And I'll even take the remnants home with me until our Albany trip so you aren't tempted to put them all back in the middle of the night."

Sarah sighed, but she knew her friend was right. And if she was honest, she couldn't even be sure what fabrics were in the bag. She glanced at the table, seeing most of her favorites were still there. "So when is it my turn to rip the bandage off your yarn stash?"

"You can come over anytime." Then Martha snapped her fingers together. "That reminds me. I had a reason for coming over here today."

Sarah moved toward the door. "Let's go have more coffee and you can tell me about it."

Martha followed behind her, hanging on to the canvas bag. She hooked it on the back of a kitchen chair, then sat down while Sarah retrieved the coffeepot to refill their cups.

"Now, then," Sarah said, setting the pot on a trivet and taking a seat across from Martha. "What's up?"

"As you know, Ian is graduating this May. I love all of my grandkids, but I've always been so close to that boy. When we had dinner at Tim and Ruth's place yesterday, they were talking about how busy they both were at work, so I volunteered to throw him a graduation party."

"That was nice of you." Sarah picked up a spoon and slowly stirred her coffee to cool it. "What can I do to help?"

Martha smiled. "That's why you're my best friend, because you know I need all the help I can get."

"I'm sure you can handle everything just fine on your own, but I love a good party."

"I was hoping you'd say that. Ian is special, so tender-hearted, that I want this party to be special too."

"What do you have in mind?"

Martha hesitated, then shook her head. "I don't know yet. I just know I want more than cake and punch and balloons. He's so creative. Did I tell you his artwork is going to be displayed in the congressional building in Washington, DC?"

Sarah sat up in her chair, surprised by the news. "When did this happen?"

"He found out on Monday. His art teacher entered her top students in an art contest sponsored by our local congressman's office. Ian won first place and his prize is to have his work displayed in the reception room of the congressman's office for one month."

"Good for him," Sarah said with a smile. "Tim and Ruth must be proud."

"They're already planning a trip to DC to see it." Martha beamed. "Ian's a typical eighteen-year-old, so he acts like it's no big deal, but I can tell he's pretty proud of himself."

Sarah could see that his grandma was mighty proud too, and for good reason. "When is graduation?"

"It's the last day of May this year, which is on a Thursday. We'll have the reception at my house that evening."

"Shall we start party planning right now?"

Martha glanced at the stove clock. "I wish I had time, but Ernie wants to drive to Pittsfield to pick up an auto part and I said I'd take him. Why don't we meet for lunch at the Spotted Dog tomorrow?"

"Tomorrow sounds good," Sarah replied. "That will give us some time to start thinking of ideas."

Martha picked up her crochet bag and the remnant bag on her way to the door. "And after lunch, we'll head to my house and go through my yarn stash. I just hope it won't be too painful." That afternoon, Sarah arrived at Jason and Maggie's house shortly after the twins arrived home from school. Sarah had decided to leave the quilt at Maggie's house so she could work on making the minor restorations to the pioneer quilt while helping the girls figure out its history.

"Mom's still at work," Amy said when Sarah walked into the house. Amy's blonde hair hung in a long braid down her back and she wore a fitted, green Celtics jersey with a long-sleeved white T-shirt underneath and a pair of blue jeans. "Do you want a snack, Gram? We've got bananas and choco-late milk."

"I'm fine," Sarah said, following her into the kitchen.

Audrey was already seated at the table eating a banana. The pink earbuds she wore matched her skirt as well as the thick, pink stripes on her short-sleeved white sweater. Still chewing, she waved to Sarah.

Amy walked over to the refrigerator to retrieve the chocolate milk while Sarah checked out a large, powder blue poster board with pictures of the pioneer quilt blocks on it, sitting in the middle of the kitchen table.

"When did you girls do this?" Sarah asked.

"Last night." Audrey dropped her banana peel on the napkin in front of her. "We downloaded the pictures on the computer and then printed them."

"I wanted to enhance them," Amy said, "to make the colors brighter and stuff, but Audrey said we shouldn't do it."

"I would have been tempted too," Sarah told her. "But it's important to document the quilt exactly as we find it. That way we'll always know what the original looked like."

Amy took a sip of her milk, leaving a tiny milk mustache behind when she lowered her glass. "So does the poster look okay?"

"It's wonderful." Sarah slid a napkin across the table toward Amy. "I like how you spaced out the quilt blocks evenly and cut all the pictures the same size. Can you make a set of copies for me?"

"Sure," Amy said. "They're all still on the computer. We can make copies any time we want."

Sarah nodded, studying the poster board in front of her once more. "Are you sure you girls placed the blocks on the poster in the same order as the quilt? Something looks a little off here."

"I'm pretty sure," Audrey said, jumping off her stool. "Let's go look."

Sarah and Audrey headed for the dining room with Amy close behind them.

Sarah walked up to the quilt, struck once more by the historical significance it represented. Westward migration had changed the country and this was a piece of that rich history. Quilts that pioneer women had taken on the journey had been used for warmth and shelter and, sadly, even as shrouds when needed. She couldn't imagine burying a loved one on a lonesome prairie and then leaving the grave site behind.

"Gram?" Audrey said, breaking her reverie.

"What, dear?" Sarah said. "I'm sorry, I didn't hear you."

Audrey held the poster board in her hands. "It looks exactly the same to me. What do you see that's different?"

Sarah looked back and forth between the poster board and the quilt on the table several times. "I guess you're right. They are the same." Yet, something still niggled at her. She had learned to trust her instincts; they rarely led her astray.

"Let's prop the poster on this chair," Sarah said, pulling out a dining room chair without any arms, "so we can take a better look."

Audrey did as she was asked, then stepped back from the chair. "Maybe we should have made the poster the same size as the quilt."

"No," Sarah replied, "that would have been too big. This quilt's large enough to fit a full-size bed. The poster board makes it easy for us to carry it around in case we need to take it with us on our investigation."

"Investigation?" Amy echoed. "You sound like this is some kind of mystery."

"Well, in a way, it is." Sarah walked around the table, taking inventory of the quilt once more. She had brought her sewing bag with her, but she didn't want to get started on any restoration work until she had fully evaluated the quilt.

"We don't know who made it or exactly when it was made," Sarah continued, "and we still need to figure out what each quilt block means. This quilt *is* a mystery until we can answer those questions and any other questions that may come up along the way."

Audrey groaned. "I'm starting to think it might have been easier to make a family tree."

Sarah smiled at her. "Are you ready to give up already?"

"No," Audrey said.

"You've already accomplished the first step," Sarah told her, "by taking these pictures."

"We did the second step too," Amy said. "We researched the Oregon Trail on the Internet last night." She cocked her head to one side as she looked at Sarah. "Did you know there was more than one trail that pioneers took out west?"

"I've heard of the California Trail," Sarah replied.

Amy nodded. "It turned southwest at Salt Lake City while the Oregon Trail turned northwest."

"And there was the Hastings Cutoff," Audrey added. "That's the trail the Donner party took and they got stuck in a snowstorm in the mountains." She shook her head. "It wasn't a pretty story."

"No, it wasn't," Sarah said, saddened by the plight that those poor, desperate people had faced. "I'm sure life on the trail wasn't easy for anyone. Can you imagine what a big decision it was for your ancestors to leave Willow Creek and head west? They probably left other family members and friends behind, with no guarantee that they'd ever see them again."

Amy sat down in a chair. "That would be so weird. I miss my friends back in Los Angeles, but at least I can chat with them on the computer and see them on the webcam."

Audrey looked thoughtful. "Imagine saying good-bye to our mom and dad, knowing we'd probably never see them again. I don't think I could do it."

"Some of them had little choice," Sarah said. She had done a little research herself last night and had been amazed at the hardships the pioneers had faced. "They came from big families and there wasn't much farmland or work to be had. Their only hope was to head west and take advantage of the fertile farmland available."

"But it took four months for them to get there," Audrey exclaimed, "sometimes even longer. I'd go crazy with nothing to do."

Sarah smiled. "Oh, there was plenty to do. Cooking and mending and finding fuel for the fire. They also helped each other out in the wagon trains, especially if someone was sick or an animal was injured. They depended on each other for survival."

"And there were books to read," Amy piped up. "I read about one lady who said she found all kinds of books on the trail that people just dumped off their wagons. She never ran out of books to read for the entire trip."

Sarah nodded. "Many of the pioneers overloaded their wagons and had to dump off things that weren't necessities. Even pieces of furniture were left on the trail."

Amy stepped toward the quilt. "So what do we do next, Grandma?"

"Well, now that you know some of the background about the Oregon Trail, you can start mapping out the journey the Hollanders took to get to their new home in Oregon. We know they started off from Willow Creek in Pennsylvania. Do you know where they settled in Oregon?"

"Mom said that most of them settled near a town called Vale," Audrey replied. "They called their new settlement Willow Bend and built a church there and everything."

"Good." Sarah rubbed her hands together. "Now we just have to figure out what they did between Willow Creek, Pennsylvania, and Willow Bend, Oregon."

CHAPTER THREE

When Sarah got home that Wednesday evening, she warmed up some leftover tuna noodle casserole in the microwave and then carried her plate to the kitchen table.

She had left some pattern books with the twins, telling them to start researching the quilt patterns to identify the blocks on the pioneer quilt, and she had told them to use the Internet as well. She knew from firsthand experience that identifying certain patterns could be like finding a needle in a haystack.

Sarah set down her fork and reached into her bag. She pulled out the copies of the quilt block pictures that the girls had printed for her before she had left.

Now she spread them out on the table in front of her. Three of them she had already identified: the mountain laurel block that signified Pennsylvania, the Cross and Crowns block that signified Oregon, and the gravestone block which she believed represented a death.

There was another gravestone block too, and it had the outline of a heart embroidered on the gravestone with the initials C.H. in the center of it. She still couldn't imagine the courage it took to trek more than two thousand miles by wagon train—and that was just counting the distance between the Missouri River and the pioneers' destination in Oregon. The Hollander family had left from Pennsylvania, adding another thousand miles to their trip.

Sarah studied the different quilt patterns in front of her. Even though she expected the twins to do their own research for this project, she needed to identify the quilt patterns herself to make sure they were on the right track. She had suggested the girls split the number of blocks they needed to identify between them to make the job easier, but she had left that process up to them.

As she ate, she began to arrange the blocks in the order they were on the quilt, wishing she had asked the girls for a copy of the front of the quilt as well.

"I'll do that tomorrow," Sarah said aloud, carrying her empty plate over to the sink and washing her plate and fork. She had just set them both in the dish drainer when the doorbell rang.

To her surprise, Tracy Calhoun stood on the other side of the door. She was a tall, statuesque woman with raven black hair and bright blue eyes. Sarah had met her a few times and liked her much better than her overbearing husband Mark.

"Hello, Tracy," Sarah greeted her. "This is a nice surprise."

"I'm sorry for not calling first. I was on my way home from work and thought I'd take a chance that you'd be home. Is this a good time?"

"It's fine," Sarah said, opening the door wider to let her in. "I just finished supper. Please come in and sit down."

Tracy walked inside, wearing a gray pinstripe jacket and matching skirt and carrying a bulging, black leather satchel in her hand. The black heels she wore clicked on the hardwood floor as she made her way into the living room.

"Where do you work?" Sarah asked.

"I'm a health management specialist at the Maple Hill Medical Center." She took a seat on the sofa. "I coordinate wellness programs and evaluate disease management protocols for our staff."

"That sounds like interesting work."

She nodded. "I enjoy it."

"So how is Sasha?" Sarah asked. Sasha Calhoun was the eighteen-year-old daughter of Mark and Tracy. She was a basketball star at Maple Hill High and a highly recruited player by several division one colleges.

"She's wonderful," Tracy said, her face softening. "I can't believe she's going to be graduating in just a few short weeks. I'm not sure I'm ready to send her off into the world."

Sarah smiled, remembering a time when she had felt the same way about Jason and Jenna. "I know what you mean, but you'll enjoy hearing about her new experiences. Where is she going to college?"

Tracy beamed. "San Diego State University. They offered her a full ride to play basketball there. She was so excited when she got the call three months ago. They want her there in June to enroll in summer school so she can start training with the rest of the team."

"Oh my," Sarah said. "That *is* a quick transition from high school to college."

Tracy nodded. "And it's what brings me here today." She unzipped the black leather satchel at her feet. "I wanted to make her a T-shirt quilt." She drew out a pattern and handed it to Sarah. "Mark learned about them on a parents' forum for the San Diego State women's basketball team. He thought that would be a perfect graduation gift for Sasha."

"I've seen these before," Sarah told her, looking at the simple block quilt pattern. "They make very nice commemorative quilts."

"I don't do a lot of sewing," Tracy explained, "so I'm afraid I won't get it finished by the time she leaves for California." She hesitated. "I was hoping I might be able to hire you to make it for me."

Sarah hesitated. Her encounters with the Calhoun family had not always been pleasant. Mark was the worst kind of stage parent. His office at the furniture store was practically a shrine to his daughter's basketball success and he had even perpetrated a hoax to hide the fact that Sasha had needed shoulder surgery during the basketball season last year. He had been afraid that news of her injury would dampen the interest of college recruiters, but Sasha had re-covered quickly and been able to finish the season.

Still, Sarah respected Tracy, and she thought Sasha was a sweet girl.

"I'll be happy to do it," Sarah said at last. "I'm between quilting projects at the moment and this T-shirt quilt is a fairly simple design, so it shouldn't take long."

Relief lit Tracy's blue eyes. "Thank you, Sarah. I really appreciate this." She reached down to unzip the leather satchel at her feet. "I was hoping you'd say yes, so I brought the T-shirts with me."

"Good. Let's take a look."

Tracy began to set the folded T-shirts on the coffee table between them. "She's been playing on basketball teams since she was in elementary school, so there were many to choose from. I decided to bring the ones that meant the most to her."

Sarah began to sort through the colorful array of T-shirts. A few sported the royal blue and white colors of Maple Hill High, but others were even more colorful. There was a lime green T-shirt with the image of a basketball and the words Massachusetts State Basketball Tournament imprinted in black letters on the front. There were two pink T-shirts from a summer basketball camp and a white T-shirt with a basketball hoop embossed on the front and the word *SWISH* printed in bright red.

"You've got quite a variety here," Sarah said. "Are they all basketball T-shirts?"

"Yes," Tracy replied. "Basketball has been such a big part of her life that she didn't have much time for other activities." She smiled. "I tried to enroll her in dance class once, but that turned out to be a disaster. Who knew that someone so graceful on the basketball court could have two left feet on the dance floor?"

Sarah studied the quilt pattern again. This T-shirt quilt was made up of ten-by-ten-inch blocks cut from the printed fronts of T-shirts. The nicer quilts had sashing in between the T-shirt blocks, made of either solid or print cotton fabric.

"What color fabric would you like me to use in between the T-shirt blocks?" Sarah asked.

"Well, the colors for San Diego State are scarlet and black." Tracy looked down at the T-shirts in front of her. "Do you think all the different colors will go well together?"

"I think I can arrange them in a way that will look nice."

Tracy smiled. "Good. Then let's use scarlet and black and I'll leave the rest of it up to you."

They settled on a price, then Sarah began to think of different ways to put the quilt together. She liked it when her clients gave her free rein to create a quilt for them. "Do you need it to be finished by a certain date?"

"Well, definitely by the time she leaves for college, which will be the second week in June. If you could have it in time for her high school graduation, that would be great. I'd love to display it at her reception."

"I think I can have it done by then," Sarah replied, calculating the days. "It really shouldn't take long to put together once I have all the pieces cut out."

Tracy smiled as she rose to her feet. "I'm so glad you can do it. Your quilts are always so beautiful."

"Thank you." Sarah walked her to the door. "I'll call you if I have any questions and you're welcome to stop by anytime if you want to take a peek at the quilt in progress."

"Thanks, but I think I'll wait until it's finished. Mark may stop by, though," she said. "He tends to get nervous about these things."

Sarah struggled to keep her smile in place as she opened the front door. The less she saw of Mark Calhoun, the better. "Does Sasha know you're having this done?"

"No, it's going to be a surprise." Tracy stepped out onto the porch. "I think she'll be thrilled when she sees it."

"I'll give you a call when it's ready."

"Thanks again," Tracy said before she headed to her car.

Sarah closed the front door and walked back to the coffee table to gather up the T-shirts. She needed to give some thought to making all these disparate colors work together. But she was always up for a challenge.

The next day, Sarah walked into the Spotted Dog. Murphy, the white corgi, ran up to greet her, his tongue licking the top of her shoe.

"Hello there," she said, reaching down to scratch him behind the ears. "My shoe probably doesn't taste too good, you silly thing."

Murphy gazed up at her, his tail wagging furiously behind him. "I'm sorry," she said. "I don't have a treat for you today, but I'll try to bring one next time."

As if he understood, the dog turned around, his tail still wagging as he trotted over to the bookstore side of the shop and disappeared behind a counter.

She looked up to see Liam approaching her, a wide smile on his handsome face. Her heart fluttered a little as she moved toward him, thrilled to see him again after a week away. "Hello, there!"

"Sarah, it's so nice to see you back in town. How's that new grandbaby of yours?"

"Sweet as can be," Sarah said, gazing into his eyes. "I had a wonderful time in Texas, but it's good to be home. Would you like to see a picture of Leah?"

His smile widened. "I thought you'd never ask."

Sarah retrieved a photo from her wallet. "This one was taken on the day Leah came home from the hospital. My grandsons picked out the outfit at the store. Don't you love the little bunny ears on the hood of her sweater?"

"She's adorable," he said, gazing down at the picture. "Reminds me of her grandmother."

"Oh, Liam," she said, a blush warming her cheeks. "She reminds me of Jenna as a baby. The boys look more like David, but I think Leah may take after her mama. She's going to change so fast though. I wish they didn't live so far away."

"I know," he said, tenderness in his voice. "But you'll see them again soon."

"I hope so," she said wistfully, then looked around the room. "I'm supposed to meet Martha here for lunch. Have you seen her?"

Liam looked around the café. "No, but I've been in the back unloading some boxes." He ran a hand over his graying hair. "Why don't you have a cup of coffee with me until she gets here?" he offered. "My treat."

"I'd love to," she said, tucking the baby's photo back into her wallet as she followed him to a table in the café.

He pulled out a chair for her. "What would you like? We have a coffee called Kenya Gold as our special blend today. It's one of my favorites."

"I'll try it." Sarah took a seat, then watched as Liam walked behind the counter to fetch their coffee.

Her gaze moved around the café, looking for any new additions to Liam's spotted dog collection. He had an eclectic assortment of spotted dogs, some on posters or other artwork and some as stuffed toys, scattered throughout the café and bookstore. She remembered last winter when he had dressed a dog in one of Sasha Calhoun's basketball jerseys to celebrate the team's success on the court.

Sarah's thoughts turned to the quilt she was to make for Sasha. She wanted to start on it soon, just to make certain it was done in time for Sasha's graduation reception. Maybe she would even have time to squeeze in a visit to Wild Goose Chase to select fabric for the quilt before she was due to meet the twins at their house this afternoon.

Liam returned with two cups of coffee, setting one in front of Sarah before taking the seat across from her. "I'll bet you couldn't find coffee like this in Texas."

She laughed. "Well, I didn't get out much. I was having too much fun with Jenna's family and the baby, but your coffee has always been my favorite." She took a sip of her coffee. "*Hmm*, this hits the spot. It's a little cool out there today."

He smiled. "It's great weather when you own a coffee shop, but I'll admit I'm looking forward to summer. Have you started your garden yet?"

"The twins planted an Amish garden in my yard as part of a class project last month."

"Oh, that's right," he said, nodding. "I remember your mentioning that."

"They planted spinach and carrots and a few other things. I have some tomato plants inside by the window, but I'm waiting for the soil to dry out a little more before I plant them and some cucumbers."

He leaned forward, lowering his voice a little. "How about we make a date of it? As soon as the ground is ready, we'll plant cucumbers and tomatoes in your garden, then head over to my house to plant green peppers and zucchini squash?"

She smiled at the idea. "That sounds like fun. I'll even bring a picnic supper to eat in your backyard if it's warm enough."

"Then we have a date?"

She nodded. "You can give me a call when you're available. I'm not too busy this month, although I do have a quilt show in Albany I want to attend and I'm helping the girls with a special project."

He arched a brow. "What kind of project?"

"Maggie's mother sent her a pioneer quilt that's been in her family for a hundred and sixty years. I believe the quilt blocks trace the family's journey west." She explained how she was helping the twins learn more about the quilt for their genealogy project.

"That's interesting," he said. "My great-great-great-grandmother Kathleen traveled on the Oregon Trail. That was shortly after she immigrated to the United States from Ireland at the time of the great famine." He shook his head. "The stories I heard of the starvation they suffered in Ireland would break your heart. They hated to leave, but it was that or starve to death."

Sarah leaned forward, always fascinated by the family histories of those around her. Liam had never told her this story before. "How old was she when they left Ireland?"

He scrunched up his face, taking a moment before he answered. "I think she was about nine or ten years old when they sailed out of Tralee. Her family stayed in New York City awhile, trying to make enough money to finance the trip west. They had relatives who had already made the trip and had sent them letters telling them of all the fertile farmland available to new settlers. Kathleen stayed in the states until she reached her twenties, then she moved back to Ireland to take care of her ailing grandmother. That's when she met my great-great-great-grandfather."

Sarah circled both hands around the warm coffee cup. "How did you find out about all of this?"

A smile tugged at one corner of his mouth. "Jeannie spent some time researching the genealogies of both of our families," he said, referring to his deceased wife. "She talked for hours with my mother and grandmother, as well as my aunts and uncles. She pieced together all the stories she heard and wrote them all down for Caitlin."

"What a wonderful legacy for your daughter," Sarah said softly. "That's what I hope this project will do for Audrey and Amy. Life was so different for the pioneers, it's difficult to imagine sometimes."

He took a sip of his coffee. "Jeannie heard stories that you'd never hear today. Like children herding cattle for miles all by themselves, then sleeping in a field before heading back to the homestead."

"It was a different world in those days," Sarah mused.

Liam's gaze moved past her shoulder. "It looks like Martha is here." He smiled at her as he got up from the table. "I suppose I'd better let you two ladies enjoy your lunch. I need to finish unpacking those boxes. I'll send Karen over here in a few minutes to take your orders."

"It was nice talking to you," Sarah said, wishing she could spend more time with him.

"Same here." A twinkle lit his eyes. "Why don't we plan on next week for our garden date? If the weather cooperates, that is. Monday or Tuesday should be free for me."

"Sounds perfect."

CHAPTER FOUR

I had an idea on the way over here," Martha said as she settled into the chair that Liam had vacated. She wore a black-and-white polka dot blouse and a pair of black slacks.

"An idea for Ian's graduation party?" Sarah asked.

"Yup." Martha hung her crochet bag on the back of the chair. "Let's order first and I'll tell you all about it." She leaned forward to peer into Sarah's coffee cup. "What are you having?"

"It's a blend called Kenya Gold. Liam recommended it and I must say it's very good."

A smile tipped up one corner of Martha's mouth. "I saw you two sitting together when I came in. I hope I didn't interrupt anything."

A blush warmed Sarah's cheeks. "Of course not. We were just having a nice talk. When I mentioned that I was helping the twins with their genealogy project, Liam told me

40

about one of his relatives who made the journey west on the Oregon Trail."

"It sounds like you're pretty excited about this pioneer quilt project." Martha brushed back a lock of her graying brown hair. "Are you sure you can spare the time to help me with the party?"

"I always have time to help you," Sarah said. "Besides, it will be fun to do some party planning. I'll have two grand-daughters graduating before long. A lot of years have passed since I've thrown a high school graduation party, so I'm a little rusty."

"You and me both." Martha chuckled. "In fact, my knees feel a little rusty every time I go up and down the stairs."

Sarah smiled as the waitress, Karen Bancroft, approached the table with a pair of menus.

"Good afternoon, ladies," Karen said, pulling out an order pad and pen from her pocket. "Our special today is the bacon and cheddar quiche. Do you know what you want to order or would you like a few more minutes?"

"I'll have the special," Sarah said, her mouth already watering.

"Make it two, please," Martha told the waitress. "And I'll have a cup of that Kenya Gold as well."

"Coming right up," Karen said, jotting the order on the pad.

When they were alone again, Sarah leaned forward, her hands clasped on the table in front of her. "So tell me about this idea."

"Well, I thought it might be fun to have a party theme that showcases both Ian's past and his future."

"That sounds neat."

"Picture this," Martha continued. "When the guests walk through the front door and into my living room, they'll see a celebration of Ian's past successes at Maple Hill High. This is where we can display the picture collage that Ruth is making for him, along with his artwork and his spelling medals, that sort of thing. We could use the high school colors of blue and white to decorate with balloons and streamers."

"That sounds like a pretty typical graduation party so far," Sarah said.

Martha smiled. "The difference is that when the guests walk through the open doorway into the dining room for cake and punch, they'll be walking into Ian's future. We'll decorate that room with the school colors of his university and have a pennant hanging on the wall. We could have paper plates and napkins and other decorations that showcase the college he's going to attend."

"That sounds great," Sarah said. "I always think it's important for kids to know there is life after high school."

"I agree." Martha hesitated. "There's only one potential problem."

"What's that?"

"Ian hasn't heard yet whether he's been accepted by the University of Massachusetts. He should know by now, but Ian said he called the admissions department and they're having some kind of computer glitch that's delayed their no-tification process."

"But couldn't they tell him over the phone if he was admitted?"

Martha shrugged. "Apparently not. Ian's an honor stu-dent and his dad is an alumnus of UMass. Tim and Ruth are sure he'll be accepted. I just don't want to take the chance of planning the party around it only to have it not work out."

Karen carried a serving tray over to the table. She handed Martha her coffee, then set a plate of quiche in front of each of them. "Here you go, ladies."

"Karen, you're a student at UMass, aren't you?" Martha said.

"I'm a part-time student in their low residency program," she replied, "which means I do most of the class work online and only have to be at the campus a few times a semester." Karen flipped her black ponytail over her shoulder. "Why do you ask?"

"My grandson applied to UMass," Martha explained, "and he's still waiting to hear whether he's been accepted. I wondered if you knew some way we could find out if he got in."

Karen thought for a moment, then shook her head. "I'm sorry, I don't. In fact, they make a point of telling incoming students not to call them to find out if they've been accepted. I suppose they don't want to be inundated with calls when they're trying to work, but it's easy to get impatient."

"I'm sure it is," Martha said, picking up her fork.

Karen looked between the two of them. "Is there anything else I can get for you?"

"I think we're fine for now," Sarah told her. "Thanks, Karen."

The waitress nodded, then turned around and walked back to the counter where a short line of customers waited to place their coffee orders.

Sarah set a napkin in her lap. "Graduation is still three weeks away. Surely Ian will know whether he got in by then."

"You're probably right." Martha sank her fork into the wedge of quiche. "Besides, we might think of an even better party theme before then. We'll have plenty of time to brainstorm on our trip to Albany."

"Did you tell Ernie about it?"

Martha nodded. "He doesn't mind a bit about my leaving. I think he's planning to go to Pittsfield with Colin that Saturday for an auto show."

Sarah was excited about their trip. She and Martha had been best friends for so long, but they never tired of each other's company. She thanked God every day for her best friend.

After lunch, Sarah followed Martha home to help her sort through her yarn stash, then headed over to Jason's house.

The garage door was open and Maggie's red Chevy Tahoe sat in the driveway. As Sarah parked her car on the street, she saw Jason carry a child's rocking chair out of the garage and place it in the back of the Tahoe.

"Going somewhere?" She asked as she walked up the front drive.

Jason turned from the car to greet her. "I wish. Maggie talked me into taking the day off to haul some of this junk…" He smiled. "I mean these *valuable antiques* to her store. This will be my third trip today."

"Is Maggie here?"

"No, she's down at the shop, trying to find room for all of this stuff." He wiped the sleeve of his shirt across his brow. "I guess I shouldn't be surprised. Her aunt Myrna lived in a huge house and it was filled to the brim with old furniture."

Sarah had never heard her son talk about Maggie's great-aunt before. "Did you visit her often?"

He shook his head. "We were invited to dinner at her place once or twice a year when we lived in California. She always enjoyed seeing the girls and she loved to spend time with Maggie." He tipped his head to one side. "So how was your trip to Texas? I called Jenna last night and she said how much she and David enjoyed having you there."

"It was even better than I'd imagined," Sarah said. "The boys are growing up so fast and they love their baby sister so much. I wish you could have been there with us."

"So do I," he said, then smiled. "But somebody has to hold down the fort in Maple Hill. I hear you got talked into helping Amy and Audrey with a school history project."

"Yes!" Sarah said. "The pioneer quilt Maggie inherited is a wonderful family keepsake. I think it's great the girls want to know everything they possibly can about it."

He nodded. "They're having a lot of fun with it. Do you really think it's some kind of picture story about the Hollanders' journey west?"

"I'm almost sure of it," Sarah said. "I've been trying to take it slow with the research, because this is Amy and Audrey's project. I'm afraid if I figure out too much too soon, I'll let something slip that they should discover for themselves. But it's so exciting."

He leaned his shoulder against the side of the Tahoe, a gleam of amusement in his blue eyes. "You haven't changed a bit, Mom. You never helped me with my homework either."

She laughed. "I helped you all the time. I just never gave you the answers."

"That's true," he admitted. "You always made me figure out the problems myself. I try to do the same with the girls, but sometimes it just seems faster and easier to show them the answer than to let them figure out how I got it."

"I suppose that would work too," she said, as she started to turn back toward the house. "I'd better let you get back to work. Maggie's probably waiting for this next load."

"You're right," he said, peering into the back end of the Tahoe. Then he called out, "Hey, Mom, wait just a minute."

Sarah hesitated as Jason walked up to her.

"Do you want to stay for supper?" he asked. "Maggie said we've got plenty of food and I want to hear all about my new niece."

"I'd love to," Sarah said. "Do you want me to get anything started in the kitchen?"

"No, thanks. Maggie made a pizza earlier and we'll just pop it into the oven when she gets home."

"Sounds good," Sarah said, then headed into the house. She found the girls in the dining room sitting cross-legged on the floor. Each had a spiral notebook open in front of her. "How's it going, girls?"

Audrey and Amy sprang to their feet.

"We've identified some of the quilt blocks, Grandma," Audrey said. "Do you want to hear what they are?"

"I sure do." Sarah rounded the table to stand next to the girls. "Shall we start at the top?"

"I'll go first," Audrey volunteered, holding her notebook open in front of her. "Of course, we know the first block is the mountain laurel tree and represents the Hollander family home state of Pennsylvania. The block next to it is called Missouri Puzzle, according to one of those pattern books you gave us."

"So we think that means they traveled from Pennsylvania to one of two places in Missouri," Amy said. "Probably either Independence or Saint Joseph. Those were the two places where most people went for supplies and to find a trail guide when they wanted to go west."

Sarah was impressed by the depth of their research so far. "I think you're right. How about the third block in the first row?"

Audrey consulted her notebook. "That's called Prairie Flower." She looked up at Sarah. "I couldn't find a town or anything called Prairie Flower in Kansas or Nebraska."

"We think it just means that they were traveling on the prairie," Amy said. "Do you think that's right, Grandma?"

Sarah nodded. "I do. The prairie went on for miles and miles with no towns along the way, just a few settlements and some supply outposts and army forts. Some of the pioneers called it the Great American Desert."

"Yeah, we read that too," Amy chimed in, then pointed to the next block. "Audrey says the next block in that row is called Drunkard's Path. But I'm not sure."

Sarah walked over to take a closer look at that particular quilt block, which was pieced from a red print calico and a solid white fabric. "This pattern can also be called Robbing Peter to Pay Paul."

"What a weird name. Now I'm really confused," Audrey said.

She isn't the only one, Sarah thought to herself. Most of the quilt blocks were straightforward, with names embroidered on them or a clear symbol, like the prairie flower to represent the long stretch of the trail over the Great Plains. But this one confused her. "We may have to research that one a little bit more," Sarah told them. "Let's move on to the next block for now."

"My turn." Amy turned a page in her notebook. "The first block in the second row is easy, since the name of the place is embroidered on it. Fort Kearney. That's an army post in the middle of the Nebraska Territory."

"And the block after that one is the gravestone," Audrey said softly. "There are two initials embroidered on the first gravestone block, C. and H." She looked up at Sarah. "Do you think that person died?"

Sarah knew from her research that life on the Oregon Trail was so perilous that she wasn't sure where to begin. "There's really no way to know the answer," she said. "Unless your great-great-aunt Myrna kept a record of it somewhere. It might have been an accident or a death due to disease. We may never know."

"Since there are two gravestone blocks on the quilt," Audrey asked, "does that mean two people from the Hollander group died during the trip?"

That made the most sense, but Sarah didn't want the girls to base their project on assumptions. "I think that's something we should research further. Your mom told us that Aunt Myrna had documents from that time. Perhaps she can convince your grandma Patty to mail copies of them to you."

"Maybe she could scan them and e-mail them," Audrey said, looking at her sister. "Then we could have them right away."

Amy headed toward the door. "I'm going to e-mail Grammy right now."

"I'll go with you," Audrey said, following her sister out of the dining room.

A few moments later, Sarah could hear the thud of footsteps as they ran up the stairs. She walked over to her bag and pulled out one of the quilting notebooks she used to keep meticulous notes of each of her projects. Just as she was labeling the top of the first page for the pioneer quilt, the doorbell rang.

Sarah set the notebook aside, ready to go answer the door, when footsteps once more pounded on the stairs and she could hear one of the girls in the front hall.

Then the front door creaked open and Sarah heard a voice that made her stop in her tracks.

CHAPTER FIVE

S urprise!"

Sarah's mouth gaped when she heard Patty's voice at the front door. She couldn't believe they had just been talking about the twins' other grandmother and now she had appeared in Maple Hill.

"Grammy!" Audrey shouted.

Sarah started walking toward the front hall just as Amy came flying down the stairs and launched herself into Patty's arms. "Grammy, I can't believe it! I just sent you an e-mail like one minute ago."

Patty laughed as she hugged the twins. "Oh, my two sweet girls! I can't believe how much you've grown since Christmas." She took a step back and looked them up and down. "You're both as pretty as ever, just like your mom."

Sarah stepped forward. "Hello, Patty."

Patty looked past the girls to where Sarah was standing. "Oh, hello, Sarah. I didn't realize you were here."

"Gram is helping us with a school project," Amy said, her voice high with excitement. "Now you can help us too! That's why I was sending you an e-mail. It's about that quilt that you sent to Mom and we're trying to figure out what it means and now you can—"

"Whoa there, sweetie," Patty said, laughing at Amy's exuberance. "I want to hear all about this project of yours, but let me sit down first and catch my breath." She tossed her purse on a marble-topped side table, then headed into the parlor, the girls following right behind her.

Sarah walked over to the parlor doorway. "May I get you something to drink, Patty?"

Patty looked up from her seat on the sofa. "Oh, that would be divine. I'd love a sparkling water with a twist of lemon, please."

Sarah hesitated, not certain Maggie had either one of those things in her kitchen, then she decided to check it out before she mentioned that to Patty. As she walked down the hallway to the kitchen, she could hear the twins chattering with their grandmother.

Sarah looked in the places most likely to contain sparkling water and came up empty. However, she did find a lemon in the refrigerator. She cut off a wedge, then added it, along with some ice cubes, to a glass of tap water before carrying it into the living room.

"I couldn't find any sparkling water," Sarah told Patty. "So I hope this will do."

"That's fine for now," Patty said, taking the glass from her. "I'll run to the store later and stock up on sparkling water and a few other necessities. I'm going to be here for a while."

"Really?" Audrey exclaimed. "How long?"

Before Patty could reply, the front door opened and they could hear Jason's and Maggie's voices.

Patty put a finger to her lips. "Shhh, don't tell them I'm here until they see me."

"Anybody home?" Jason called out.

"We're in the parlor," Audrey replied, then stifled a giggle with her hand.

A moment later, Jason and Maggie walked into the parlor. When they saw Patty, they both stared at her and Maggie dropped the paper sack she had been holding in her hand.

"Surprise!" Patty shouted, then leapt off the sofa with her arms outstretched.

"Mom?" Maggie said, as if she couldn't quite believe her eyes. An orange rolled out of the bag at her feet and careered toward the coffee table.

Patty laughed. "Yes, it's really me. I know I should have called first, but I know how much you love surprises." She walked over to Maggie and gave her a big hug. "How are you, honey?"

Maggie hugged her back. "I'm fine, Mom. I just can't believe you're here. Where's Dad?"

"Oh, he's on a fishing trip in Canada, but he's going to meet up with me later. I'll tell you all about it at supper." She turned to Jason. "And there's my handsome son-in-law," Patty said. "You look just as surprised as Maggie."

"That's putting it mildly," he said, reaching out to hug her.

Sarah bent down to pick up the orange and placed it back in the bag Maggie had dropped. She was debating whether to stay for supper when Jason walked over to take the bag from her.

"I should probably go," she said softly to him.

"No, you're staying for supper," he whispered, a wry smile on his mouth. "We've got plenty of pizza for both grandmothers."

Forty minutes later, the six of them sat at the kitchen table as Maggie pulled the pizza out of the oven.

A savory aroma of spicy tomato sauce and baked pizza dough filled the air as she carried the pan to the table and set it on a trivet.

"That looks so good," Audrey said.

Maggie handed the pizza cutter to Jason. "Will you slice it while I get everyone something to drink?"

"Sure." He stood up and ran the round slicer over the pizza until there were eight large wedges. "Hand me your plates," he told them, "and I'll dish up a slice for you."

Patty held up both hands. "None for me, thanks. I had two fish tacos when I arrived at the airport in Boston and I'm still stuffed."

"Aren't you and Larry vegetarians?" Jason asked Patty.

"We were, but Larry loves fishing too much to give it up, so now we're pescetarians."

"Pesky what?" Audrey asked, looking confused.

Sarah hid a smile behind her hand as Patty began to explain.

"A pescetarian is a vegetarian who also eats fish," Patty explained to Audrey. "I was a little reluctant to make the change at first, but it does make life more convenient when you have more dining options on the road."

Maggie brought a pitcher of tea to the table. "Okay, we've waited long enough, Mom. Tell us what brings you here."

"Do I need an excuse to visit my daughter?" Patty asked playfully.

"Of course not," Maggie replied, reaching out to squeeze her shoulder, "but we could have picked you up at the airport if you had let us know you were coming."

"I needed a rental car anyway," Patty said. "I don't want to make you or Jason cart me around. I know you're both busy, but I'm looking forward to some quality time with all of you, especially my two granddaughters."

Amy handed her plate to Jason, who dished up a slice of pizza for her, then placed another slice on Audrey's plate. "So how long are you staying?" he asked, reaching for Sarah's plate.

"Three weeks," Patty replied.

The plate slipped from his grasp and he almost dropped it. Then he looked up at Patty. "Three weeks?"

She beamed. "Isn't that wonderful? When Larry told me about his fishing trip, I decided this would be a perfect time to come to Maple Hill. We've got that family reunion in Willow Creek at the end of the month and Larry will drive there from Canada so we can go home together."

"Three weeks?" Jason said again.

Maggie cleared her throat and gave him a warning glance. "That's great, Mom. I'll get the guest room ready for you. Is there any special food you'd like to eat? I don't think I have any fish in the freezer..."

Patty waved away her concern. "Don't you worry about a thing, Maggie. I can take care of myself while I'm here. And I can do all the cooking too! It will be like a vacation for you."

Sarah listened to the conversation as she ate her pizza, not saying much. Patty's personality could be a little overwhelming at times and she wasn't always tactful, but Sarah had learned not to take it personally.

Three weeks, Sarah thought to herself. She didn't blame the woman for wanting to spend time with her family, but Sarah would never think of imposing on Jenna and her family for that long—especially uninvited.

Still, she needed to give Patty the benefit of the doubt. Just because they hadn't always gotten along well in the past didn't mean they couldn't eventually become friends. They would certainly be seeing a lot of each other while Sarah was helping the twins with their project.

"I still can't believe you're here," Maggie said, staring at her mother. "Jason and I have been moving all the things you sent me to my shop. Every time I look at them I think of

Aunt Myrna, so I think I'll just display most of them instead of putting them up for sale."

"They're yours to do with as you wish," Patty said. "What did you think of the quilt?"

"It's amazing," Maggie said, looking over at Sarah, then back to her mother. "And it arrived at the perfect time. Amy and Audrey are working on a genealogy project for their history class and they're going to talk about the Hollander family's journey west on the Oregon Trail."

Patty clapped her hands together. "Well, isn't that wonderful? Aunt Myrna would be so proud of you girls."

Amy swiped at her mouth with her napkin. "That's why I was sending you an e-mail, Grammy. Mom said that Aunt Myrna had some letters and stuff that talked about their trip. I wanted you to send them to me to help with our project."

"But now they're back in California," Audrey mused, her face forlorn, "and Grammy's not going back home until after our project is due."

"Hold on, girls," Patty said. "I've got exactly what you need in my bag."

Maggie turned to her mother. "How?"

"I brought the letters for the reunion, dear. In fact, I had a printer in California make them into a booklet and ordered several copies so I could give them out to the family. Every Hollander deserves to know his or her heritage."

This news made Sarah's pulse pick up. Not only did she have authentication of the pioneer quilt, but now there would be a written history from the time period when the quilt was made. She couldn't believe her luck.

"So tell me more about this project," Patty said, settling back in her chair.

Amy and Audrey took turns explaining the project and how the quilt chronicled the Hollander family's journey west. Sarah added a comment or two, caught up in their excitement.

"That all sounds wonderful," Patty exclaimed. Then she sat up in her chair and snapped her fingers. "I've got an idea! Why don't you give the same presentation at the reunion that you're going to give in your history class?"

Amy and Audrey glanced at each other, appearing less than thrilled with the idea.

"Think about it," Patty encouraged them. "You could be giving all of our relatives new information about the family. They'd love you for it." Then she turned to Sarah. "And it would be wonderful if you could join us at the reunion."

Sarah blinked. "Me?"

"Of course," Patty replied. "As someone who works with vintage quilts, you could give the twins' presentation a unique perspective. I'd pay you, naturally, since you wouldn't be joining us for the rest of the reunion activities."

"Mom," Maggie began, casting a quick glance at Sarah. "I don't think Sarah wants to go all the way to Willow Creek, Pennsylvania, to give a one-hour presentation."

Sarah wanted to hug her daughter-in-law. "It sounds like a special family occasion. I wouldn't want to intrude. The girls will do a fine job of telling everyone about the quilt."

Amy whirled around to face Sarah. "Gram, you have to come with us! You know everything about quilts and they might start asking us a bunch of questions."

"Please," Audrey begged. "It would be so much fun to have both of our grandmas there."

Sarah looked over at Jason, who simply shrugged his shoulders.

"It's up to you, Mom," he said.

"Please, Grandma," Amy said again.

"Please," Audrey echoed.

It was an offer Sarah couldn't refuse, not when her granddaughters wanted her there so much. "I'll be happy to contribute to the presentation," she told Patty, "but I can't accept any money for it."

"That's up to you," Patty said. "I'll make sure there's a reservation for you at the hotel in Willow Creek. It's filling up fast."

Sarah took another bite of her pizza, wondering if she had made the right decision. But if it made the girls happy it would be worth it. Then another thought occurred to her.

Sarah looked over at Patty. "There is one thing I would like, if you don't mind."

"What's that?" Patty asked.

"One of those booklets you mentioned," Sarah told her. "I think those letters just might hold the answers to some of the mysteries in that quilt."

CHAPTER SIX

That evening, Sarah returned home with the intention of getting started on Sasha's quilt. But by the time she had folded all the laundry and put it away, she was feeling a little tired. It had been a long day and she didn't want to take the chance of making a mistake when she started cutting into Sasha's favorite T-shirts.

Instead, she decided to get out her notebook and start adding information about the pioneer quilt. After dinner she had remembered to ask the girls to print out a copy of the front of the quilt so she could see how all of the blocks went together.

She pulled that photo from her bag, along with the notebook and sat down at the desk in her sewing room. The first thing she did was list what she knew about the quilt's background. Then she began to list the pattern of each quilt block in order, starting with the first row, which she labeled with the number one.

1A. Mountain Laurel Tree—appliqué block, dark green leaves, brown trunk, ivory background fabric. Probable significance: Pennsylvania was the home state of the Hollander family.

1B. Missouri Puzzle—pieced block, orange, brown, and green calico print and solid brown triangles. Probable significance: the launch point of the journey west on the Oregon Trail.

1C. Prairie Flower—pieced block, light blue calico print, solid light pink calico, yellow calico, green calico. Probable significance: the endless prairie seen on the trail.

1D. Drunkard's Path—pieced block, red calico print and solid white fabric. Significance unknown.

Then she moved on to the second row of the quilt, identifying each block from left to right.

2A. Fort Kearney—appliqué block, navy blue calico on a white background, embroidered with the words *Fort Kearney* in navy blue thread. Probable significance: the wagon train stopping at Fort Kearney in the Nebraska Territory.

2B. Gravestone—appliqué block, embroidered with black thread on a white background. Initials C.H. in the center of the gravestone inside an embroidered heart. Probable significance: the death of a family member along the trail.

2C. Chimney Rock—appliqué block, embroidered with the words *Chimney Rock* in navy blue thread. Gray calico on white background. Probable significance: the passing of Chimney Rock on the trail in Nebraska Territory.

2D. Bible verse—appliqué block, embroidered with navy blue thread. Verse reads: *The Lord will keep you from all harm, he will watch over your life; the Lord will watch over your coming and going both now and forever more. Psalm 121: 7–8.* Probable significance: Faith that God would see them through their journey.

Sarah recognized that verse as part of the Traveler's Psalm, which seemed a fitting addition to the pioneer quilt. The family had relied on their faith to get them through hostile territory, protect them from wild animals, and face whatever hardships awaited them in the future.

She paused a moment to yawn, covering her mouth with her hand, then resumed documenting the quilt. The twins hadn't told her about their research on the third and fourth rows of the quilt yet, but Sarah recognized most of the patterns well enough to include them in her notebook.

3A. Delectable Mountains—pieced block, light brown calico, dark brown calico, yellow calico. Probable significance: the wagon train traveling through a mountain range.

3B. Fort Hall—appliqué block, the words *Fort Hall* embroidered in navy blue thread, fabrics of light blue and navy blue calico. Probable significance: the wagon train stopping at Fort Hall along the trail.

3C. Double Wedding Ring—pieced block, pink calico, yellow calico, blue calico, green calico, and solid ivory fabric. No date or names recorded. Probable significance: a wedding on the trail.

Sarah couldn't imagine marrying someone in such harsh conditions, but she had learned from her research that a surprising number of weddings had taken place on the trail. The most difficult part for most couples was finding a circuit preacher somewhere along the trail to marry them. She moved on to the next block, another yawn escaping her.

3D. Bible verse—appliqué block, embroidered with navy blue thread. Verse reads: *Finally, brothers, whatever is true, whatever is noble, whatever is right, whatever is pure, whatever is lovely, whatever is admirable— if anything is excellent or praiseworthy—think about such things. Philippians 4:8.* Probable significance: Unknown.

Sarah read the verse again, trying to determine the significance of it in this context. It was difficult to tell when she didn't know what the family had encountered at this point in their journey.

She put down her pen, too tired to continue. Maybe in the light of day, the significance of the verse would be clear to her.

Then she remembered the booklet that Patty had sent home with her. "I might find it in there," she said aloud, rising from the chair.

She took a moment to stretch the tight muscles in her back before she closed the notebook and walked out of the sewing room to prepare for bed.

By the time she pulled back the bedclothes, Sarah knew she was too tired to do any reading tonight. She knelt at her bed and bowed her head. "Heavenly Father," she prayed aloud, "thank you for this day and all the blessings in it. Watch over Jenna and her family and Jason and his family. They are all so precious to me. And please, Lord, help me be patient with Patty and help us come together as friends during her time here. Amen."

Sarah stayed on her knees in silent contemplation for a few minutes more, giving to God all the things in her heart and mind. Then she climbed into bed, turned off the lamp on her nightstand and fell into a deep, peaceful sleep.

On Friday morning, Sarah walked into Wild Goose Chase a few minutes after it had opened for business. The owner and one of her good friends, Vanessa Sawyer, waved as she carried a bolt of fabric to the cutting table. "Hey, Sarah, you're back! How's Jenna doing?"

Sarah walked over to her. "She's great and so is the baby. I've got a picture of her." She pulled Leah's baby picture out of her bag and handed it to Vanessa.

"Look at her," Vanessa breathed, smiling at the photo. "Oh, Sarah, she's beautiful."

Sarah wasn't about to argue. "And she's such a good baby. I got an e-mail from Jenna this morning saying that Leah only got up once to eat last night."

"She's an angel." Vanessa walked over to Sarah and gave her a hug. "Congratulations, Grandma. You must be so proud."

"I am," Sarah said. "And so blessed. But enough about me," Sarah said, tucking the baby photo back in her bag. "What's new in your life?"

Vanessa smiled. "I'm just preparing myself for the kids to get out of school in a few weeks. They've already got spring fever and have been staying up too late every night. I practically have to drag them out of bed in the morning."

Sarah nodded. "Jason used to be the same way. He used to play baseball with the neighborhood kids on school nights and was supposed to come home as soon as the street lamps turned on at dusk. More than once, Gerry had to go drag him off the baseball field so he could take a bath and go to bed."

Then she looked down at the golden apricot fabric that Vanessa was unrolling from the bolt. "This is gorgeous," she said, fingering the silky material. "What are you going to do with it?"

"I'm invited to a few graduation receptions this year," Vanessa explained, "so I thought I'd make myself a new dress." She held a swath of the fabric in front of her, letting it drape around her collarbone. "What do you think?"

"It's perfect," Sarah said, admiring the way the color looked against Vanessa's coffee-colored skin. "If you have any leftover fabric when you cut out the dress, I'd love to add it to my remnant stash." Then she laughed. "Old habits are hard to break. Forget I said that. I just cleaned out my stash, or I should say, Martha cleaned it out for me."

Vanessa smiled. "I understand. I have my own stash at home and can't stand getting rid of anything. You just never know when those remnants are going to come in handy."

Sarah watched her cut the fabric, the scissors sliding through it as if it were butter. "Anyway, I came in today to find some fabrics for a new quilt I was hired to make."

Vanessa lifted a dark eyebrow. "What kind?"

"It's a T-shirt quilt," Sarah replied. "Have you seen one before?"

"My niece had one made for her graduation last year. I thought it was a cute idea. With your sewing skills, it shouldn't take you long to put it together."

"That's what I'm hoping. I need to have it done in time for Sasha Calhoun's graduation reception."

Vanessa laughed. "I bet that girl has an entire closet full of T-shirts with all of her years playing basketball. How did you choose which ones to use?"

"Sasha's mother chose them for me. And this quilt is supposed to be a surprise, so we'll have to keep this between you and me."

"You've got it." Vanessa folded up the fabric she had just cut. "Sasha was one of Lena's coaches for her youth basketball team last summer, so we're invited to the reception. I can't wait to see what her T-shirt quilt looks like."

Sarah walked over to the rows of fabric bolts on the south wall. "I just want to make it unique. The pattern is so simple, which it has to be with all the different colors in those T-shirts, but I'd like to do something to give it a little pizzazz."

Vanessa thought for a moment. "You could use glitter thread and do some embossing on the border."

Sarah nodded, appreciating the idea. "That's definitely something to consider. I'm going to use red and black for the sashing and border. Those are the school colors for San Diego State, where Sasha's going to play basketball."

"Black should work with about any color."

"That's what I'm thinking," Sarah said as she flipped through the bolts of black fabric on the shelf in front of her. "And I can use the red as an accent color."

"I just got in some new fabrics," Vanessa told her, waving her to the back room, "and I haven't had time to put them out yet. Come and take a look."

Sarah followed her, appreciating how neat the storage area was. There were several boxes stacked by the steel door and some fabric bolts on a table, each one still covered in plastic.

"Here you go," Vanessa said, lifting more fabric bolts out of an open box and setting them on the table. "These are the blacks and grays that I ordered."

Sarah saw the one she wanted as soon as it hit the table. It was a black on black paisley print that had a soft sheen to it. She peeled back the clear plastic wrapping so she could get her fingers on the fabric. It was a cotton blend, with just enough polyester to make it wrinkle-free and give it a rich luster.

"I think this will be perfect," Sarah said, holding the bolt in her arms. "A lot of Sasha's T-shirts are cotton blends, so this will be a nice match."

"I've got a matching fabric in red," Vanessa said, pulling out another bolt."

Sarah couldn't believe her luck. "That's perfect!"

Vanessa carried both bolts out of the back room. "How much would you like?"

Sarah thought about it while she followed Vanessa to the cutting table. "Go ahead and give me two yards of the black and three yards of the red. I think I'll use the red for the quilt backing too."

While Vanessa cut the black paisley, Sarah went in search of the other fabrics for the quilt. She had decided to make a triple border using an ombré effect, which meant starting with one color tone that then shaded into another and finally into a third, the three fabrics graduating from light to dark.

After several minutes of analyzing fabrics, she selected several different shades of gray and silver, deciding to mix and match them when she got home to see which combinations she liked best.

"Did you find what you wanted?" Vanessa asked as Sarah set the bolts on the cutting table.

"I think so." Sarah thought for a moment, then said, "I'll take a yard of each fabric."

As Vanessa measured and cut the fabric for Sasha's quilt, Sarah began thinking about the pioneer quilt still laid out on Maggie's dining room table. She had wanted to finish cataloging the quilt blocks in her notebook this morning, but she had gotten stuck on the first block in the fourth row. It was a pattern she hadn't seen before and one she couldn't find in the pattern books she owned.

She dug into her bag, hoping Vanessa might be able to help. "I have a question for you."

"I'm all ears."

Sarah slid a photocopy of that particular block in front of Vanessa. "Part of this quilt block is a Snake Trail, which is similar to Drunkard's Path. But I don't recognize the tree in the middle. Do you?"

Vanessa looked at it for a long moment before she shook her head. "Sorry, I have no idea. Where did it come from?"

Sarah told her about the pioneer quilt and how she was helping the girls identify the different quilt blocks. This particular block, made of a Dresden blue print calico, was a pieced block with a thin, winding row of white fabric in the Snake Trail style, but with a tree in the middle.

"I checked some of my favorite pattern Web sites on the Internet this morning," Sarah said, "and I still couldn't find it."

"That's strange." Vanessa began unrolling fabric from the last bolt. "Maybe it's an original design."

Sarah had considered that possibility. "There are a few unique appliqué designs, with Bible verses and important family milestones, but this is the only pieced block that doesn't fit a traditional quilt block pattern."

Vanessa gave a sympathetic shrug. "I wish I could help."

Sarah made a mental note to take a picture of the mystery block with her to the quilt show next Saturday. Some of the best quilters in the area would be there and one of them just might be able to identify it.

"Hey, I'm headed to a quilt show in Albany next Saturday," Sarah said as Vanessa rang up her order. "Martha's going with me, but I have room for you too, if you're interested."

"I'd love to go, but we've got a family wedding in Pittsfield that day." Vanessa sighed. "Between the graduation receptions and the weddings this month, I'm busy almost every weekend."

"Well, let's plan to go to a quilt show or a conference together one of these days. We need to get you out of this store once in a while."

"I'd love to go on a fabric tour," Vanessa said, then laughed at herself. "My idea of a vacation from my fabric store is to visit different fabric stores in other towns. Does that sound normal to you?"

"Perfectly normal," Sarah assured her, laughing as she gathered up her bags and headed for the door. "Thanks, Vanessa."

"Bye," Vanessa called after her. "And tell Jenna congratulations for me."

Sarah left the store, eager to get home and start reading the booklet Patty had given her. It might help her figure out the mystery pattern in the fourth row and move the twins one step closer to completing their project.

CHAPTER SEVEN

April 28, 1849

Dear Beth,

It is a bright Tuesday morn, although the smell of rain is still in the air. We are sixteen days out of Pennsylvania and I am already tired of living out of a trunk. I am told that we will buy a big wagon once we reach Missouri, along with a team of oxen that will pull us the rest of the way.

Yesterday, we forged a small river and had fish for supper. Tomorrow, my brother hopes to make better progress on our journey. I wonder if we shall ever see each other again, Beth, and I keep you in my prayers every night. I shall plant a tree in your honor when I get to my new home.

Yours sincerely,
Emma

Sarah turned to the next page of the journal, realizing it was almost time for lunch. She had started reading the booklet when she had arrived home from the fabric store, hoping to find some tidbits that would help her decipher the quilt. She was somewhat surprised by this first letter. There were few details of the trip or the people taking it. She turned to the next letter in the booklet, also written by Emma and marked with the same date as the first letter.

April 28, 1849

Dear Beth,

I have included a letter for you to show your family, but this one is for your eyes only. It seems forever since I said good-bye to you on that chilly May morn in Willow Creek. We both cried, but your new husband was there to comfort you as the wagon pulled away. I pray that I, too, may soon have a husband who cares for me as Elmer cares for you. I know you think me foolish to find a husband in such a manner, but his letters to me have been sweet and he seems a learned man.

Now that Mother is remarried, I do not feel welcome in my stepfather's home. I am almost four-and-twenty and fear I will end up an old maid if I do not follow my heart into the wilderness. He waits there for me and writes of the wildflowers that grow outside his cabin door. Perhaps he will bring them to me for a bridal bouquet when we meet at Salt Lake City. My heart flutters in my chest just to think about it and I'm half-giddy, half-sick by the idea of marrying a man I have never met before in my life.

His name is Benjamin Carson and he is five years my senior. None of the boys named Benjamin at school ever plagued me, so I take that as a good omen that he will have an even temper and be a man of good humor. Father used to laugh all the time and get mother laughing too, even when she was cross with him.

I hope Benjamin likes girls with dark brown hair and green eyes. I hope he doesn't find my nose too pert or my smile too crooked. You have always told me that I am pretty, Beth, but none of the boys at home thought me pretty enough to marry. I do hope Benjamin Carson has no regrets when he sees me. And I hope he's not a cross old man with white whiskers and no teeth.

Sarah smiled to herself, already enthralled by the girl who had penned these words over a hundred sixty years before. She settled into the kitchen chair and continued reading.

I have so much in my heart that I want to share with you, Beth. They are words I cannot say to my needle-nosed sister-in-law nor my henpecked brother. Maude resents that I am another mouth to feed on the journey even though I gave Carl all of my savings to make this trip. They shall be happily rid of me when I marry Benjamin and make a home for the two of us in his log cabin.

You may think me foolish, but I am not one to sit and wait for happiness to find me. I would rather wander in the wilderness than rot away in Willow Creek in a home where I am not welcome. I shall pray for you tonight, Beth, and ask that you pray for me and for Benjamin. Pray that he has all of his teeth and that I am pleasing to his eye.

Your hopeful friend,
Emma Hollander

Intrigued, Sarah quickly flipped through the booklet, eager to see if Benjamin was the man of Emma's dreams.

Her eye landed on another letter by Emma, dated July 1849, and she began to read it.

July 23, 1849

Dear Beth,

We are camped outside of Salt Lake City and tomorrow morning I will meet Benjamin for the first time ever. The wagon train will stay long enough for the wedding, then take its leave. My heart beats so fast I can hear it in my ears. I know I shall not rest tonight...”

Sarah stopped reading, realizing something was wrong. She sorted through the quilt block pictures on the table, then found the one she was looking for. Fort Hall. According to the map of the Oregon Trail that she had found on the Internet, Fort Hall was directly north of Salt Lake City by several hundred miles. Why would the Hollander wagon train have gone north after the wedding instead of continuing west?

“I must have missed something,” Sarah told herself. She needed to read the letters in order, from the beginning, to figure out this contradiction.

But that niggling sensation that something wasn't quite right about this quilt grew stronger.

Sarah closed the cover of the green booklet, then rose from the table to make herself some lunch.

She used a slice of leftover meatloaf from the refrigerator and whole wheat bread to make a sandwich, then turned back to the beginning of the booklet. She settled down to eat her sandwich and began to read the second letter, dated in May, and written with broad, black strokes.

May 9, 1849

Dear Pastor Simpson,

We continue to ask for your prayers and the prayers of the congregation as we make our way toward a wild and untamed land. We shall reach Nebraska City soon and hire a guide for our journey. All of us have agreed that he must be a godly man and live by his commandments.

You have entrusted Charlotte and me with the mission of building a new church in Oregon and we shall do our best to earn that trust. We have already encountered some trouble along the journey, but we shall be more watchful now so that disaster does not befall us.

God be with you,
Josiah Hollander

As soon as she saw the name Charlotte, Sarah wondered if she was the C.H. represented on one of the gravestone quilt blocks. She could read these letters all day, but she needed to get started on Sasha's quilt.

"Just one more," she told herself, turning to the next page.

May 11, 1849

Dear Ma,

I do not know when you will receive this letter, but I promised to write to you whenever I had the time to put pen to paper. The days are full with toil and travel, never knowing if it is God's will that we reach our destination. I often look back over my shoulder, wishing I could see you and Willow Creek again. I have only been gone a few weeks, but it seems like a year or more.

The mud is our enemy today and we've been stuck for over an hour waiting for the rain to stop. That is why I can write to you today, but it may be another week until we head south to Nebraska City. There we shall hire a guide and gather supplies for the journey ahead. I will try to write to you then. Tell my brothers and sisters to mind you and give Grandma a kiss for me.

> *Your loving son,*
> *Amos Hollander*

"That's odd," Sarah said to herself. "If they're heading south to Nebraska City, then why is there a Missouri Puzzle block on the quilt?" She had read that Nebraska City was another launch point for the westward migration, but there was nothing to indicate that city on the quilt.

That made two contradictions now between the quilt and the Hollander family letters.

As curious as she was to figure it out, and to see if Emma married the man of her dreams, and if Amos got over his homesickness, and if Josiah made it all the way to Oregon, she needed to get started on Sasha's quilt. With a sigh of resignation, she closed the booklet and finished her sandwich.

Then she got to work.

The next day, Sarah pinned one of Sasha's T-shirts to her cutting board and marked the measurements with a ruler.

She was just about to begin cutting when a knock sounded at the back door. Then she heard it open.

"Mom?" Jason's voice called out.

She removed a T-pin from between her lips and said, "I'm in here."

Jason met her in the doorway of the sewing room. "Are you too busy for a visitor?"

She smiled up at him. "I'm never too busy for you. Come on in and I'll work while we talk."

Jason sat in her office chair while Sarah returned to the cutting board on her table. She was just about to cut through the neckline of Sasha's state championship T-shirt when she heard Jason yelp.

"Mom, what are you doing?" he asked, looking horrified. "That's a state championship shirt."

"I know," she said, calmly cutting through the neckline down to the mark she had made with the fabric pen. "I'm making a T-shirt quilt for Sasha Calhoun. It's a way for her to display all of her favorite T-shirts instead of their being stuffed in a closet somewhere."

He arched a brow. "A T-shirt quilt?"

She smiled as she continued cutting. "So what brings you here today? Are you running errands?"

"No." Jason heaved a long sigh. "I just needed a break from Zumba. It's some sort of new dance exercise that Patty is teaching Maggie and the girls. The music was giving me a headache."

Sarah cut through the last mark on the T-shirt, hearing the weariness in his voice. "How's it going over there?"

"Not too bad, actually," he said. "Patty helped Maggie at the store yesterday and took the girls shopping, so I haven't seen her much. She fixed a pescetarian-friendly meal last night that was pretty good. I've always liked fish and I'll probably be eating a lot of it for the next three weeks."

Sarah folded up the first T-shirt square and laid it on the ironing board. "Well, I'm glad you stopped by. I've been reading letters from the booklet Patty gave me and it makes me appreciate having you and Maggie and the kids so close by." She reached for the next T-shirt from the pile. "And I miss Jenna, but all I have to do is hop on an airplane to see her."

"My mother-in-law apparently had the same idea," he quipped, then gave her a wry smile. "Are you sure you want to go with us to this reunion? I don't want you to feel like Patty or the girls pushed you into it."

"I'm looking forward to it," Sarah said. "You know how much I like to talk about quilts."

"That's true."

"I just wish this one wasn't such a mystery," Sarah continued as she set the ruler on the front of the next T-shirt. "I can't identify one of the blocks and there seem to be some contradictions between the letters and the quilt."

"What do you mean?"

She told him about the letters written by Emma, Josiah, and Amos, then let Jason skim them for himself.

"That *is* a little strange," he said, handing her the booklet. "But maybe their plans changed along the way."

"I suppose that's possible." She considered the possibility that the quilt had been made in advance of the trip. That would explain the discrepancies; if someone had made the quilt in anticipation of taking a specific route that had changed once their journey began. But what about the gravestones on the quilt? How could someone make those quilt blocks before the trip, especially if they chronicled deaths that occurred during the journey? That information might be found in the booklet, but maybe she could find an even better source.

An hour later, Sarah finished cutting out the last of the T-shirt blocks and put the waste fabric in a paper sack. Jason turned away from her computer, where he had been playing an online crossword game.

"I suppose I'd better go home," he said, rising out of the chair.

"Do you mind if I come with you?" Sarah asked him. "I have a few questions for Patty."

He smiled. "Grab your dance shoes and let's go."

"I don't know who made the quilt," Patty told Sarah. She stood at the kitchen counter preparing a vegetable lasagna. "I don't think Aunt Myrna ever knew either. All I know is that it's been passed down through the generations and now it's Maggie's."

"I'm surprised you didn't want it," Sarah said, watching Patty slice thin strips of zucchini and layer them like noodles in the pan.

"The quilt really doesn't match my décor," Patty explained. "Besides, it would go to Maggie eventually and this way I get to have the pleasure of giving it to her. The girls are getting some good use from it too. They've been researching all sorts of things on the Internet and trying to find the names of different quilt patterns. It seems one has them particularly stumped."

"I've got a couple of questions about the quilt too. The places on the quilt don't seem to match the letters the pioneers sent to their friends and family in Willow Creek."

Patty looked at her. "What do you mean?"

Sarah explained the discrepancies. "I just find it very strange. That quilt is meticulously made and the detail work is amazing. I find it hard to believe the places on the quilt are wrong."

Patty pursed her lips. "Are you saying my ancestors lied?"

Sarah blinked, surprised by the charge. "No, of course not. I'm just trying to find a reason for the contradictions."

Patty sniffed as she turned back to her lasagna. "Maybe your interpretation of the quilt is wrong."

Sarah bit her tongue, not wanting to argue with her. There was no reason to argue for something she couldn't prove yet. But now she was even more determined to find out the truth. Identifying the quilt maker might be a good first step to doing just that.

"No matter what the reason for the discrepancy," Sarah said tactfully, "the girls should know who made the quilt for their presentation. Did your aunt Myrna have a list of names of the family members who traveled west?"

Patty walked over to the tomato sauce on the stove and gave it a stir. "I don't think she ever compiled a list, but I believe there were at least three families who made the trip and one bachelor."

That was good to know, Sarah thought to herself. She had already read letters from thee of them. Emma Hollander was traveling with her brother Carl and his wife Maude. Amos didn't mention traveling with anyone in his letter to his mother, so he might be the bachelor. Josiah had mentioned a woman named Charlotte.

"Can you tell me about a Josiah and Charlotte Hollander? Were they married or brother and sister?"

"They were married," Patty replied. "They had six children, but their four oldest children were already married when Josiah and Charlotte decided to travel west, so only the youngest two went with them."

"Can you imagine traveling with children in a wagon train?" Sarah said, in awe of their fortitude. "Sometimes I had trouble keeping my two kids corralled in a car."

Patty placed the pan in the oven. "Maggie was always good for me, but we Hollanders have always been excellent travelers."

Sarah pushed herself away from the table, wanting to check in with the twins and see how they were coming with their project. "Thanks for your help, Patty."

Patty turned away from her to rinse a spoon under the sink faucet. "You're welcome."

Sarah left her in the kitchen and headed to the living room. Amy was sitting on the floor with her back leaning against the sofa and a laptop cradled between her crossed legs. Audrey sprawled across the rug on her stomach. A book was open in front of her and she was wearing her pink earbuds again.

"Look at you two," Sarah said as she walked into the room. "Hard at work on a Saturday afternoon."

Audrey pulled the earbuds out of her ears and sat up. "That's because Mrs. Hiland decided everyone has to do a power point presentation along with their genealogy report."

"It's so not fair," Amy added.

Sarah sat down on the sofa. "It doesn't sound that bad. You can use a lot of the quilt blocks in your power point and you have all those letters in the booklet to use real life quotes from your ancestors."

"But who wants to read a bunch of boring letters?" Audrey asked.

Sarah smiled to herself, knowing she might have felt the same way at their age. "Let's finish identifying the quilt blocks," she told them, "and then we can talk about those letters."

CHAPTER EIGHT

When Sarah arrived home that evening, she walked straight to her sewing room and found her quilting notebook. The twins had done a good job researching and identifying the patterns on the pioneer quilt and she had agreed with their findings—including their puzzlement with the first block in the bottom row of the quilt.

She sat down at her desk with the picture of the quilt and opened her notebook, briefly reviewing the notes she had made earlier about the first three rows of quilt blocks. Then she started cataloging the blocks in the last row, starting with the one she couldn't identify.

4A. Unknown—pieced and appliqué block, a continuous winding Snake Trail pattern in white fabric on blue calico around the outer edge of the block, with an appliqué tree in the center. Probable significance: the Snake River?

She breathed a small sigh of frustration and moved on to the next block, hoping to add more information to 4A when she found some answers.

4B. Gravestone—appliqué block, embroidered with black thread on a white background. Gray, white, and green cotton shirting. No initials. Probable significance: the death of a family member along the trail; strange that no initials were embroidered on this block.

4C. Bible verse—appliqué block, embroidered with navy blue thread on yellow shirting. Verse reads: *Blessed is the one who perseveres under trial because, having stood the test, that person will receive the crown of life that the Lord has promised to those who love him. James 1:12.* Probable significance: nearing the end of the journey and reflecting on the trials they had faced.

4D. Cross and Crowns—pieced block, purple calico and solid white fabric, with the purple used to piece a cross shape and four crowns set diagonally between the arms of the cross. Bottom right edge of block is embroidered with the words *Willow Bend.* Probable significance: the pioneers establishing a settlement in Willow Bend, Oregon.

Sarah studied the quilt blocks, still trying to figure out the contradictions between the quilt and the letters. She knew from experience that if she kept digging long enough she would eventually find the answer. The first thing she needed to do was identify the quilt maker. It was most likely one of the women on the trail. Perhaps several of them had even worked together to make the quilt. But had they made it during the journey or after?

The answers she sought might be in the booklet. Before she had left Jason's house, she had talked the girls into reading it, suggesting that they take turns reading the letters that their Hollander ancestors sent back to friends and family in Willow Creek. Then the two of them could compare notes and put the most interesting parts from the letters into their presentation.

She hoped that once they started reading, they would become enthralled with this unique window into the past. It was a blessing for them to hear stories from their ancestors in their own words and she wanted the girls to appreciate it.

When she was ready for bed, Sarah took the booklet into her bedroom with her. After her evening prayers, she settled against her pillow and opened the book where she had left off.

A quick glance through the rest of the booklet showed her that five people had regularly sent letters back home. She had already read Emma, Amos, and Josiah's accounts of the first leg of their journey. Now she began to read a letter signed by a man named Charles Hollander.

May 19, 1849

Dear Matthew,

I am writing this letter to urge you to come join us on the journey west. If you travel by steamboat and horseback, you will soon catch us on the trail, as we will be lumbering along with a team of oxen pulling our schooners.

If I had not promised my parents to help Grandmother find her way to the Oregon Territory, I would be on a horse myself, traveling as fast as it could run. The men returning from the gold camps claim that gold nuggets can be scooped up with a shovel in California. I fear that if we tarry too long on the trail, the gold will all be gone by the time I get there.

Grandmother tells me I have gold fever and tries to persuade me to settle on the free land in the Oregon Territory. Unmarried settlers can claim three hundred twenty acres each, and Grandmother says that I can add her three hundred twenty acres to mine when she dies. But the land will be there forever and the gold may not last.

This is why I beseech you to leave Willow Creek behind and come and find your fortune with me. A year of hard work and we could live the rest of our lives as men of leisure. Do not tarry in your decision, Matthew, for we are to cross the Missouri River tomorrow. If you do not want to hunt for gold with me, then you may take my place with my Grandmother. As her great-nephew, I am certain that she would bequeath her acres to you if you work the land for her.

Come west, cousin! Your fortune awaits you!

Yours truly,
Charles

Sarah noted that Charles Hollander wished to go to California at the height of the gold rush. She wondered if he had ever made it there or if he had chosen to listen to his grandmother. She turned to the next letter in the booklet, penned by Harriet Hollander.

May 20, 1849

Dear Cornelia and family,

We have finally reached our first destination. Nebraska City is a wild place. There are fights breaking out on the streets and too many saloons. I shall be glad when we move on from here, but we must take care to buy healthy livestock for the long journey ahead of us, so we may not depart for a few days more.

I and the other women bought the food today that we will need to sustain us for the next four months. I purchased three hundred pounds of flour, eighty pounds of sugar, forty pounds of corn meal, one hundred pounds of bacon, twenty pounds of coffee, ten pounds of salt, thirty pounds of beans, and thirty pounds of dried fruit to prevent the scurvy.

The total cost to feed Charles and me for the journey was over two hundred dollars. He chafed at the amount, but he's never gone hungry before as I have. We do not need the luxury of a fancy saddle if we are starving to death. It may look nice to the young ladies, but the leather is tough to chew.

The trail guide that my cousin Josiah hired today is a man named John Grant, a fur trader who knows the territory well. He told us that we would see more bison than we could count on the prairie, so we can depend on some fresh meat along the trail.

I have not yet told Charles that I also purchased a rifle. He will find out soon enough if a wild animal or other varmint attacks us. I will turn sixty-four years old next week and the rifle is a gift for myself. I've always wanted to learn to shoot and this journey seems the perfect time to do it.

Good tidings and blessings to you all!

All my love,
Mother

Sarah closed the book, admiring the gumption Harriet showed at taking such a journey. She couldn't imagine pulling up stakes and leaving her home and most of what she owned behind. Then again, Harriet might have feared her grandson was about to do something foolish and hoped to set him on the right path by going on the trip with him.

She let out a long sigh as she settled onto her pillow, wondering if Harriet might have sewn the quilt. But if she had, why was there a quilt block with a Missouri Puzzle pattern and no mention of Missouri in her letter?

Sarah fell asleep trying to figure out the answer to that question.

On Sunday morning, Sarah stopped by Bradford Manor Nursing Home to have coffee and a cinnamon roll with Leland, then made her way to church. Leland Montgomery had been her father's schoolmate when they were boys, then became a good friend after her parents married. He had moved to Bradford Manor from his home in Illinois and had no family left, so Sarah liked to spend time with him whenever she could.

She was a little late leaving the nursing home, so by the time she arrived at Bridge Street Church there were cars parked up and down the street and the parking lot was full as well. Sarah parked a block away, then hurried as fast as she could in her black, low-heeled pumps. The organ was playing as an usher opened the front door for her.

"Thank you," she whispered, taking a moment to catch her breath and pat down her hair before she walked into the sanctuary.

"Sarah!"

She turned around to see Martha coming up the stairs from the basement. "Hey, there. What are you doing?"

"I brought some cookies for the coffee hour," Martha explained. "It was my daughter Kate's turn to host it this week, but she wasn't feeling well so I volunteered to take her place."

"That was nice of you."

Martha moved closer to her and whispered. "I need to talk to you after the service. Are you staying for coffee?"

"I can," Sarah said, not having made a decision either way. "Is something wrong?"

Martha hesitated. "No, not really. I'll tell you everything after the service."

Intrigued, Sarah followed Martha into the sanctuary. Sarah took one of the few empty spots at the end of a middle pew while Martha made her way down the other side of the aisle to sit with Ernie.

Sarah settled into the pew as the organist began to play the prelude to the service. She spotted Jason and his family several rows up, along with Patty, who turned around and gave Sarah a wave. Then Patty leaned close to Maggie and whispered something in her ear.

There was no reason to think Patty was saying anything negative about her, so Sarah told herself to concentrate on the service.

"Welcome," Pastor John said, standing at the pulpit. "This is the day the Lord has made! Let us rejoice and be glad in it!"

As the organist began to play the opening hymn, Sarah glanced over at Martha, wondering what her friend wanted to tell her. She would find out soon enough over cookies and coffee. Sarah just hoped it wasn't anything serious.

An hour later, Sarah greeted the pastor on her way out of the sanctuary, then made her way downstairs. Jason and his family were already there, seated at one of the long Sunday school tables with Patty.

Maggie waved to her. "Sarah, we saved a place for you."

Sarah waved back, then made her way through the cookie line. She was still full from the glazed cinnamon roll she had eaten at Bradford Manor, but she placed two small snicker-doodle cookies on her plate anyway, wanting something to nibble on with her coffee.

"You can sit by me, Gram," Amy said, scooting her chair over as Sarah approached the table.

"Hello, everyone," Sarah said, setting her plate on the table.

The twins were dressed in identical blue dresses, something they seldom did. They each wore a matching white knit shrug over their dresses and Audrey had a blue silk ribbon in her hair.

"You girls look nice." Sarah sat down at the table. "I like your dresses."

"Grammy got them for us," Amy told her.

Sarah could tell from the girl's tone that she wasn't exactly thrilled with the gift. "They're very pretty."

"I took the girls shopping in Pittsfield yesterday after you left," Patty said. "We had so much fun that we're going to do it again next weekend."

"But not next Sunday," Maggie told her, then smiled at Sarah. "We're having a Mother's Day dinner at our house and we'd love for you to be there, so mark your calendar."

"I will," Sarah said, pleased by the invitation. Since Patty was so rarely in Maple Hill, she had assumed that Maggie would want to spend that day with just her mother. "May I bring anything?"

"No need," Patty interjected. "Maggie and I will be making a delicious meal. Have you ever had California spring rolls, Sarah?"

Sarah thought for a moment, then shook her head. "I don't believe so. What are they?"

"They're fish or shrimp rolls wrapped in rice paper," Patty explained. "The wasabi paste gives them a wonderful flavor."

Jason took a sip of his coffee. "We've been eating a lot of wasabi. Patty even put it in the scrambled eggs this morning."

Patty laughed. "He loves it," she said. "It's been so much fun to introduce him to some new foods. Was he a picky eater growing up?"

"No, not at all," Sarah said, smiling at her son. "I couldn't cook fast enough for him when he was a teenager. His stomach was a bottomless pit."

"It still is sometimes," Maggie said, giving her husband's flat stomach a loving pat.

"I think that's my cue to get more cookies," Jason said, rising out of his chair. "Anyone else want some?"

"None for me," Patty said. "Some of us need to watch our waistlines."

Sarah saw Martha emerge from the kitchen carrying another platter of cookies. "I think I'll go see if Martha needs some help," she said, leaving her cookies and coffee at the table as she headed into the kitchen.

Martha smiled when she saw her. "You've got perfect timing. I just put the last of the cookies out there, so my job is done until it's time to clean up."

Sarah could hear the steady hum of voices from the other room, but they were alone in the kitchen. "So what's going on with you?"

Martha walked over to close the door between the kitchen and the fellowship hall. "I just wanted to update you on the latest with Ian."

They sat down at the table, Sarah fearing the worst. "Was he rejected by UMass?"

"No," Martha said, surprising her. "He told me he got accepted."

Sarah was confused. "That's great news, isn't it?"

"There's more." Martha leaned closer, lowering her voice to almost a whisper. "I was talking to him about his graduation party and mentioned the theme I was planning for him. I've always been able to tell when something is bothering him and he finally admitted that he was accepted to UMass weeks ago, along with several other schools in the area."

"I don't understand. Why didn't he say anything earlier?"

"Because he wants to go to school in California instead," Martha said. "And he wants me to keep it a secret from his parents."

CHAPTER NINE

W hat are you going to do?" Sarah asked.

Martha twisted her fingers together, worry clouding her eyes. "I agreed to keep his secret."

"Oh." Sarah fretted how Tim and Ruth would react if they found out Martha had kept this from them.

"You know I don't have favorites among my grandchildren," Martha said earnestly, "but I've always had a soft spot for Ian. He was such a sensitive little boy and he's grown into a kind, young man."

"He is special," Sarah agreed, thinking of how popular he was with the younger children at church. He had been a Sunday school teacher throughout high school.

"The problem is that he hasn't applied to any California schools yet," Martha told her. "I'm just worried that Ian still might not be telling me the whole truth. He even mentioned getting a job for a year to make some extra money while he decides what he wants to do."

"That doesn't sound like a bad plan," Sarah said. "A lot of kids go to work right out of high school."

Martha nodded, her brow furrowed. "I just worry that he won't make a decision and will regret not going to school right away."

"Well, no matter what he decides to do, his graduating high school is a big milestone. We should celebrate his accomplishments."

Martha's brow cleared and a smile lit her face. "You're right, of course. I am very proud of him. He's worked hard in high school and he deserves a great party."

Amy opened the kitchen door. "Gram?"

"I'm right here, dear." Sarah half rose out of her chair so Amy could see her.

"We're leaving now and Grammy thought you might want your cookies and coffee," Amy said, walking toward her with the plate and cup. "Hi, Mrs. Maplethorpe."

"Hello, dear," Martha said. "I like your dress."

"Thanks." Amy set the plate in front of Sarah. "Audrey picked it out and Grammy likes it when we match, so she bought two of them. Grammy thinks it's funny when people can't tell us apart." Then her mouth twitched. "Sometimes she can't tell us apart either."

Sarah picked up a cookie. "That's because she doesn't get a chance to see you girls very often."

"Yeah, I know," Amy said, and waved good-bye as she walked out the kitchen door into the fellowship hall.

When they were alone again, Sarah reached out and laid her hand on Martha's forearm. "So it's settled. We're going to give Ian the best graduation party in town. And I know worrying is part of a grandma's job description, but I'm sure everything will work out."

Martha nodded. "You're right. It's just that I've never heard him mention wanting to go to college in California before, so this new idea of his has come completely from left field."

"How long will you have to keep his secret?" Sarah asked her.

"Not long, I hope. Ian asked me not to tell his parents until he got chance to do it himself."

Sarah patted Martha's arm. "In the meantime, I think we should start making a shopping list for his graduation party."

The tension lines faded from Martha's face. "Thank you for listening. You always make me feel better."

"I'm just taking my turn," Sarah said with a smile. "I'll let you know the next time I'm in need of your shoulder. And that may be soon with Patty here."

Martha lifted a brow. "Is she causing problems?"

"No," Sarah said slowly, "not really. But when I mentioned that there were some discrepancies between the pioneer quilt and the letters her ancestors wrote on the Oregon Trail, she thought I was insulting her family by calling them liars."

"You would never do such a thing." Martha shook her head in amazement. "So what did you say?"

"Well, after she said my interpretation of the quilt had to be faulty, I changed the subject."

"She didn't!"

Sarah took a bite of her cookie, enjoying the hint of cinnamon she tasted as well as Martha's reaction. "She most certainly did."

Martha leaned back in her chair and folded her arms across her chest. "I recognize that expression on your face," she said. "You're going to prove her wrong, aren't you?"

"I need to find the truth for Audrey and Amy's project," Sarah said, then acknowledged what Martha probably already knew. "And, I'll admit, it stung a little when she called my work faulty. But it won't be easy. This is a one-hundred-and-sixty-year-old mystery. Most of the clues are long gone except for those in the quilt and the letters."

"If anyone can do it, you can," Martha said confidently. "Let me know if I can help."

Sarah held up the second cookie in her hand. "You can make me some of these cookies to eat while I burn the midnight oil. They're delicious."

Martha laughed. "Consider it done."

On Monday afternoon, Sarah arrived at Hawthorne Middle School early to pick up the girls. Cars lined both sides of the street as parents awaited their children. When she had been in school, almost every kid in town walked home and the ones from the country rode a bus.

She sat in the car with the window cracked, enjoying the scent of spring in the air. After a few moments, children began to spill out of the front door of the building, many of them sporting backpacks on their shoulders.

A yellow school bus came to a stop between her car and the front of the school. The motor rumbled loudly and she hoped the bus wouldn't block Amy's and Audrey's view of her car.

A knock sounded on her driver's door window and she turned to see Ian Carper grinning at her. The generous dusting of freckles on his face had faded slightly over the winter, but he still maintained that shock of strawberry blond hair that no beauty salon could ever duplicate.

"Hey, Mrs. H," Ian said as she rolled down her window. "Are you waiting for the twins?"

"I am." She rested her bent elbow on the car door. "What are you doing here?"

"Mom had a dentist appointment, so I volunteered to pick up Trina. When I saw you parked here, I thought I'd come over and say hello."

Sarah knew most teenage boys wouldn't bother to seek out their grandmother's friends, but that was part of what made Ian so special.

"So I hear Grandma recruited you to help plan my graduation party?"

"She did. We're still in the idea phase, so if you have any suggestions I'd love to hear them."

He shrugged. "It doesn't really matter to me. I'm just excited to finally be done with school. This last month is taking *forever*."

Sarah laughed. "It won't seem that way when you're out. There might even be days when you miss your old high school."

Ian braced one hand on the hood of her car and leaned in, a wide grin on his face. "Not me. I like Maple Hill well enough, but I want to see the world."

Maybe that was the reason he wanted to go to California, Sarah thought to herself. "Where do you want to go?"

He shrugged, his grin still in place. "Someplace warm in the winter might be nice for a change. I've had my fill of shoveling snow out of our driveway." He looked up and called out, "Hey, Trina, I'm over here!" Then he pushed himself off the car. "See you later, Mrs. H."

As Ian walked away to meet Trina, she saw the twins round the front of the parked bus and hurry toward the car. Amy beat her sister and slid into the front seat.

"No fair," Audrey cried as she opened the back door. "I called shotgun."

"But I got here first." Amy snapped on her seat belt, then looked over at Sarah. "Hi, Gram. Can we stop for a snack before we go to the historical society?"

Sarah hitched a thumb over her shoulder. "I made some snack packs for you. There are pretzels and raisins and some caramel corn." She glanced in the rearview mirror so she could see Audrey's face. "They're in the basket on the floor. Do you see them?"

Audrey bent down for a moment, then handed a resealable plastic bag over the seat to her sister. "Here you go."

"Thanks," Amy said, as Sarah shifted into gear and pulled cautiously away from the curb.

She moved slowly, having to wait several times as children walked across the street in front of her. She was beginning to think it would have been faster for the girls to walk to the historical society instead of being picked up.

At last, the student traffic cleared and she made her way downtown. Although the weather was still cool, the sun shone in a clear sky. As the girls munched on their pretzels, she wondered if Liam still wanted to get together for their gardening date. She hadn't heard from him yet and the ground was definitely dry enough now.

"What exactly are we looking for again?" Audrey asked from the backseat.

"I think it would be helpful for your project if you had more information about the pioneers who wrote those letters and, if possible, if you knew which one of them made the quilt." Sarah turned a corner and headed toward the white clapboard building with the hitching post in front. "I know the historical society has access to some census records."

"Census what?" Audrey said, snapping a pretzel between her teeth.

"You know," Amy replied as she fished the raisins out of her snack bag. "It's that thing where the government counts people every ten years. We talked about it in class a few weeks ago."

"So how is that going to help us with our project?" Audrey asked.

Amy looked at Sarah expectantly, waiting for the answer.

"Census records can tell us where and when someone was born and where and when they died, for one thing," Sarah explained. "These are public records, so any one can see them."

Sarah parked, then switched off the ignition and instructed the girls to seal their snack bags and leave them in the car. She let the twins lead the way as they climbed up the steps to the front door of the building. Once inside, she steered the girls toward the front desk where Irene Stuart sat with a book open in front of her.

As the historian, Irene loved questions about the past and her brown eyes lit up when she saw them. "Hello!"

The girls slowed their step and Sarah said, "Go ahead, girls. Tell Irene what you need."

Irene smiled at the twins. "I can guess why you two are here. Mrs. Hiland's class does a big genealogy project every year and her students start coming in about this time. Am I right?"

Amy bobbed her head up and down, her blonde ponytail swinging behind her, but she didn't say anything.

Finally, Audrey cleared her throat and stepped closer to the desk. "We need to find some census records. Please."

"I see." Irene rounded the counter, wearing a brown tweed suit that matched her hair and eyes. "Did you have a particular state in mind?"

Audrey glanced over at Sarah. "Well, I don't think it was a state yet. We're trying to find stuff about some pioneers on the Oregon Trail."

"They came from Pennsylvania," Amy added, "and settled in Willow Bend, Oregon."

Irene nodded. "I think I may have what you need. Follow me, ladies."

Sarah and the girls followed Irene past the large fireplace, where antique cooking pans and utensils were displayed, to the computer station in the corner.

"I've recently been able to gain access to several state archives, including Oregon. That means I have their census records online." Irene leaned over a chair and let her fingers fly over the keyboard.

A moment later, a Web site popped up on the screen.

"There you go," Irene said, stepping away from the computer. "The Oregon State Archives Census Records."

Sarah motioned for the girls to sit down, then turned to Irene. "Do you know how far back the census records go?"

Irene tapped one finger against her chin as she considered the question. "I believe Oregon became a state in 1859, so they probably started taking a census a few years before that. Many of the states and territories in the US were taking a census count by the mid- to late-nineteenth century."

"This is cool," Audrey said, sitting in front of the keyboard. "Who should we type in first, Gram?"

Sarah pulled out a chair beside her and sat down while Amy plopped into a seat on the other side of her sister. "Just put in a name of one of the letter writers."

Audrey glanced over at her sister, then said in a small voice. "We haven't actually started reading them yet."

"We were going to," Amy said quickly. "But then Grammy rented a movie last night and it lasted past our bedtime, so Dad said we had to go straight to bed."

Sarah wasn't sure what to do. This was their project, but she didn't see the need to make a second trip here when she had the booklet in her bag. "I'll tell you the names," she said, "if you promise to start reading the letters this evening."

"I promise," Audrey said.

"Promise," echoed Amy.

Sarah pulled out her notebook, where she had listed all the names she had found in the letters so far. Then she tore out a fresh sheet for Amy and handed it to her. "You should write all this down so we each have a copy of it."

"Okay," Amy said, then reached for a stray pencil lying on the computer table.

Sarah turned back to Audrey. "What kind of information does the Web site ask for?"

"Just a minute and I'll find out," Audrey said, moving the mouse over the screen. "I'm clicking on the historical records index."

Amy leaned in close as a new screen popped up on the computer monitor. "It looks like there's a box to type in a name and another one for a year. There's also a box called *County* and one that says *Record Type*."

The girls definitely knew more about computers than she did, so Sarah decided to let them take charge of the search. "The first letter was written by Emma Hollander."

"Okay," Audrey said. "Let's try Emma Hollander and the year 1849, right?"

Sarah nodded, then waited with the girls while the computer went into thinking mode.

Amy sighed when another screen popped up. "There's no record for her."

Sarah wasn't really surprised, since Emma had written about marrying Benjamin Carson, but she thought it would be worth a try. "The second letter was written by Josiah Hollander."

"Can you spell Josiah for me?" Audrey asked.

Sarah spelled the name, then watched her input it and the year 1849 into the computer. A moment later, the words *No Records Found* appeared on the screen.

Amy slumped back in her chair. "What if we don't find anything?"

Sarah smiled at her granddaughter. "We're just getting started. You don't give up in basketball when the other team scores the first points, do you?"

"No," Amy mumbled.

"Well, the computer is ahead of us by two to zero, so maybe we need to change our strategy."

Amy sat up. "Hey, Audrey, just put in the name this time and leave the year blank."

Audrey rolled her eyes. "There's probably tons of people who lived in Oregon named Emma Hollander."

"Maybe, but I don't think the name Josiah's been popular for a really long time."

"I'll try it," Audrey said, her tone skeptical. Then a moment later, she grinned. "We got one!"

CHAPTER TEN

A ctually, we got two," Audrey clarified, pointing to the computer screen. "But one is a birth certificate for 1932, so we know it can't be that one."

"I think we should write it down anyway," Amy said to Sarah, who sat with her notebook open on her lap. "The baby Josiah from 1932 might be one of our relatives too."

Sarah jotted down the name on a fresh page in her notebook. She liked the enthusiasm the girls were showing for this project.

"The other one is a death certificate," Audrey said slowly. "Josiah Wallace Hollander. Date of death is June 13, 1869." She turned to Sarah. "That would have been twenty years after they went to Oregon."

Sarah nodded. "Does it say anything else?"

Audrey turned back to the screen. "It says the county name is Malheur."

"I wonder if that's the county where Willow Bend is." Amy said, popping up from her chair. "Do you think they have an atlas here?"

"I'm sure they do. Why don't you ask Irene to help you find one?"

Amy left the computer station to search for the historian while Audrey turned to Sarah. "Let's try another name."

"How about Emma Hollander again, only this time without the date?"

Audrey pointed to the screen, where the familiar words *No Records Found* stood out in bold black letters. "I already tried it again. She's not there."

Sarah was disappointed. Her methodical reading of the letters in chronological order left her itching to find out what had happened with the hopeful bride-to-be.

"Who else can we try?" Audrey asked.

"Put in Amos Hollander," Sarah said, checking her notebook, "and see what comes up."

Audrey typed the name into the computer. "There's a marriage record for Amos Hollander and Bessie Dauber in 1851."

"What county?"

Before she could reply, Amy came running up to them with an atlas the size of a large sheet pan in her arms. She set it on the computer table and flipped it open. "Here it is," she said, stabbing a finger at the eastern edge of the state. "I found Willow Bend and it's right smack in the middle of Malheur County."

"That's where Amos got married," Audrey announced. "Malheur County."

Amy's brow crinkled. "Who's Amos?"

Sarah smiled as she smoothed out a wrinkled page of the atlas. "You'll know when you read those letters."

"Tonight, Gram," Amy assured her. "I'll read all of them tonight."

Audrey snorted. "No way. There's too many. You'll be snoring before you read the first three."

"I never snore," Amy retorted.

"How do you know?" Audrey gave her a sly smile. "Maybe I recorded it with your new camera."

Two red spots burned in Amy's cheeks. "Did you?"

"Why are you so worried if you never snore?" Audrey asked her sister.

Sarah leaned toward them, hoping to get them back on track. "Girls, we have work to do."

"But, Grandma," Amy cried, "she recorded me while I was sleeping."

Sarah met Audrey's gaze. "Did you do that, dear?"

Audrey looked sheepish. "No, I was just teasing."

Amy's shoulders slumped with relief. "That was *not* funny, Audrey."

Sarah checked her watch. "Okay, you two, I need to get you home for supper soon, so let's keep working. The next name on my list is Charles Hollander."

Audrey typed his name on the keyboard. *No Records Found.*

"Okay," Sarah said, marking it in her notebook. "How about Harriet Hollander?"

A moment later, Audrey said, "She's in here. There's a record of her death on May 7, 1869, in Malheur County."

Sarah jotted that name down in her notebook, then looked over the list. There were three more people who had been mentioned in the letters so far: Carl, Maude, and Charlotte Hollander.

Audrey performed all three searches and came up with three hits. Each of them had a death certificate in Malheur County. Charlotte had died in 1871 and Carl and Maude had both died in the year 1892. Each of the three had Malheur County listed as their place of residence at the time of their death.

Amy counted up the names on her notepaper. "So there are at least six Hollanders who made it to Willow Bend," she said. "Josiah, Charlotte, Amos, Harriet, Carl, and Maude." She looked up at Sarah. "I wonder what happened to the other two?"

"The answer might be in those letters," Sarah told her. "That's why it's so important for us to read them and find every piece of information we can. The more information you have, the more accurate your presentation will be."

"Does that mean we're done here?" Audrey asked.

Sarah looked through her notebook. "Let me take a look at my notes." She had been placing the focus on the letter writers, but what about the recipients? They might have followed their friends and relatives out to Oregon at a later date. In fact, Charles's letter to his cousin Matthew had encouraged him to come west as soon as possible.

"Let's try the name Matthew Hollander," she told the girls, "just to see what we find. Only this time we'll add the county of Malheur to the search box."

Audrey didn't find any records to place Matthew Hollander in Malheur County during that time period. Sarah suggested she remove the county name and try again, knowing he could have come to Oregon and settled elsewhere, but there were no records found.

Next Sarah suggested that Audrey input the name Simpson in the search box, along with the county of Malheur, to see if the pastor back in Willow Creek had ever followed his flock to Oregon. But there were no records found of anyone named Simpson during that time period.

After they completed their research at the historical society, Sarah drove the twins back to their house.

"Are you coming in, Gram?" Amy asked as she opened the back door of the car.

Sarah hesitated, and then decided to broach an idea that she had been mulling for the past couple of days. "Would you girls mind if I took the pioneer quilt home with me for a little while?"

Audrey pulled her backpack off the floor in front of the front passenger seat. "It doesn't matter to me. We have the pictures and we can always come over to your house if we need to see it again."

"I don't care either," Amy said, ducking into the backseat to grab her backpack.

Her decision made, Sarah turned off the car and followed the girls into the house. There was no sign of Jason or Maggie, but Patty was in the dining room setting the table.

"I thought you girls would never get home," Patty said as Amy and Audrey walked inside. Then she saw Sarah behind them. "Oh, hello."

"Hi, Patty. How are you?"

"I'm having the time of my life." Her eyes twinkled. "It's so nice to spend time with my family again."

"Where are Mom and Dad?" Audrey asked.

Patty smiled. "I sent them out to eat tonight, my treat. Jason has seemed a little stressed lately so I thought he and Maggie could use a night out together."

"That was nice of you," Sarah said, genuinely touched by her thoughtfulness.

Amy gazed warily at the fine china on the table. "So what are we going to have for supper?"

"A four course meal," Patty said, rubbing her hands together. "I want to show you girls the proper etiquette for fine dining. I know you never get a chance to experience that in Maple Hill, but you need to be prepared."

Then Patty looked over at Sarah. "I'm sorry, but I've only fixed enough food for the three of us. I didn't realize you'd have the girls out for so long this afternoon or I would have asked you for supper."

"That's no problem," Sarah said sincerely. "I need to be going anyway. I just wanted to stop in and pick up the pioneer quilt." Then she looked at the table. "Did you move it somewhere?"

"I put it upstairs," Patty replied as she placed a linen napkin beside each plate. "I didn't want it to get damaged out here in the open where anything could happen to it. Besides, it's a shame that we never sit in this nice dining room."

"Then you won't mind if I borrow it? It will be easier to restore the quilt at my house since all my tools are there."

"Oh, of course," Patty said. "We do want that quilt looking nice for the reunion." She headed for the door. "You wait right here while I run upstairs and get it."

Amy looked over at Sarah. "Have you ever had a four course meal before, Gram?"

Sarah's heart melted at the trepidation she heard in the girl's voice. "Many times. Usually, there's an appetizer, a soup or salad, the entrée or main dish, and a dessert. That might vary a little, but in very nice restaurants each course is served one dish at a time and then those plates are cleared away before the next course is served."

Amy tilted her head to one side. "It sounds to me like it just takes longer than having all the food on the table at once."

Sarah bit back a smile. "I'll let your Grammy Patty explain it all to you. I'm sure she's spent a lot of time planning this meal for you."

"What should we do next for our project?" Audrey asked.

"Well, after you read the letters, you should plot the Hollanders' route on a map. Why don't we meet here on Thursday afternoon after school? Will that be enough time?"

"I think so," Audrey said, nodding.

"Maybe you can use the computer to make a nice map," Sarah suggested, "then you can figure out how you want to show the route that they took."

"Cool," Amy exclaimed. "I like using the graphic art software on the computer. I'm sure that would work for making a map."

"Just remember that the map of the United States won't be the same in 1849 as it is today. You'll have to find an accurate map from that time period and use it as a guide for making your own map."

"We can do that," Audrey said as Patty came bustling back into the dining room. She carried a bulging cardboard dress box with the sides taped closed.

"Here you go." Patty handed the white dress box to Sarah. "Do you know how long it will take you to restore it?"

"I'm not really sure. I've just started another project, but I promise it will be done in time for the reunion."

"Wonderful," Patty said as she walked Sarah to the door. "I'll let Maggie know that you have it. I'm sure you'll take excellent care of it."

"Of course," Sarah said. "Have a nice supper with the girls."

"Thanks," Patty stood in the open doorway as Sarah made her way down the porch steps. "I'm sure we will."

Sarah drove home and carried the dress box into the house. She set it on the kitchen table, then placed her bag and notebook on the counter before checking the phone for messages.

Still no call from Liam.

Liam was a man of his word, so she knew he would call her eventually. She had plenty to keep her busy in the meantime. Sarah carried the dress box into the sewing room and set it on her desk. Then she opened a drawer and pulled out the letter opener, using it to slice through the tape on both sides of the box.

Sarah lifted the lid and saw that Patty had wrapped the quilt in white tissue paper. She began to unroll the layers of tissue paper, the bulk of it pooling on the floor by the time she reached the end.

Then she picked up the neatly folded quilt and carried it into the dining room. This was her spillover room when she had multiple projects going on at the same time. Even if she had only one project, she often liked to work in the dining room just for a change of scenery.

The telephone rang as she smoothed out the quilt. Her heart skipped a beat at the sound and she hurried into the kitchen to answer it. "Hello?"

"Hello, Sarah."

She would know that Irish brogue anywhere. "Hi, Liam. How are you?"

"I'm busier than I want to be," he said, "but not too busy for our date tomorrow night if you're still available."

"I am," she replied, "but we can reschedule if you have things you need to do."

He chuckled. "There may be other things I *need* to do, but our date is at the top of the list of things I *want* to do."

A blush warmed her cheeks. "Shall we meet at your garden or at mine?"

"I'll come to your house first," he said. "I've already picked up some beans and green pepper plants at the greenhouse this afternoon, but I forgot to get seed packets for the cucumbers and zucchini."

"I've got some on hand," Sarah told him. "And plenty of tomato plants. There should be plenty for both of us."

"Sounds fine," he said. "After we finish planting your garden, I'll drive us over to my house and we'll plant mine before we have our backyard picnic. It's supposed to be sunny and warm tomorrow, so the weather will be perfect."

Sarah walked over to her refrigerator and opened the door. "Do you have any special food requests for the picnic basket?"

"As long as it comes from your kitchen," he said. "I'm sure it will be delicious."

They discussed a time for Liam to arrive at her house tomorrow afternoon, making sure there would be plenty of daylight left for both the planting and the picnic.

When Sarah rang off, she was already planning the picnic menu in her mind. It might not be a four course meal, but she would make sure it was the best picnic in town.

Later that evening, Sarah sat at the kitchen table with the booklet and her notebook in front of her. Now that she had instructed the girls to start reading the letters, she wanted to stay one step ahead of them. She opened the booklet to where she had left off.

The next letter had been written by Emma and was still dated in the latter half of May.

May 26, 1849

Dear Beth,

We have left Nebraska City and are finally on our way! Carl bought a team of six oxen to pull the schooner that he also purchased. It is packed full to the brim with furniture and our supplies. There is not even enough room to sit during the long days or to sleep in at night. We walk alongside the wagon all day, then sleep under the stars at night. The sky looks bigger here than it did at home, perhaps because there are no trees or hills to block the view.

With each step I take, I tell myself that I am moving closer to my future husband. He shall find me with sore feet and holes in my boots, but that is part of the cost of the journey and I pay it without complaint. Maude does enough complaining for us both, even though she charges me with watching the children. I try to make life on the trail easier for her, but nothing I do seems to please her.

Every evening, my nephews and nieces and I gather fuel for the fire. There is little wood here, so we find dried buffalo chips along the trail and gather them for the fire. I try to make a game of it and the children race to see who can fill their bucket first. Then we cook supper, unless the wind is blowing too hard or the rain puts out the blaze. Mostly we eat bread and bison meat. I did not care for the flavor of the meat at first, but hunger is the perfect seasoning.

I am eager to cook for my new husband and have asked the ladies in our wagon train for some of their favorite recipes. Perhaps I would be wiser to ask the men for their favorites instead!

The prairie goes on forever, dear friend, and the wind never stops blowing. Some days it sounds as if the wind is talking to me as it blows through the tall grass. Sometimes I talk back to make the children laugh, but I am really talking to you and wishing you were here. I wake at night from dreams I cannot remember and stare at the stars, wondering if Benjamin is looking at them too.

We follow the river west, but the water is thick with dirt. Harriet advises us to stir in a bit of cornmeal to clean it, but I still do not like the taste of it. I added too much cornmeal the first time and ended with a bowl of cornmeal mush for breakfast!

I hope the water is clean and sweet in Salt Lake City. I hope my husband is clean and sweet too. There are many more steps I must take along the trail until I find out.

Your friend,
Emma

Sarah wrote down the date of the letter and the information that the group was traveling the prairie in the Nebraska Territory. This letter conformed with the third block in the first row of the quilt, Prairie Flower. She was eager to see if some of the other letters did as well.

CHAPTER ELEVEN

May 30, 1849

Dear Pastor Simpson,

Josiah and I are on our way to build a new church in the Oregon Territory, yet every day I feel as if I am walking in God's sanctuary and find myself in awe of his handiwork. The sky here goes on forever and the sunsets welcome the night with a blanket of glorious colors. The land is a sea of grass that rolls like waves in the ocean.

The bison roam in huge herds too numerous to count. They drink at the rivers and streams, along with the deer, and both provide a hearty meal of fresh meat for us after a weary day on the trail.

Our children laugh and play in the tall grass, relishing their adventures in this new and unfamiliar land. Thomas likes to help his father drive the oxen, shouting "Haw" when he wants the oxen to turn to the left and "Gee" when he wants them to turn to the right. After supper last night, Thomas gave little Hattie a ride on his shoulders and she kept shouting "Haw!

Haw!" until he finally turned to the left. At only four years old, she already has her ten-year-old brother well trained.

Josiah and the other men take turns guarding the precious cargo in our wagons each night. We hear tales of hostile Indians and desperate people who have lost everything, including their conscience, who prey upon the wagon trains.

Harriet has taken to toting a rifle and can shoot almost as well as any man in our party. Maude keeps herself busy sewing a wedding quilt for Emma, leaving the bride-to-be to chase after Maude's six children, who seem determined to get lost in this wilderness.

Amos and Charles play their fiddles by the fire every evening and fill the night with music. The children dance and sometimes we adults sing along, but most nights we are all too bone tired to do anything but sit and listen and remember our loved ones back home.

My Josiah ends every evening with a prayer that God will see us through this journey. I pray that we can keep the promise we made to our church family in Willow Creek.

Your faithful friend,
Charlotte Hollander

Sarah breathed a wistful sigh as she came to the end of Charlotte's letter, then read through it once more to look for any hints to illuminate their journey.

The one thing that stood out was that Maude was sewing a wedding quilt while Emma chased after her brother and sister-in-law's children. If Maude was a quilt maker, perhaps she had put together the pioneer quilt that now lay on Sarah's dining room table.

Sarah got up from the kitchen table and walked into the dining room. She was eager to get her hands on the quilt and see what secrets it could tell her. Once again, she was struck by the fine workmanship and the neat, even stitches of the hand-quilted blocks.

She took a seam ripper and sat down at the table, carefully inserting the pointed edge of the seam ripper into one of the loose threads on the Mountain Laurel block.

One by one she pulled the threads free, noting that they were thinner than the stronger and smoother six-cord threads that became popular in the late nineteenth century, after the invention of the sewing machine.

If she hadn't already authenticated the quilt, this would be one more clue that the quilt had been sewn prior to that time.

When Sarah had removed half of the threads from the loose fabric piece, she carefully lifted one end to peer underneath.

The cotton batting had grayed a little, but was in fair shape for its age. The fabric piece was good quality cotton. She gently lifted the edges of the pieces around the exposed batting, but could see nothing on the underside of those fabrics to give her any more clues about the quilt.

She did the same thing with the rest of the blocks in that row. All were made of quality fabric with almost perfect execution of cut and style. There were no clues beneath the fabric of those blocks either.

As she began sewing the first block back in place, several lines from Charlotte Hollander's letter returned to mind.

She set the booklet next to her as she sewed, trying to figure out what was bothering her. At first, she had assumed the quilt had been made to chronicle the trail the Hollanders had taken to Oregon, but this quilt contained more than a time line. There was a message here—one she hadn't deciphered yet. Charlotte talked about "precious cargo" and the promise they had made to the church. And Josiah's first letter had spoken about trouble along the journey and being more watchful so disaster didn't befall them.

Was there a connection between their promise to build a church and the impending danger?

Sarah shook her head, realizing that didn't make a lot of sense. Why would anyone cause trouble about building a church? Especially when trouble had occurred before they had even crossed the Missouri River?

When she had finished sewing the Mountain Laurel block back in place, Sarah set her needle and thread aside, needing a break. Her gaze fell on the mystery block in the fourth row. It seemed somewhat familiar to her now, but she had studied it so many times that wasn't surprising.

"What are you?" Sarah said aloud, walking around the table.

She traced one finger over the winding white fabric of the snake's body, searching her memory for the treelike pattern. She thought it might be a variation of a pattern she had seen before, but nothing came to mind.

After a few minutes, Sarah walked out of the dining room and returned to the kitchen. She walked over to the kitchen table and placed the booklet on it, telling herself she would read only one more story before getting ready for bed.

Settling into a chair, Sarah pulled the booklet toward her.

May 31, 1849

My dear Cornelia,

I laugh now to think of all the people in Willow Creek who called me daft for undertaking this journey. I have never felt so young before! The fresh air of the prairie has healed my lungs of their affliction. I no longer struggle to breathe at night or wake tired in the morn. It is a miracle and a sign for me that I am following God's path for my life.

My grandson does not like the fact that I am now a better shot than he. He still talks of the gold hills of California while I try to plant seeds of the future prosperity waiting for him in the Oregon Territory. Proverbs 28: 19–20 says "Those who work their land will have abundant food, but those who chase fantasies will have their fill of poverty. A faithful person will be richly blessed, but one eager to get rich will not go unpunished."

I plan to have our trail guide speak to him. John told me he has seen men return from the gold hills with empty pockets and broken spirits. He's a hardened man, but I sense a good heart beneath the gruff exterior. If I was thirty years younger, I might set my cap for him. Yet, with no husband to feed and no children to chase after, I can do as I please. Charles likes to fuss at me, but he'd prefer I sit in the rocker he placed in the back of the schooner. With all the bumps in the trail, I would probably fly off and break my head! So no rocker for me. I'll walk the rest of the way to the Oregon Territory and plow my land there myself if I cannot convince Charles to come to his senses.

Hope you and the family are well. I miss you all.

With love,
Mother

When Sarah saw that the next letter was written by Harriet's grandson, she couldn't resist reading it.

June 1, 1849

Dear Matthew,

My hope is that you do not receive this letter. My reason is selfish, for if you are on your way to meet our wagon train, then this letter might miss you. Grandmother continues to insist that I belong in the Oregon Territory with her. I am a man grown and tell her that daily. Lately, she will not cook for me or mend my clothes. She tells me that if I do not need her, then I should manage those things for myself.

Each day I think about the gold and leaving the wagon train and not coming back. At the next outpost, I will use the remainder of my money to buy a horse. Our trail guide John talks of his travels as a fur trapper and I am keen to find my own way in this world.

Come with me, Matthew, and we shall live a life of ease. Or, if you want to join up with the wagon train, I shall give you my schooner and my team of oxen for you to take Grandmother the rest of the way. She would perish on the trail without me so I cannot, in good conscience, leave her yet.

Last evening, we heard the sound of gunfire just outside the circle of wagons. Grandmother had shot off her rifle, claiming there was a man sneaking into our camp. When no intruder was found, John threatened to take her rifle away. In the end,

John let her keep the rifle in spite of my strongly urging him to take it from her.

Today, we are further delayed. Josiah is too deliberate in his planning and I dream of turning my schooner toward California and leaving them all behind. We could go there to-gether, Matthew. It is your choice, free farm land or gold for the taking. For me, the choice is an easy one. I hope your choice will be revealed to me soon.

Your cousin,
Charles

Sarah pondered the words of each of the letters as she made some final notes in her notebook before heading off to bed. She had no way of knowing whether Charles's or Harriet's version of events was more accurate, but she found herself rooting for the grandmother.

The next day, Sarah had on her prettiest pair of gardening gloves for her date with Liam. They were a pink floral print in a soft cotton jersey fabric with PVC dots on the palm side of the gloves to provide extra gripping power. She had com-bined them with dark blue jeans and a butter yellow cotton blouse that matched her yellow garden boots.

She was already in her garden when he showed up in his pickup truck. When he climbed out of the driver's seat, she could see that he had worn blue jeans as well, along with a blue chambray shirt and a pair of brown leather boots.

He reached into the bed of the pickup and pulled out a tray of seedlings, then carried them into the backyard.

"I see you've started without me," Liam said with a smile.

"I'm just breaking up some of the dirt clods from the last rain," she said, tapping at the soil with a hoe. "The girls got the ground ready when they planted their Amish garden, so it's ready to go." Sarah walked over to inspect the green pepper plants he had bought at the greenhouse. "Very nice. Those are just the right size." She pointed toward the other end of the garden. "I've got the tomato seedlings ready to plant too."

"Why don't I dig the holes while you plant," he suggested.

She handed him the trowel. "That sounds fine with me."

Sarah picked up the first tomato plant and popped it out of the plastic container. She gently loosened the roots from the compacted dirt and knelt down on the red knee pad she used in the garden. Liam scooped out a trowel full of loose dirt so Sarah could set the plant inside the hole before Liam pushed the dirt back around it.

"We make a good team," she said, reaching for another tomato plant. "But it seems like you're the one doing most of the work."

He grinned as he overturned another trowel full of dirt. "You call this work? I can't remember when I've had so much fun."

Sarah smiled, enjoying herself as well.

"Besides," Liam continued, "I'm just working up an appetite for that picnic supper." He pointed the handle of the trowel toward the wicker basket sitting on her back porch. "Any hints on what's inside the basket?"

"None," she teased. "Not until we're done with both gardens and it's time to eat."

"Then I'd better start digging faster," he said, slicing into the soil once more.

Half an hour later, Sarah had a neat row of spindly tomato and green pepper plants in her garden. A few rows away, there were fresh mounds of dirt where she had planted her cucumbers and zucchinis and staked the bean plants.

"Now that's what I call teamwork," Liam said. He used a rag to clean the blade of the trowel. "Where do you want me to put this?"

"You can set it in the garage while I get the picnic basket. Then we'll be ready to go."

Liam lived a few blocks away in a red brick bungalow with a detached garage and a chain-link fence around the backyard. She could see the small area of dirt he had dug up for a garden as they pulled into the driveway.

"Time for round two," he said, switching off the ignition.

Sarah grabbed the picnic basket and climbed out of the truck. "Where do you want me to put this?"

"You can set it on the bench just inside the back door," Liam said as she opened the back gate of his truck. "The door is unlocked."

Sarah carried the picnic basket to the house and opened the door to a neat little mudroom with white walls and an old wooden washboard hanging near the deep sink. A wide bench stood opposite the sink with Liam's shoes and boots lined up on the floor beneath it.

She set the picnic basket on the bench, then walked back outside where Liam was setting the seedlings by the garden.

As she approached him, Sarah pulled the zucchini seed pack from her pocket. "Are you sure you don't want any tomatoes or cucumbers? I've got extras of both and I don't want to see them go to waste."

"I suppose they might be good in a salad. I can always take them to the café if I've got too many."

As in her garden, the soil in Liam's plot was already loose and ready to go. This time they worked a little faster, with Sarah on her kneeling pad planting six to eight zucchini seeds in each hill while Liam nestled green pepper plants into the ground a few rows away.

"So I see Maggie's mom is back in town," Liam said. "She stopped in for lunch today."

"Yes, she arrived for a surprise visit last Thursday and is staying with Jason and Maggie until the end of the month."

"That *is* some surprise," he said wryly. "How did Jason take the news?"

"Like a good son-in-law," Sarah said, pushing some loose dirt over the zucchini seeds. "I know he's glad the girls get to spend time with their other grandmother, it's just that Patty can be a little..." Her voice trailed off.

Sarah didn't want to sound petty or talk about Patty behind her back. The woman might be a little irritating sometimes, but Sarah knew that Patty loved Maggie and Jason and the twins every bit as much as she did.

"What I mean," Sarah clarified, "is that you never know what she's going to do or say next. Yesterday, she prepared a four course meal for the girls."

Liam chuckled. "She is one energetic woman. I could barely keep up with her at the bookstore today."

A dog started barking in the neighbor's yard behind them as Sarah moved down the row. "What do you mean?"

"Patty was doing some research and wanted to find as many books as she could on the subject." He set another green pepper plant into the soil. "Frankly, I was surprised she didn't ask you to help her."

"Help her do what?" Sarah asked, growing even more confused.

Liam pivoted on his knees to face her. "Patty was looking for books on vintage quilts and the Oregon Trail. She told me her family owns a pioneer quilt and there were some questions about it that she wanted to answer."

Sarah sank her fingers into the dirt. "How strange." Only it wasn't strange at all. While Sarah was setting out to prove that she was right about the quilt, Patty was out to prove her wrong.

Liam started to say something else, then his gaze moved past her and he rose quickly to his feet. "What in the world?"

CHAPTER TWELVE

Sarah followed his gaze and saw a young man hopping over the chain-link fence into Liam's backyard. He wore a gray sweatshirt with a hood pulled loosely over his head and a pair of dark blue jeans—and stocking feet.

He stumbled as he hit the ground, then regained his footing and shot forward, his head turning back as if to see if anyone was behind him. The movement caused the hood of his sweatshirt to fall off his head, revealing a shock of strawberry blond hair.

"It's Ian!" She said in surprise.

"You're right." Liam set down the trowel in his hands. "But what is he doing?"

It was obvious that Ian didn't see them as he headed toward the fence on the other side of the yard.

Sarah took a few steps in his direction, waving her hand in the air to get his attention. "Ian!"

He stopped and turned, his mouth gaping a little when he saw her. "Mrs. . . . H?"

She moved closer to him, seeing the sheen of sweat on his brow and the grass and mud stains on his socks. One of his white athletic socks had a small hole in the toe. "What's going on?"

"Um," he hedged, glancing once again toward the back fence. "Nothing . . . really." His words came in short bursts, his chest heaving as he tried to catch his breath. "I'm . . . just . . . taking a . . . shortcut."

Ian might be good at his classroom studies, but he wasn't a good liar. He bent over at the waist, struggling to catch his breath. Sarah knew he had struggled with asthma as a child, but Martha had told her that he had outgrown it.

Liam now stood beside her. "You act like someone's chasing you, boy. Are you sure you're all right? And where are your shoes?"

The dog started barking again and panic flared in Ian's eyes. "Can we . . . talk about this . . . inside?" He twisted his head around again as the barking grew louder. "I hate . . . to ask . . . but . . ."

Liam didn't hesitate. "Let's go."

Sarah and Ian quickly followed him to the back door, Ian still looking behind him every few steps. Something was obviously going on.

They walked into the mudroom and Liam opened the door that led into the kitchen. He waved Ian and Sarah inside, then grabbed the picnic basket before he joined them.

"Please have a seat," Liam said, setting the picnic basket on the table. Then he turned to Sarah. "Would you like something to drink?"

"No, thank you," she said, still worried about Ian. His breathing had eased now, but his face was red and covered with perspiration. "Are you all right, Ian?"

His gaze dropped to the table. "I think I've ruined everything."

Sarah and Liam exchanged glances. She didn't like the despair she heard in his voice. "Do you want me to call your parents?" she asked.

"No!" Ian lifted his head and met her gaze. "I mean, can we wait a little while? They're going to find out soon enough anyway, but I'm not ready to face them yet." He buried his face in his hands. "I don't know what I'm going to do."

Liam filled a glass at the sink and set it in front of Ian. "Are you hungry? Sometimes a man can think better on a full stomach."

Sarah took his cue and walked over to the picnic basket. She opened the lid and began to set out the food she had prepared earlier. "I have cold fried chicken, cornbread muffins, potato salad, and pickled asparagus. And there are some chocolate chip cupcakes for dessert."

"That sounds like quite a feast," Liam said as he walked over to the cupboard and pulled out some plates.

Ian didn't say anything as Liam set a plate in front of him, along with making a place for Sarah and himself.

She began to open the lids on the food as Liam added silverware to their place settings, along with some paper napkins.

Ian scooted his chair forward. "That chicken does smell good."

"Help yourself," Sarah told him, taking a seat across from him. "I made plenty of food."

Ian picked up a fork and stabbed a chicken thigh. "This may be the last decent meal I eat for a while," he said with all the drama an eighteen-year-old boy could muster. He set the thigh on his plate, then scooped up a large spoonful of potato salad. "Once my parents find out what's been going on, they'll bring down the hammer."

Liam reached for a chicken leg. "That sounds pretty serious."

Sarah placed some pickled asparagus spears on her plate, wanting Ian to open up to them. Martha had sensed that there was something more going on with her grandson and she was right. But if Ian didn't tell someone, nobody could help him.

Ian tore off a bite of chicken, barely chewing it before gulping it down. "It's not criminal or anything," he clarified. "Although Sasha's dad might disagree."

Sarah lowered her fork. "Sasha Calhoun?"

Ian nodded. "We've been seeing each other for a couple of months now." He looked between the two of them. "I know what you're probably thinking. Sasha's one of the most popular girls in school so what's she doing with me?"

"We're not thinking that at all," Sarah said, feeling free to speak for both of them.

"It's weird, I know," Ian continued. "We got paired up in English class to do a project together. At first, I was bummed because she's a jock, so I figured I'd have to do all the work myself. But I was wrong about her. She's smart and funny and cute." He licked a chicken crumb off his thumb. "I finally worked up the nerve to ask her out and I couldn't believe it when she said yes."

Sarah knew a love-struck teenager when she saw one and Ian was head over heels. But she was certain Martha didn't know about his girlfriend or she would have mentioned it. "Did you tell anyone you were dating?"

He shook his head. "Sasha made it clear that we had to keep it a secret from everyone. She said her dad would flip if he found out."

"I take it he found out," Liam said wryly, reaching for another chicken leg.

Ian heaved a long sigh. "Mr. and Mrs. Calhoun had gone out for supper, so Sasha invited me over to study. We were in the family room when we heard the front door open. They had come back early because Mrs. Calhoun wasn't feeling well."

Liam leaned forward in his chair, listening intently to the boy's story.

"I'd left my tennis shoes in the front hall because I stepped in some mud when I was walking over to her house," Ian continued. "Anyway, Mr. Calhoun must have seen them, because he started yelling for Sasha, asking if she had a boy with her."

Sarah had heard Mark Calhoun get upset once before. It had been last January during the half-time break at a girls' high school basketball game. Sarah had been on her way to talk to the principal when she had heard Mark's outburst through the walls of Principal Wagner's office. Mark had been angry that his daughter was benched for the game because of a bad grade, or at least, that's what he had claimed.

Later, Sarah had found out that Mark's plan to hide Sasha's shoulder injury had spun out of control and he had taken his frustration out on the principal.

Ian set down his fork. "I wanted to stay and talk to him, you know? Try to make him understand that I really care about Sasha. But she panicked and insisted I climb out the window. She was sure that if he found out who I was, we would never be able to see each other again."

If it was any other father, Sarah might think that was a bit of teenage melodrama, but she believed it was possible Mark would forbid a relationship between them.

"So I ran," Ian admitted. "Mr. Calhoun must have seen me running in the backyard because he opened the back door and was shouting for me to stop. I kept running, thinking he'd chase after me." Ian shook his head. "I should have stopped."

"Do you think he knew it was you?" Liam asked.

Ian shrugged. "I have no idea. He only saw the back of me as I was running away, so probably not."

"Do you think Sasha will tell him?" Sarah asked carefully, not wanting to say or imply anything that would upset the boy now that he was confiding in them.

"No," he replied without hesitation. "She'll never tell. She's kept a lot of secrets from him over the years."

Sarah's heart went out to the young couple, even though she knew it wasn't right for the two of them to be alone in the house. What bothered her most was that Ian had apparently kept their relationship from his family too. Martha obviously didn't know about it.

In fact, now Sarah wondered if his decision to turn down an offer from the University of Massachusetts had something to do with his relationship with Sasha.

"Have some more chicken," Liam said to the boy, pushing the bowl toward him.

Ian eagerly reached for another piece.

Liam looked over at Sarah and smiled. "You've outdone yourself. This meal is delicious."

"Thank you," she replied, knowing this wasn't quite the date they had planned. She watched Martha's grandson devour the food on his plate and prayed for God's guidance.

When Ian finished his last piece of chicken, Sarah asked, "What are you going to do now, Ian?"

He wiped the napkin over his mouth, then crumpled it in his hand. "I don't know. I guess I'll wait for Sasha to call me. And I guess I'll have to buy some new shoes unless she can find some way to get my old shoes to me."

"I think you should tell your parents," Sarah suggested. "They might be able to help."

"I will, Mrs. H. I promise. But please don't say anything to them. I've got to talk to Sasha first. I don't want to tell anyone before I talk to her first."

Despite the desperation in his tone, Sarah knew she couldn't make that promise. "I won't say anything to your parents, but I can't keep a secret from your grandma. Someone in your family needs to know what's going on."

His shoulders relaxed as he leaned back in his chair. "That's all right, you can tell Grandma. I know she'll keep my secret."

Sarah served the chocolate chip cupcakes and then she and Liam gave Ian a ride back to his house. There was no sign of Mark Calhoun lurking about as they made their way to the pickup truck and climbed inside. Sarah sat squished between the two of them, hoping she was making the right decision in not going inside with Ian and persuading him to tell Tim and Ruth what had happened.

"Thanks again," Ian said, his hand braced on the edge of the open car door, "for the chicken and everything."

Liam leaned forward to look at Ian. "As the father of a daughter," he said, his tone genial, "I just want to tell you one thing. Mark Calhoun will never approve of your relationship as long as you sneak around behind his back. I know that's the way Sasha wants it, but sometimes a man has to step up and do what's right."

Ian nodded. "I know. I just want to talk to her first."

"Good luck to you," Liam said, his brogue thicker than usual.

"Take care, Ian," Sarah said.

Ian nodded, then closed the car door and walked into the house.

"Poor kids," Liam said as they drove away. "Do you think they realize they're only making things worse this way?"

"I doubt it," Sarah replied. "They're so young. And I think Sasha probably has something to do with Ian's indecision about college. No wonder he wants to go to school in California, since that's where she'll be." Then she realized she was still sitting in the middle of the seat next to Liam. Feeling self-conscious, she took off her seat belt and tried to scoot nonchalantly over to the passenger seat that Ian had just vacated. "Did you ever keep a secret like that from your parents?"

Liam smiled, his gaze on the road in front of him. "Believe it or not, I wasn't a big talker when I was Ian's age. Ma used to joke that she had to pry my mouth open with a crowbar to get me talking. But I never lied to them, if that's what you mean. My father was a patient man, but he didn't tolerate lying."

Sarah watched the sunset as they headed west toward her house. Ribbons of color streamed through the branches of the trees on top of the hill. "Mark can be so ... intense. I guess it doesn't surprise me that Sasha might lie to avoid a scene with him."

Liam didn't say anything for a long moment. "But what about her mother? They've always seemed close to me."

Sarah agreed, but that didn't make her feel much better.

As Liam turned onto Hillside Avenue, he glanced over at her, an amused gleam in his green eyes. "And here we thought the most exciting part of our date would be planting vegetable gardens."

She laughed. "Instead, we found ourselves in the Maple Hill version of *Romeo and Juliet*. Let's just hope that this romance has a happy ending for everyone involved."

Later that evening, Sarah prepared for bed, saying a special prayer for Ian and Sasha. Then she climbed into bed with the Hollander family booklet.

She had thought about calling Martha as soon as Liam had dropped her off, wanting to tell her about Ian, then she decided it was too late. She would call her first thing in the morning or, better yet, she would stop over at her house.

As she settled beneath the covers, Sarah plumped the pillow behind her head, then opened the booklet to the page where she had left off.

The last letter she had read had been written by Charles Hollander and talked of a delay in their journey. This next letter had been penned by Amos Hollander, the homesick bachelor.

June 10, 1849

Dear Ma,

How I wish I was home with you and my brothers and sisters at this moment. We have had nothing but rain for three days and I have been soaked through to the skin. Each time a wagon is stuck in the mud, we halt the wagon train and work together to pull it free. My wagon was stuck twice today and when we pulled it free the second time I almost turned it around to head back to Willow Creek.

Some days I feel as if we are traveling in circles, although John assures me that we will get to the Oregon Territory before the first snowfall. Josiah has doubled the number of men who watch the wagon train during the night. Harriet warned him that we might be in danger after seeing a man skulking about.

Although I would never call any good woman a liar, I do not know whether to believe her or Charles, who claims his grandmother is losing her eyesight and probably mistook a coyote for a man.

Please tell Elizabeth happy birthday for me. I cannot believe she is already twelve years old. By the time I see her again, if ever, she may be a woman full grown. Please remind Walter to watch the fence on the pigpen as the boar likes to chew through it. I advise that you leave that boar in Pennsylvania if you and the family ever join me in Oregon. He is nothing but trouble.

My dear mother, I shall do my best to make a place for you all and promise to work hard. Please pray for me and for all of us. We hear word that there is cholera farther down the trail and we have already passed some unmarked graves. Our trail guide, John Grant, tells us that graves cannot be marked or they will be robbed for the goods that might be inside with the body, such as clothes and family mementos. A grave dug in the path of the wheel tracks soon hardens, making it more difficult for the wild animals to find. I know not how many of these graves *we have passed over, but I take comfort in the fact that God knows where to find all of his children.*

Do not worry about me, Mother, for I am as strong and healthy as when I bid you goodbye in Willow Creek. It seems forever ago and I hope we meet again soon on this earth.

Your loving son,
Amos

Sarah read the letter again, her heart aching for the families who had to bury their loved one in unmarked graves, never to be seen again. She took solace in her visits to the Maple Hill cemetery, where she could place flowers on the graves of her parents and husband. It was a time for reflection and remembrance.

She leaned over to switch off the lamp on her nightstand, then closed her eyes and whispered a quiet prayer into the darkness. "Heavenly Father, you are always with us, even when we are lost. Thank you for your divine guidance and help me to always follow in the path you set before me. Amen."

CHAPTER THIRTEEN

I'm in big trouble," Martha said on Wednesday morning.

Sarah stood on Martha's front porch, ready to tell her about her conversation with Ian the night before. But maybe Martha already knew. "What happened?"

"Let's go into the kitchen and I'll tell you," Martha said, ushering her inside.

Sarah followed her into the front hall, waving to Ernie who sat in the living room in a recliner watching television. "Hello, Ernie."

"You've got great timing, Sarah," he said. "Martha's got a batch of snickerdoodle cookies in the oven right now. I was going to steal a few, but I guess you beat me to it."

Sarah laughed. "Don't worry, Ernie, I'll share. Your wife makes wonderful cookies."

"That's why I married her," Ernie said, turning his attention back to the television set.

Sarah joined Martha in the kitchen, inhaling the sweet cinnamon aroma of the baking cookies. "My mouth is watering already."

"They'll be ready in a couple of minutes, so we can have some with our coffee." Martha walked over to the coffeepot and poured two cups, setting both on the table.

Sarah pulled out a chair and sat down, feeling as at home in Martha's kitchen as she did in her own. "So tell me what happened."

"I got a call from Ruth around ten o'clock last night. She's upset with me for not telling them about Ian."

"So they know about his school dilemma?" Sarah asked, wondering just how much Ian had confessed to his parents.

Martha nodded. "She had just heard him come in the front door and found him in the kitchen heating up something for supper. That's when he told her everything."

Sarah was surprised that Ian had still been hungry after devouring half a picnic basket full of food but pleased that he had finally told his mother the truth.

"But get this," Martha continued. "Ian also told his folks that he's been secretly dating Sasha Calhoun! He's serious about her and thinking about following her to California." Martha shook her head. "I knew that boy was keeping something from me."

"At least you don't have to keep his secret anymore."

Martha nodded. "And that's why I'm in trouble. Ruth was upset that I hadn't told her before now. She even questioned whether I was keeping other secrets from her as well." Martha took a sip of her coffee. "I guess I can't blame her. We worked it out before the phone call was over, but I'm making a double batch of cookies this morning, one batch for you and one for Ruth, to apologize for hiding Ian's secret from her."

Sarah leaned forward, her hands curled around her coffee cup. "I saw Ian last night at Liam's house."

"What in the world was he doing there?" Martha asked.

Sarah told her the story, stopping only when the oven timer went off and she had to wait for Martha to remove the cookie sheet from the oven before continuing.

"So that's why he finally opened up to his folks." Martha pulled off her orange oven mitts. "I still can't believe my Ian is dating Sasha Calhoun. She's a good three inches taller than he is."

Sarah smiled. "Well, I think that might be the least of their problems at the moment."

Martha chuckled at herself. "You're right. Things like height don't matter when you're in love. But how can they be in love? They're only eighteen years old."

"You and Ernie were only eighteen when you got married," Sarah gently reminded her. "And most of our friends followed quickly after."

Martha sat down. "But that's different," she insisted. "*Times* were different back then. People got married at a young age all the time. It was almost expected."

Sarah nodded. "Times have definitely changed. So many young women are working toward their college degrees and getting established in their careers before they settle down with a husband and children."

"And young men don't seem to be in any hurry either." Martha stood up and walked over to the counter, testing the cookies with one finger. Then she began to slide the spatula under each cookie to move them to a cooling rack on the counter.

"I guess Ian is an exception," Martha continued. "He's ready to throw away an opportunity to go to a good university for a girl. I don't even know if he really wants to go to college in California."

Sarah picked up a cookie, still warm from the oven and took a bite. The sweet, baked dough practically melted in her mouth. "Just remember, this too shall pass. By the time we throw Ian's graduation party, everything might be resolved."

"I hope so." Martha took a bite of her cookie, chewing for a moment before she let out a small chuckle. "Of all the girls in Maple Hill, Ian falls for Sasha Calhoun. My little guy really knows how to pick 'em. She's a sweet girl, but that father of hers…"

"I know." Sarah didn't need Martha to elaborate. "It's possible Sasha's confided in her parents by now, or at least her mother, although Ian seemed convinced that she would never tell."

"You're making a quilt for Sasha, right?"

Sarah nodded. "A T-shirt quilt. I need to start working on it again to have it ready in time."

Ernie walked into the kitchen, his hand casually trailing along the wall. "Are those cookies ready yet?"

"There're some on the cooling rack," Martha said, then told him about Ian's troubles.

Ernie braced himself on the counter and stacked up five cookies in one hand, then he turned toward the table. "Sasha Calhoun? How did he snag her?"

"He's a handsome young man," Martha said in Ian's defense, forgetting that she had said almost the same thing to Sarah a few minutes before. "Sasha or any other girl would be lucky to have him."

Ernie popped a cookie into his mouth and then grabbed another one from the cooling rack before making his way toward the door. "I just hope that Mark Calhoun fella keeps his head about all of this. Maybe I should have a talk with Ian."

"Don't say anything," Martha warned. "We need to let Tim and Ruth handle this. But we can talk to Ian when he stops by after school today."

"Better save some of those cookies for him, then," Ernie suggested, moving back to the counter to grab two more cookies. "Or better yet, make another batch. That boy can go through cookies faster than anyone I know."

After Ernie left the room, Martha turned back to Sarah. "I think I know where Ian got *that* from."

Sarah smiled, dipping her cookie into her coffee. "Are we still on for Albany on Saturday?"

"I'm counting on it," Martha replied. "I want to buy the supplies for Ian's party there once we decide on a theme. Any ideas?"

"I'm still thinking about it. Maybe we'll be inspired when we're shopping. I'm also hoping to find some inspiration with this pioneer quilt. It's got me baffled."

She told Martha about some of the letters. "I love how life on the trail is coming alive through those letters," Sarah said, "but I can't help but feel that they're keeping something back."

"Maybe they were trying to protect their loved ones back home from bad news or keep them from worrying."

"I suppose that's possible," Sarah said. "But that doesn't explain why the path the quilt indicates is different from the route they mention in their letters. Although, I'm starting to understand the Drunkard's Path quilt block. Amos and Charles both mentioned delays, and that it was going to take longer to get to their destination. Perhaps they had to change their route and that's what the Drunkard's Path block represents."

"Do you know who made it?"

Sarah nodded. "I'm thinking it might have been a woman by the name of Maude Hollander. Two of the letters mention her working on a wedding quilt for her sister-in-law and I know she made it all the way to the Oregon Territory because the girls found her name in the census records."

"Is it possible she signed it anywhere?"

Sarah shook her head. "I haven't found a signature yet. I think the next step is to create a family tree. If Maude did make the quilt, she probably passed it down to one of her children, and so on, until it finally ended up with Patty's aunt Myrna."

"And then on to Patty," Martha said, "who gave it to Maggie."

Sarah nibbled at her cookie, thinking it through. "According to Patty's aunt, the quilt was made by one of the Hollander women who made the first journey west. More Hollanders probably followed at some point, but that first journey was the one chronicled in the quilt."

"Do you have a list of the women who made that journey?"

Sarah nodded, knowing them by heart. "Emma and her sister-in-law Maude, Harriet, and Charlotte. Emma is the only one of the three who isn't listed anywhere in the Oregon public records."

"That doesn't sound so bad," Martha said. "You have a twenty-five percent chance of picking the right one just by guessing. Once you gather some more information, it should be easy."

Sarah knew she was right, but there was one problem. Talking to Patty never seemed to be easy.

"I don't understand," Patty said. "Why do you need to know so much about my family?"

Sarah had wanted to talk to Patty after leaving Martha's house this morning, but Patty had chosen that day to hike on Greylock Mountain. She still had on her jogging gear, when

Sarah stopped by that evening, including a camelback water system that she had worn on her back to provide plenty of water for her hike.

Audrey and Amy weren't around either. Jason had taken them to the 4-H meeting where Martha was giving a demonstration on crocheting.

"If I can create a family tree," Sarah explained, "that will help me determine who made the quilt."

"And why is that so important?" Patty said. "Unless you're now questioning whether the quilt itself is authentic."

Maggie walked into the parlor carrying a pitcher of tea. "I'm sure that's not the reason, Mom." She refilled each of their glasses. "Sarah's just trying to help the girls with their project."

"That's right," Sarah affirmed. "There were four Hollander women who made the initial journey to the Oregon Territory. One of them must have made the quilt."

"I'm sure Aunt Myrna had those genealogy records stored somewhere, but I never came across them," Patty said. "All I can tell you is that my great-great-grandmother was one of the pioneers."

"Really?" Sarah wondered why Patty hadn't bothered to mention this before. "Which one?"

"Charlotte Hollander. She and Josiah were my great-great-grandparents. They're also the ones who built the new church in Willow Bend to carry on our family's faith traditions from Willow Creek."

Sarah jotted this information down in her notebook. "They both sound like very fine people in their letters. Josiah was the leader of the group from what I've read so far."

"Yes," Patty affirmed. "My side of the family has wonderful leadership abilities. I'm sure that's why Aunt Myrna put me in charge of the upcoming reunion. She knew I would make sure everything went off without a hitch."

Maggie sat down beside her mother on the sofa. "Do you want me to help you with that camelback, Mom? It looks uncomfortable."

"No, it's fine," Patty assured her. "Your father and I go hiking in California all the time, so I don't even notice it anymore."

Sarah glanced through her notes, then looked up at Patty. "So which of their children was your great-grandparent?"

"Henry Arthur Hollander," Patty said without hesitation. "He was the oldest of their children. And his son, Archibald Hollander was my grandfather."

Sarah drew lines between the names to connect them. "Do you know what happened to Emma Hollander? Did she ever make it to Oregon?"

Patty shook her head. "I'm sure I knew at one time, but I can't remember now."

"And Charles Hollander?"

"I have no idea," Patty said.

Maggie turned to her mother. "I thought you knew all about the Hollanders."

"I know about *our* branch of the Hollander family," Patty clarified. "Aunt Myrna is the one who kept track of the other branches."

Sarah wished there was someone to fill in the blanks. "I've read in the letters that Carl and Maude Hollander had six children. Do you know how they were related to Josiah and Charlotte?"

"That I do know," Patty stated. "Carl and Josiah were first cousins, although Josiah was several years older. Back then, there were such large families that it wasn't unusual for a child to have fifty or sixty cousins." She sighed. "My great-grandfather Henry married Olive Wentworth. She was the youngest of twelve children. Can you imagine how many grandchildren her parents had to account for? They probably had trouble remembering all their names."

"But that would be so much fun," Maggie said, "to have so many cousins. I always had a blast with the kids my age at the Hollander family reunions, but we only saw each other once a year."

Patty smiled at Sarah. "Can you imagine having ten more Audreys and Amys running around? I love my granddaughters, but just keeping them entertained these last few days has left me exhausted. I needed that hike today to reinvigorate myself."

"I keep telling you, Mom," Maggie said, "that you don't have to entertain the girls. They love just spending time with you."

"I know, dear," Patty said, "but I see them so rarely that I want our time together to be special." She turned to Sarah. "I'm sure you feel the same about your daughter and her family in Texas."

"Yes, I do," Sarah admitted. "Especially now that Jenna has a new baby. I talk to Thomas and Jonathan on the phone as often as I can, but they grow so quickly and I don't want to miss a minute of it."

"Exactly," Patty said, their eyes meeting in a rare moment of camaraderie.

"I get it, Mom," Maggie said to Patty. "I really do. And I appreciate all the things you're teaching them, but you don't have to do it all in one visit. You and Dad are both retired now. You can visit as often as you'd like."

Patty reached over and patted Maggie's leg. "I know, dear, and I appreciate the open invitation. I'll tell your father we should come more often. I'm sure there are one or two decent lakes around here where he could fish."

Sarah took her leave and headed home, appreciating the few tidbits of information she had been able to collect about the Hollander family. It was dark by the time she walked through the back door into her kitchen. She switched on the overhead light, then set her bag on the counter.

The house was chilly and Sarah rubbed her hands together as she made her way to the living room to start a fire. A short time later, she had a nice blaze going. She curled up on the sofa with the Hollander family booklet, pleased to see the next letter was by Emma.

June 20, 1849

Dear Beth,

Today I wonder if I will ever meet my Benjamin. We are at a standstill given the cholera that seems to be all around us. Our trail guide has taken ill and it has fallen upon me and the other women to nurse him. He is a stubborn man, but I will put up with no nonsense. If he does not survive, we cannot continue this journey on our own. His name is John Grant and he knows this wild country well. He is a little wild himself, with a bushy brown beard and long hair that needs a good pair of scissors as much as it needs a comb.

I keep hoping Harriet will succeed in taming him, using either her sharp tongue or her rifle. She has become an expert with both, but she seems to enjoy his wit and flirts with him shamelessly even though he is decades younger than she.

I talk of jests and flirting, but in my heart I fear for my nieces and nephews and the other children. We have passed too many small graves along the trail and I know that cholera can hit them the hardest. Maude is fussier than ever and, in this instance, I cannot blame her. She plagues Carl all the time, questioning the wisdom of making this journey. Fortunately, my brother will not waver. He knows the best future for their family is in the Oregon Territory. I just pray that they all make it there.

As for me, dear Beth, I am making my wedding dress in every spare moment, of which there are few, and I say a little prayer with each stitch. Every day that we draw closer to Salt Lake City, I wonder what awaits me. We've already passed Chimney Rock and I know that soon we will see mountains.

John claims they are higher and more majestic than any I have ever seen before, but I will not believe him until I see it with my own eyes. He likes to jest with us sometimes, even in his illness, but I will not be easily fooled by anyone.

I do not know when I shall be able to write again. Perhaps I will be a married woman when I next dip my quill in the ink-well and write your name. If that happens, my name will be different, but my affection for you will never change.

Your best friend,
Emma Hollander

Sarah set the booklet in her lap, enjoying the familiar crackling and snapping noises of the wood in the fireplace. She didn't use it as often as they had when Gerry was alive. He had chopped wood every year and stacked it in the garage. They had even roasted marshmallows in the fireplace a time or two, when the children were young.

The heat from the flames made her tired and she closed her eyes for a moment, remembering those happy times they had shared together.

The sound of the doorbell woke Sarah. She sat up, disoriented for a moment, then she realized she had fallen asleep in front of the fire.

When the doorbell rang again, she leapt off the sofa and hurried to the front door, patting her hair into place. It was late, almost eleven o'clock. She had no idea who could be stopping by so late.

CHAPTER FOURTEEN

Sasha Calhoun stood shivering on Sarah's front porch when she opened the door.

"Sasha!" Sarah exclaimed as a cold gust blew into the house. "What are you doing here?"

Tears filled Sasha's green eyes. "Please, Mrs. Hart, may I come in?"

Sasha didn't need to ask twice. Sarah pulled her inside and steered her toward the fire. The girl wore a short-sleeved, pink T-shirt, and her bare arms were as cold as ice. Sasha had on a pair of faded blue jeans, but the sandals she wore left her feet bare as well.

"The first thing we're going to do is get you warmed up," Sarah told her, settling Sasha on the sofa. She picked up the crocheted afghan on the back of the sofa and tucked it around the shivering girl. "I'll be right back."

Sarah hurried into the kitchen and poured a cup of milk into a mug, then heated it in the microwave for a little over a minute. When she took it out, she stirred in a spoonful each of sugar and cocoa powder, then carried the hot chocolate into the living room.

"Drink this," Sarah said gently, "it will warm you up."

Sasha didn't say anything as she took the cup from her and put it to her lips. She took a small sip at first, then a little more.

Sarah sat down in the rocking chair, waiting until Sasha was ready to talk. There had to be some reason that Sasha was out in this cold night without as much as a jacket.

"Thank you," Sasha said at last, daintily wiping the chocolate milk mustache from her upper lip. "I feel a little better now."

"Can you tell me what's going on?"

Sasha's eyes filled with tears. "I didn't know where else to go. Ian told me once that you rented rooms to people, so I was wondering if I could stay here for a little while."

"You want to rent one of my rooms?"

Sasha nodded. "I don't have a lot of money, but Ian said he would help me cover the cost." Her lower lip quivered. "I don't have anywhere else to go."

Sarah moved to the sofa, circling one arm around the girl's shoulders. "Sasha, what happened? Why do you want to leave home?"

"I don't want to leave," she replied, "but I don't have a choice." Her voice was choked with tears. "My dad said I had to go."

"Oh, Sasha," Sarah murmured as the girl buried her face in Sarah's shoulder and began to sob. She gently patted her back while the girl's athletic frame shook with her sobs.

It was obvious that the secret was now out. She wondered how Mark had discovered it and why Tracy had let him kick their daughter out of the house.

"He just doesn't understand," Sasha said through her tears. "He won't even try. I think he hates me!"

Sarah continued to comfort her, stroking the girl's long brown hair. "Honey, you know that's not true. Your parents both love you."

"Dad only loves the daughter he wants me to be." Sasha sniffed, then pulled back far enough for Sarah to see her tear-stained face. "As long as I was playing basketball and was the high scorer in every game, he was happy. But anytime I tried to do something else, like a normal high school girl, he'd get upset."

"How did he find out about you and Ian?" Sarah asked her.

"He looked at my cell phone," Sasha said, her tone full of indignation. "And he read all of my private text messages. There wasn't even anything bad in there. He told me I didn't have time for a boyfriend. So I told him that I'll have plenty of time when I turn down the offer from San Diego State. And that's when he kicked me out." Tears filled her eyes, her indignation melting into a pool of despair. "When I called Ian, he told me to come here."

A knock sounded at the door and Sasha stiffened, her eyes widening with apprehension. "If that's my dad, please don't let him in."

Sarah couldn't make her any promises, but if it was Mark Calhoun on her porch, she had a few things to say to him in private. She walked over to the door and peeked through the window. "It's Ian."

"Oh, good," Sasha said, relief flooding her voice.

Sarah opened the door to let him in. "Hello, Ian."

"Is Sasha..." His gaze fell on the sofa. "Sasha!"

She stood up as he hurried toward her. They hugged for a long moment, then he took a step back and said, "I'm so sorry this happened."

Sasha shook her head. "It's not your fault. And it doesn't matter now anyway. Dad finally knows and I'm out of the house. End of story."

Ian turned to Sarah. "Sasha can stay here, right?"

Sarah hesitated. The girl was eighteen, but she was also still in high school and not yet ready to be on her own. "Give me a minute," she said.

The two of them resumed talking, their heads together and their voices low.

Sarah headed into the kitchen and picked up the phone. Then she dialed the Calhoun residence.

Tracy Calhoun arrived at Sarah's house less than ten minutes later. Her blue eyes were red rimmed when Sarah opened the door to let her in.

"Oh, Sasha," she cried, running to her daughter and embracing her. "Why did you run out like that?"

"Dad told me to go," Sasha replied. "I didn't have any choice."

Tracy stepped back and reached out to tuck a stray lock of hair behind her daughter's ear. "Of course you had a choice, honey. You had to know how your father would react."

Sarah cringed. She had been hoping that Tracy would take Sasha's side, not make excuses for Mark.

"I didn't think he'd kick me out of my own house," Sasha exclaimed. Ian stood next to her, offering his silent support.

Tracy sighed as she looked at her daughter. "But it was a blow—to both of us. I have to be honest here, honey, I'm not sure you're making the wisest decision with this choice."

"I knew you'd take Dad's side," Sasha said.

"I'm not taking sides," Tracy clarified. "I'm trying to figure out what's best for my family."

"Ian and I want to be together," Sasha insisted. "And we can't if I go to San Diego."

"But you're both so young," Tracy cried. "You have the rest of your lives to be together. If you're meant to be, then four years apart won't matter."

Sarah knew Tracy meant well, but if someone had told her at eighteen that she should spend the next four years all the way across the country from Gerry, she would have rebelled as well. When you first love someone, even a day away from that person can seem like an eternity.

"My mind's made up, Mom," Sasha told her. "I'm not going to San Diego State. I'm going to stay here in Maple Hill and find a job so Ian and I can be together."

"What?" Ian exclaimed, turning to face Sasha. "You can't mean that, Sasha. You've got a full-ride scholarship to play basketball at a great college. I won't let you give up on your dream."

"It's not my dream anymore," Sasha told him. "Now I just want to be with you."

Ian stared at her a long moment, then pulled her close for a hug.

Tracy rubbed her temple with her fingertips. "It's late and we're all tired. Maybe you and your dad do need a small break from each other right now." She turned to Sarah. "May I rent a room here for Sasha for the next few days? I know it's a lot to ask to take in a teenager..."

"I'll be happy to have her," Sarah said, aware that this was a problem that couldn't be fixed in a day. It had been a long time coming from everything Sarah had gathered, and it had the potential to tear Sasha's family apart.

Tracy turned back to her daughter. "I thought this might happen, so I packed a small bag for you and brought it with me. But please promise to call me, day or night, if you need anything or just to talk."

Sasha nodded. "Okay."

"Promise?" Tracy asked again.

"I promise," Sasha said quietly.

Ian stepped forward. "I'll make sure she's all right, Mrs. Calhoun. I know you don't really know me all that well, but I just want Sasha to be happy."

Tracy nodded, her mouth tight. Then she turned to go.

Sasha followed her mother out the door and retrieved her bag from the car. When she returned to the house, she handed a week's rent to Sarah. "Will this be enough?"

"It's more than enough," Sarah said, handing some of the money back to her. She kept only enough to buy extra food for the next few days. This was an unusual situation and Sarah didn't want to profit from it. She just wanted to help.

"You should probably head home now," Sarah told Ian. "It's late and your folks are probably worried."

He nodded and looked at his girlfriend. "I'll see you tomorrow. And please promise me that you'll reconsider going to San Diego."

"Right now, I just want to go to sleep," Sasha said wearily.

Sarah watched Ian walk out the door, wishing he would realize the importance of following his own dreams too. She just hoped he was listening to his heart instead of his hormones.

After Ian left, Sarah showed Sasha to her room. She had two rooms available for boarders upstairs and both of them happened to be empty this month. As they made their way up the stairs, Sasha sniffled quietly behind her, still upset after the meeting with her mother.

When they reached the top of the stairs, Sasha stopped to look at the small, open sitting room. It contained a love seat and two overstuffed chairs, along with a television and a bookcase along one wall.

"This is nice," Sasha said. "It looks like a good place to do homework."

"You'll have the upstairs all to yourself," Sarah told her. "My only rule is no visitors up here without permission." She hadn't played chaperone since Jason and Jenna were teenagers, but she would have to get into the routine again for as long as Sasha was here.

Sasha followed Sarah to the first bedroom. The soft yellow walls and the green and pink Nine Patch quilt on the twin bed gave the room a peaceful serenity that she thought Sasha could use about now.

"You can put your clothes in the closet or the dresser," Sarah said, pointing out the tall oak dresser opposite the bed. "There are extra blankets in the bottom drawer if you get cold tonight."

"Okay." Sasha set the bag her mother had packed for her on the foot of the bed. The girl looked around the room as if trying to get her bearings.

"And this way to the bathroom," Sarah told her, leading Sasha to the bathroom next to her bedroom. There were freshly laundered white hand towels stacked on the marble topped vanity and two large white towels hanging from the towel rack next to the shower.

"You'll find everything you might need in here." Sarah opened the door of the linen cupboard. "Shampoo, soap, toothpaste, hair spray. There's a hair dryer and a curling iron under the sink too."

"You've thought of everything," Sasha said. Her eyes were red rimmed from crying and her complexion was pale.

"It's late," Sarah said. "I'll let you get ready for bed. Just let me know if there's anything you need."

"Thank you." Sasha followed Sarah to the stairs. "And thank you again for letting me stay here. I don't know what I would have done without you."

Sarah smiled. "Things will look better in the morning. They always do." Then she thought of something else. "What time do you need to get up for school?"

Sasha thought for a moment. "I usually set my alarm for about seven o'clock."

"There's an alarm clock on your nightstand if you need it," Sarah told her.

"That's all right." Sasha pulled a cell phone from her pocket. "I use the alarm on my phone." Then her phone began to buzz and the shadow of a smile crossed her face. "Ian just sent me a text. He just got home and wanted to tell me good night." She looked up at Sarah. "Isn't he the sweetest guy ever?"

"He's very nice," Sarah said, realizing Sasha truly did care about him and wasn't just rebelling against her father. "Can I get you anything before bed? Maybe another cup of hot chocolate?"

"Thanks, but I'm good," Sasha said as she began to text on her phone, her thumbs flying over the miniature keyboard.

Sarah made her way downstairs, hoping that Sasha and Ian didn't text each other all night. The girl looked exhausted and could use some sleep, but she wasn't in any position to take Sasha's cell phone away from her.

This was a sticky situation, Sarah told herself as she turned off the lights downstairs and headed for her bedroom. Sasha was legally an adult, but Tracy had entrusted Sarah with her care until their family problems could be worked out. Sarah would have to find a balance between serving as a parental figure and as a landlord.

When she said her prayers that night, she included Sasha and her family in them.

"Almighty God," Sarah began. "Be with the Calhoun family as they deal with difficult issues. Bless Sasha and her father and mother. Give them patience and understanding and guide them back to each other. And please give me wisdom, Lord, as I try to be a peacemaker." She took a deep breath, then said, "Amen."

 CHAPTER FIFTEEN

S arah awoke early that Thursday morning, her mind still dwelling on the events from the night before. She climbed out of bed and wrapped a robe around her nightgown, then made her way into the kitchen to start the coffee.

As she filled the glass carafe at the sink, she looked out the window to see another beautiful day dawning. She loved the month of May, with each day stretching longer until dusk, and the flowers, trees and shrubs all around Maple Hill blooming with beautiful colors.

She poured the water into the coffee machine, added grounds to the filter, then turned it on. As the coffee brewed, she walked to the stairs, listening intently, but she could hear no movement overhead.

It wasn't quite seven o'clock yet, so she was glad that Sasha was still asleep. She padded into her sewing room and retrieved the Hollander family booklet. The aroma of brewing coffee filled the air as she sat down at the kitchen table. She needed to get through these letters more quickly if she wanted to reconcile the journey chronicled by the quilt with the one the Hollander pioneers had written about in their letters home.

She was due to meet with the twins tonight and help them with their project. Sarah couldn't wait to see what they thought of the history in those letters and why they differed so much from the quilt.

When the coffee was done brewing, Sarah poured herself a cup, then grabbed a bran muffin from the freezer and warmed it in the microwave. She carried both the muffin and the coffee back to the table with her and began to read the next letter in the booklet.

June 28, 1849

Dear Pastor Simpson,

My heart is heavy as I write this missive to you. My youngest child, the light of my life, my sweet, little Hattie has been taken from me. I cannot bear to write the words without my soul shattering. Why has the Lord forsaken me, Pastor? Why did we ever undertake this journey? Every day I ask myself if Hattie would still be with us if we had not left Willow Creek. It is a question with no answer, but I ask it of myself and of Josiah over and over again.

Thomas weeps daily for his sister and blames himself. She was walking alongside him as he helped his father steer the oxen on the trail. She tripped on something, we know not what, and fell. Before anyone could reach her, the wagon wheel rolled over her and crushed her small body.

She died in my arms, Pastor, and I do not remember what happened for the rest of that day and into the night. Josiah tells me that I was wild with grief and could not be comforted. I would not let anyone touch her and cradled her in my arms for hours until I finally fell into a faint sleep, weak from exhaustion.

The next day we buried her. I would let none of the other women help me prepare her body. I washed her myself and combed her long, red hair. Then I wove her hair into the braids that she loved so much. I placed her favorite blue dress upon her small body but left her feet bare. She always loved to run in the tall grass with bare feet, despite my warning of snakes and thorns. Now, nothing can hurt her.

I wept as I wrapped her in my mother's wedding quilt and carried her to the small grave that the men had dug. It is in the middle of the trail and will be unmarked. Pastor, I cannot put into words the pain that I felt when they laid her body there. I left not only my daughter on that lonely prairie but my heart as well. Our trail guide said a prayer, as Josiah was too overcome with grief to speak. As the service for Hattie ended, my poor Thomas fell onto the grave, calling his little sister's name. She was the shining light of our family and we all feel lost in the darkness without her.

I turn in my Bible to the Psalms and recite this passage over and over again. "'My heart is in anguish within me; the terrors of death have fallen on me. Fear and trembling have beset me; horror has overwhelmed me. I said, 'Oh, that I had the wings of a dove! I would fly away and be at rest. I would flee far away

and stay in the desert; I would hurry to my place of shelter, far
from the tempest and storm.'"

I do not know if we can continue on our mission, Pastor. I
feel as if God has forsaken us and I want to turn back home. We
will have failed you and our church brothers and sisters, but I
do not know how we can go on.

Yours in grief,
Charlotte Hollander

Sarah had tears in her eyes when she finished reading
Charlotte's letter. The grief Charlotte had expressed had
been so real and raw. She wondered how Charlotte and
Josiah had continued on their journey. It was impossible for
her to know what she would have done in the same situation.
Just the thought of losing one of her children or grandchildren made her throat tighten with emotion.

She took another sip of her coffee, trying to collect herself
before turning to the next letter in the booklet.

July 2, 1849

Dear Ma,

I write to you with the sad news of the passing of Hattie
Hollander. She died in an accident on the trail and was buried
there three days ago. Josiah and Charlotte and little Thomas
were all overcome with grief. I dug the grave for the poor girl
and patted the soil firmly over her so that the wolves and coy-
otes would not find her body.

Emma left one lone wildflower upon the grave as the wagon
train started to move west once again. The wind will blow
the flower away soon enough, but I hope that a tiny seed was

planted there to mark the grave of that happy child. We will all miss Hattie's smiles and her lively chatter.

Fort Kearney is now a day away and I hope that a sojourn there will refresh our spirits. Josiah and Charlotte have agreed to wait until we arrive there to decide if they will continue with us to the Oregon Territory. Their burdens are heavy and their hearts torn, but as you have always reminded me, time is a great healer.

If we leave Josiah and Charlotte at Fort Kearney and Emma at Salt Lake City, that means Carl, Maude, Harriet, Charles, and I will be the only Hollanders that remain to carry on this journey. I feel we must persuade Josiah that he continue his mission; we cannot abandon it now.

Whatever happens, I will do my best to make you proud, Mother, and ask once again for your prayers.

Your devoted son,
Amos

Sarah finished the letter, confused by something she had read. Amos had mentioned that they would arrive at Fort Kearney in one day, but that made no sense when Emma had written almost two weeks earlier that they had already passed Chimney Rock. Sarah closed the booklet and walked into her sewing room to retrieve the historical map of the Oregon Trail that she had printed out earlier.

Sarah set the map on top of her desk and found Chimney Rock, marking it with one of the T-pins she used for her quilts. Then she found Fort Kearney on the map and marked it with another T-pin.

According to the map, Chimney Rock was located hundreds of miles north and west of Fort Kearney. If they had been there two weeks before Amos wrote that letter to his mother, that meant they had backtracked on the trail and lost both time and miles on the journey.

She headed to the dining room, wanting to check the quilt but almost certain that the quilt block depicting Fort Kearney came *before* the quilt block depicting Chimney Rock. *That* would make sense and gave her one more reason to believe that the quilt had recorded the actual journey. So why did the letters differ so much?

Was it possible that both Emma and Amos had been lying? She found it difficult to believe that Emma would deceive her best friend and that Amos would lie to his mother who meant so much to him.

But what other possible explanation could there be? And even if she could prove that was the case, Sarah was still left wondering why.

Even stranger, there was a gravestone block on the quilt set between the Fort Kearney and the Chimney Rock quilt blocks, yet the initials on the gravestone were C.H., not H.H. as she had expected after reading about the accidental death of Hattie Hollander.

"Mrs. Hart?" Sasha called out.

Sarah left the dining room and met Sasha at the bottom of the stairs. "Good morning. How did you sleep?"

"Okay," Sasha said. "I was pretty tired, but I have a little bit of a headache this morning."

Sarah wasn't surprised. Someone who had cried that much and that hard was bound to be a little dehydrated. "You need some water," she said, steering the girl toward the kitchen. "And some orange juice might help with that headache too."

"I don't usually eat breakfast," Sasha told her.

"Well, I don't start the day without it in this house." Sarah poured her a glass of orange juice and checked the clock on the stove. "I have some instant oatmeal, so it won't take too long."

"I guess that sounds okay," Sasha replied, "if you're sure it's not too much trouble."

"Not at all." Sarah prepared the instant oatmeal and popped it into the microwave. While it cooked, she filled a big glass with water and set it in front of Sasha.

"I'm not sure I can drink that much," Sasha told her.

"Just do your best. The more you drink, the better you'll feel."

A minute later, the microwave dinged, signaling that the oatmeal was done. Sarah took it out and stirred it with a spoon. The porridge was a little thick, so she added some milk, then gave it another stir.

"Here you go," Sarah told her, setting the bowl in front of her. "Be careful, it might be hot."

Sasha took a cautious bite. "Wow, this is good." She spooned up another bite, blowing on the spoon for a moment before putting it in her mouth.

Sarah added more orange juice to her glass, happy to see Sasha finish all of the oatmeal and drain the orange juice before getting up from the table.

"Thanks for breakfast," Sasha told her. "My headache does feel a little better."

"I'm glad to hear it." Sarah picked up the dirty dishes as Sasha grabbed her backpack.

"I'd better get going."

"Let me give you a key before you go," Sarah said, moving into her sewing room. She kept her spare keys for her boarders hidden in the bottom drawer of her desk.

A moment later, she returned to the kitchen and handed a key to Sasha. "I'm not sure I'll be home when you get back from school, so just let yourself in. Help yourself to a snack if you're hungry."

"Okay." Sasha took the key from her and dropped it into the pocket of her jeans. Then she headed toward the back door.

"Have a good day," Sarah called after her.

"Thanks, I'll try." Sasha closed the kitchen door behind her, leaving Sarah alone in the kitchen once more.

It was going to be tricky to work on Sasha's quilt while the girl was living in the house. Sarah would have to work on it during the day and put it away before Sasha got home from school. Sarah didn't know how long the girl would be living here, but graduation was coming up soon and she had promised Tracy that the quilt would be finished by then.

Sarah spent most of the morning and early afternoon working on Sasha's quilt, stopping only long enough to phone Martha and fill her in on the latest details involving Sasha and Ian.

Later that afternoon, Sarah headed over to Jason's house to meet the twins and talk to them about the route the Hollander pioneers had taken to Oregon.

"Wait until you see what we did," Amy said when she met Sarah at the front door. She wore a lime green tracksuit and white tennis shoes with lime green trim.

"I like your outfit," Sarah told her.

"Thanks. Grammy got one for me and one for Audrey, but hers is blue."

Amy led the way into the dining room. Audrey and Patty were already there. Audrey wore an electric blue athletic suit with white tennis shoes and matching electric blue trim. Patty wore a tracksuit as well, only hers was powder blue and her silver gray hair was pulled back into a high ponytail.

Their attire made Sarah smile, thinking they looked more like triplets than twins with their grandmother.

"Hello, Patty," Sarah said.

Patty looked up. "Nice to see you again, Sarah. May I get you something to drink? I have some new herbal tea that is quite good if you'd like a cup."

"That sounds nice," Sarah replied as her gaze moved to the far end of the dining room where an easel was set up near the window. It had a large map of the Oregon Trail on it.

"Did you girls make that?" Sarah asked, impressed with the size and scope of the map.

"We've been working on it for days," Patty said as she moved toward the doorway. "Do you girls want anything to eat or drink?"

"I'll have a strawberry banana smoothie, please," Audrey told her.

"Me too," Amy added. "And can I have extra strawberries in mine, Grammy?"

"Coming right up," Patty said, then she disappeared down the hallway.

"Grammy makes us whatever food we want," Amy told Sarah. "And she takes us shopping almost every day. We're even going shopping in Pittsfield tonight after you leave."

Audrey scowled at her sister. "Amy, that's not nice to say. You're going to make Gram think we're just waiting for her to leave."

Amy turned to Sarah, concern lining her face. "Oh, I didn't mean that, Gram."

"I know you didn't, dear," Sarah assured her. "Don't worry about it. I'm glad you're having such a good time with your Grammy." Then her gaze moved back to the historic map on the easel. "How did you make the map so big?"

"Well, first we used the graphic software on our computer to design it," Amy explained, "and then we printed off each section on a separate piece of paper."

Audrey walked over to the easel. "Grammy took us downtown to buy some poster board and this easel. Then we used invisible tape to connect all the pieces of the map together so it all looks like one piece."

"You did an excellent job," Sarah said. She couldn't even see the taped seams from where she stood and hoped their history teacher would be impressed as well.

"We've been reading the letters too," Audrey said. "They're not as boring as I thought they'd be."

"The one where the little girl got run over by the wagon was really sad," Amy said solemnly. "I stopped reading them after that one."

"Me too," Audrey admitted as Patty returned to the room carrying a tray of beverages.

"Here's your tea," Patty said, handing a cup to Sarah.

"Thank you, Patty," Sarah said.

Patty turned to the twins. "And two smoothies for my two best girls." She had put little pink umbrellas in each of the tall glasses.

"Thanks, Grammy," the girls said in unison.

"You're very welcome." Patty turned toward the map. "Now, what did I miss?"

"We were just talking about the letters," Sarah told her. "So far, I've noticed that the route mentioned in the letters actually differs quite a bit from the route depicted on the quilt."

"We noticed that too!" Audrey exclaimed, exchanging a high five with her sister. "It's just weird."

Sarah was glad they were so observant. "I think we should mark each route and see what they look like." She turned to Audrey. "Do you have any colored tacks?"

"I think Dad has some in his office," Audrey said, setting her smoothie aside. "I'll go look."

After Audrey left the room, Patty looked over at Sarah. "Isn't it possible the quilt maker just placed the blocks randomly on the quilt?"

"It's possible," Sarah admitted, "but not very likely. The workmanship in this quilt is some of the best I've ever seen. At this point, I think the quilt maker may have been Maude Hollander. There's more than one letter writer who talks about her quilting on the trail and she's one of the women who made it all the way to the Oregon Territory."

Patty sighed. "It just seems that you're making the girls go to a lot of extra work. The letters clearly detail the journey, so why bother comparing them to the quilt?"

"Because if the quilt is correct," Sarah said slowly, "then there must be a reason your ancestors lied about their route to the people back in Willow Creek. I find that intriguing, don't you?"

Patty didn't respond and, a moment later, Audrey returned to the room with a box of colored tacks.

"I'll mark the quilt trail in green," Audrey said, opening the box and setting it on the dining room table, "And Amy can mark the trail in the letters in red."

Audrey picked up a green tack. "They both start in Willow Creek, she said, placing a tack there while her sister did the same. "Then the next quilt block shows them in Missouri, which means they probably bought their supplies in Saint Joseph or Independence."

"And the letters describe them buying all that stuff in Nebraska City," Amy said, placing a red tack in that spot. "They don't mention Missouri at all."

The girls continued placing the different colored tacks on the map and explaining the differences between the routes. Patty looked on but didn't say anything, her foot tapping silently against the floor.

Amy put a red tack at Chimney Rock, then another at Fort Kearney. "This is as far as I got in the letters, but look." She picked up a pencil and drew a line, starting with the first tack she had placed all the way to the last tack at Fort Kearney. The winding, backtracking line showed exactly why Sarah questioned the veracity of the letters.

While she was drawing that line, Audrey had continued placing her green tacks along the route shown by the quilt until she reached the mystery block. "I'm not sure where they went next," she said, then placed a green tack in the state of Oregon, "but here's where they ended up if they followed the landmarks on the quilt."

"Oh my, it looks like you girls have some work left to do to figure this out," Patty said. "Though the letters must be right. The Hollanders have always been an honest people. If they did take that zigzag route, there must have been a good reason."

Sarah agreed with part of Patty's statement. There must have been a good reason for them to obfuscate their route, and she and the twins needed to keep digging until they found that reason.

CHAPTER SIXTEEN

That evening, Sarah arrived home to find Sasha and Ian sitting together on the front porch swing, their heads bent close together.

The air still had a chill in it as she climbed out of her car and walked to the front of the house. When the couple saw her, they quickly moved apart.

"Hello," Sarah said, making her way up the porch steps. "How was school?"

"Fine," Sasha replied, then quickly stood up. "I didn't let Ian in the house, Mrs. Hart. We've just been sitting out here the whole time."

Sarah smiled. "It's a bit chilly out here. Why don't you two come inside, and I'll fix you something to eat."

"Thanks, Mrs. H," Ian said, "but I have to go home soon. Can Sasha and I just stay out here a few more minutes?"

"Of course," Sarah said, moving toward the door. "I'll go in and start supper."

Sasha sat back down on the swing and the two of them were mooning over each other before Sarah even made it into the house. She remembered what it was like to be young and in love. Now that they thought the world was against them, they would probably grow even closer.

By the time Sarah had chicken stew warming on the stove, Sasha came into the house and was speaking into her phone.

"Okay, I will," Sasha said. "Yeah. Me too. Bye."

Sasha hung up the phone and slipped it into her pocket. "That was my mom. She just wanted to check in with me and said to tell you hello."

Sarah was glad that Sasha and her mother were still communicating. "Have you heard from your dad?"

"No." Sasha walked over to the stove and bent down over the stew. "This smells great. I'm starving."

"It should be ready." Sarah handed her a bowl and a spoon. "Go ahead and dish up some for yourself."

Sasha picked up the ladle near the stove and filled her bowl. Then she turned to Sarah. "Do you mind if I eat this upstairs? I need to start on my homework."

"No, that's fine," Sarah said as she dished up a bowl for herself. "Just let me know if you need anything."

"I will," Sasha said as she headed toward the stairs.

Sarah carried her bowl of stew into her sewing room and set it down on her desk. She had been eager to continue reading the pioneer letters ever since she had returned from Jason's house. Patty seemed determined to stick up for the integrity of her ancestors and Sarah really couldn't blame her, but the truth was important too. Sarah wanted her granddaughters to know their full family history, both the good and the bad.

Sarah's own family had a great-great-great-uncle who had robbed banks and spent time in prison. He had disappeared shortly after his release and none of her ancestors had ever heard from him again. Every family had a black sheep, she supposed, but they were also part of the fabric of a family's history.

Sarah settled in to read more about the Hollander pioneers and the journey on the Oregon Trail.

July 17, 1849

Dear Pastor Simpson,

We are making our way west through the mountains as I write this letter. We grieve for our little Hattie every day and Charlotte weeps for her every night. These mountains are beyond description. Their height and majesty serve to remind me of God's magnificent presence in our lives and soothe my weary soul. I know now that we made the right decision at Fort Kearney. Returning to Willow Creek would not have brought our sweet daughter back to us. Indeed, our hearts might have ached even more to live in that place that holds so many memories of her. So now we continue on to fulfill our mission and settle in the Oregon Territory.

Despite our new determination, danger is still with us. We do our best to ward off the evil in our midst, but not everyone on the wagon train is watchful. I pray that we come through these mountains unscathed and I will do my best to protect our special cargo.

This mission keeps me from despairing in my grief, but there are some days I still find it difficult to even draw breath. If I have one solace, it is when I look into the heavens each night. I stand under a glittering canopy of stars and know that these same stars light the night sky above Hattie's grave on the prairie. I know that God will see us through this and I pray for the peace that surpasses all understanding.

Your humble servant,
Josiah Hollander

Sarah took another bite of her stew and realized it was growing cold. After taking a few moments to finish her supper, she started to read the next letter, excited to see she had finally caught up to Emma's letter from Salt Lake City.

July 23, 1849

Dear Beth,

We are camped outside of Salt Lake City and tomorrow morning I will meet Benjamin for the first time ever. The wagon train will stay long enough for the wedding, then take its leave. My heart beats so fast I can hear it in my ears. I know I shall not rest tonight, for tomorrow I shall be a bride.

Carl has sent word to Benjamin that we have arrived. I haven't been able to sit still for more than a moment today as I keep thinking of chores that need to be done before I leave my family behind to start a new life.

My wedding dress is complete and fits me perfectly. I shall be wearing it the first time Benjamin sees me and I hope it will help him fall in love with me. I hope he wears a black suit and a tie and clean boots. John has tried to jest with me about the wedding, but I am too nervous to find anything funny today.

Charlotte was kind enough to make me a white lace handkerchief for my wedding. She seldom smiles anymore, but she is sweet and kind. She sings softly to herself, mostly hymns, and they seem to comfort her.

Harriet has suggested that I buy a rifle before the wedding in case my husband turns out to be a scoundrel. I am not quite sure if she is in jest or serious, but I refuse to think ill thoughts of Benjamin. I have waited too long and come too far to have second thoughts now.

I wish you could be at my wedding tomorrow, Beth, to help calm my nerves. I shall be better when I see Benjamin, for it is the unknown that creates fear. In a few more hours, I shall be Mrs. Carson and my new life will begin.

I shall pray tonight that God blesses my marriage and that he watches over the man who is to be my husband.

> *Your friend,*
> *Emma Hollander*

Sarah quickly turned the next page, eager to see what Emma had thought of her new husband.

July 24, 1849

Dear Cornelia,

We ate a wedding feast today, but there was no bride or groom to share it with us. Emma was to marry a man named

Benjamin Carson, but when Carl went to fetch him, he was told that Mr. Carson left Salt Lake City a week ago with no intention of ever returning. Poor Emma could not believe the news and even accused her brother of lying to her. She insisted on going into the city herself to find Mr. Carson, and our trail guide John was kind enough to escort her.

They came back to the camp at dusk and Emma refused to speak to anyone. She spent the whole of the evening in Carl's schooner, and even her nieces and nephews could not cajole her into joining the rest of us for the evening meal we had prepared to celebrate the wedding.

John did not give us many details of their trip into town, but he told us that there will be no wedding and that a man who treats a woman that way should be hung from the tallest tree. I contend that Mr. Carson did Emma a favor by revealing the yellow streak on his underbelly before the marriage. Emma is young and strong, both excellent traits for a single woman in the Oregon Territory. I have no doubt she will meet a bachelor there who will want her for a wife.

Our journey continues and so do our troubles, it seems. My grandson still plagues me about my rifle and I have offered to give it to him when we make our land claim in the Oregon Territory, but his heart is still set on California. The more days that pass, the more worried I am that Charles will not come to his senses before it is too late.

It is getting dark and my eyes are tired. I shall write again when I can. All my love to you and the family.

Your devoted mother,
Harriet Hollander

Sarah set down the booklet, feeling bad for Emma Hollander as if the woman had been left at the altar yesterday instead of more than a hundred and sixty years before. Was it possible she went on to Oregon and there was simply no census record of her there?

Sarah needed to dig deeper to find the answers that she couldn't discover in the letters. Tomorrow, she would make another trip to the Maple Hill Historical Society.

On Friday afternoon, Sarah sat at the computer workstation in the corner of the historical society building. She was most curious to figure out the initials C.H. on the gravestone quilt block. Maybe finding more information on the children who had made the trip west would give her a lead.

Josiah and Charlotte had mentioned their children by name—Thomas and Hattie. Emma had referred to Carl and Maude's children but hadn't mentioned any of their names. Amos and Charles were both bachelors and Harriet a grandmother, so there were no other children along with this particular group.

She decided to start from the beginning of the journey. She brought up the Pennsylvania online census records and searched for Carl Hollander. A moment later, his name popped up in a marriage record and she jotted the results down in her notebook.

Carl Hollander and Maude Downing, married July 21, 1839, in Willow Creek, Pennsylvania.

Sarah circled Maude's maiden name, then searched for Maude Downing. After several minutes, a result popped onto the screen. Maude was listed there, along with her parents, her grandparents, her eight siblings, and best of all, her children.

Sarah picked up her pen and added the names to her notebook: *Mary, Albert, Violet, Joseph, Anna, and Arabella Hollander.* None of them started with a C, so she decided to dig deeper.

She accessed the Oregon census records again and looked up each name. To her surprise, every one of Carl and Maude's six children were listed in the Oregon census. That meant none of them had died on the journey.

So if Maude had made the quilt, who was the C.H. on the gravestone block? She tapped her pencil against her notebook, thinking of all the possibilities. Then she remembered some of Emma's comments about her sister-in-law. It sounded as if Emma had charge of Maude's children while Maude spent much of her time on Emma's wedding quilt.

Perhaps Maude had needed the rest if she was expecting a baby, Sarah thought to herself. Was it possible that she had lost a newborn baby with the initials C.H. during the four-month journey to the Oregon Territory? Sarah was speculating now, but infant mortality had been very high during that time period—especially on the Oregon Trail, where there was poor nutrition, no medical care, and little time for recovery when the wagon train needed to keep moving westward. It made her think of Jenna and Leah, how they had received the best medical care during labor and delivery. "Thank you, Lord," she whispered, "for guiding the doctors and nurses as they care for people each day. And for blessing us with the medical knowledge to prevent and treat diseases that were so prevalent in the past. Amen."

After closing the browser window on the computer, Sarah gathered her things to leave.

"Did you find what you needed?" Irene called out to her. She stood on a ladder in front of a bookcase, handing down a large volume to her husband Chris, who stood at the base of the ladder.

"Some of it," Sarah replied. She waved to them both, then made her way outside. It was a gorgeous spring day, much nicer than the day before.

Sarah was tempted to go for a drive around Greylock Mountain, then remembered that Sasha would be home from school soon. Part of her liked having a teenager in the house again and she enjoyed cooking for two, but she had lost some of the independence she enjoyed so much.

Tomorrow, she and Martha were headed to Albany for the day. She had mentioned that date to Sasha last night before they went to bed and she had promised to talk to her mother about the fact that Sarah wouldn't be home all day.

She knew Sasha was old enough to stay there by herself, but she wanted Mark and Tracy Calhoun to be informed since they had entrusted Sarah with the care of their daughter.

"Dear Lord," Sarah prayed as she turned her car toward Hillside Avenue, "please help me be a peacemaker between Sasha and her family. Give me the right words to say to open all of their hearts. Amen."

CHAPTER SEVENTEEN

I can't believe we're finally here," Martha said as they pulled into Albany on Saturday morning. "I needed to get out of town for a bit after all the family drama this week."

They had left Maple Hill around eight thirty that morning, first stopping at the Spotted Dog to buy some coffee to go. Albany was just a little over an hour away when traffic was light, and Sarah and Martha had spent much of the time talking about everything under the sun—the Hollander quilt, Ian and Sasha, even the weather.

Sasha had still been asleep when Sarah had left that morning. Ian had stopped by for another sojourn on the porch swing last night, which was a pretty tame date by today's standards. Sasha and her mother had plans to go to lunch today and Sarah hoped that their lunch would be a first step toward reconciling their family.

"I've got a big day of yarn shopping planned," Martha continued, as they turned onto Albany Shaker Road and proceeded toward the parking lot of the Desmond Hotel.

"When do you want to meet up?" Sarah asked her.

"Oh, that's for you to decide. I'm just along for the ride. And for lunch," Martha quickly added. "We can't forget about lunch."

Sarah smiled as she checked her watch. "The quilt show starts at ten, so let's meet at one o'clock for a late lunch. By then I'll know if I need more time at the show or if I'm ready to go."

Martha nodded. "Don't forget that we need to stop by that big party store and buy decorations for Ian's party before we leave town."

"I won't," Sarah said as Martha pulled up to the front entrance of the hotel. "Have fun at the knitting store."

"I will. You have fun at your conference. And good luck identifying that quilt block!"

As Sarah climbed out of Martha's car, she checked her bag to make sure she had the picture of the mystery block with her. She couldn't wait to show it around to fellow quilters and get their opinion on it.

The Desmond Hotel had a lovely, peaceful ambiance and the stately conference rooms were the perfect place for a quilt show. Sarah followed the signs to the Albany Quilt Show and soon mingled with fellow quilters, many of whom she recognized.

"Hey, Sarah," called someone behind her.

She turned to see a short woman waving at her. "Gwen," Sarah said with a smile, "this is a nice surprise."

Gwen Winters was around thirty and often won prizes for her quilting work at the Eastern States Exposition in Springfield, Massachusetts.

"How are you?" Gwen asked, walking up to her.

"Fine, thanks. Are you exhibiting one of your quilts today?"

Gwen smiled, tucking a strand of her long, black hair behind her ear. "No, I decided to just come for the show. I find looking at other people's quilts to be so inspiring for my own work."

"I know what you mean." Sarah pulled the picture out of her bag. "Speaking of other people's works, I'm trying to identify a pattern on a vintage album quilt that I'm restoring." She held out the photo. "Does this look familiar to you?"

Gwen looked at the picture, her brow furrowed. "Well, the outside of the block looks like a variation of the Snake Trail pattern."

"I thought so too," Sarah said. "But it's the tree in the middle that I can't quite figure out."

Gwen's eyes widened. "I've seen this tree pattern before. This is a redbud tree."

Sarah nodded, finally making the connection. "You're right. It's an obscure pattern and this is a variation as well, but I knew I had seen this somewhere before."

Gwen looked up at her. "So why do you think it's included with the Snake Trail pattern?"

Sarah shook her head. "It doesn't really make sense, does it?"

"It sure doesn't." Gwen shrugged her narrow shoulders. "I wish I knew the answer. In fact, now I'm intrigued. Where did you get the quilt?"

Sarah gave her a short history of the pioneer quilt and the letters that had accompanied it, drawing the attention of another quilter.

"That is absolutely fascinating," a tall, blonde woman said, then introduced herself. "I'm Cassidy York and I collect pioneer quilts, but I've never heard of one quite like that."

"It's a lovely piece," Sarah told Gwen and Cassidy. "The workmanship is some of the best I've seen and each block seems to have a special meaning. It's only this one block that I don't quite understand."

Cassidy looked at the picture, then shook her head. "You've got me stumped." Then she smiled. "No pun intended. But I do know that early settlers used the blossoms of the redbud in their salads. I've got an old pioneer cookbook and there's a recipe in it that calls for redbud blossoms."

Sarah nodded, appreciating the information but still struggling to figure out why the quilt block was part of the Hollander pioneer quilt. She could understand the Snake Trail reference, given that they were traveling near the Snake River. But what was the possible significance of the redbud tree?

Sarah decided to let that question simmer in the back of her mind for a while as she made her way around the quilt show. A wide variety of exhibits displayed both vintage quilts and brand-new ones of all different colors, patterns, and sizes. Before she knew it, three hours had passed and she was due to meet Martha for lunch.

Martha was waiting in her van under the carport at the front entrance when Sarah left the hotel. "How was the show?"

"Fantastic. I saw some great new techniques and so many wonderful quilts. I took some pictures to help me generate ideas for my next project."

"When will that be?"

Sarah sighed. "As soon as I figure out this pioneer quilt and finish Sasha's T-shirt quilt. The latter is going to take a little longer than I had planned now that she's living with me. I don't want to spoil the surprise by letting her see it."

Martha pulled out from under the carport and made her way back to the street. "So what's next on the schedule? Lunch and then back to the quilt show?"

Sarah thought for a moment, then shook her head. "No, I think I've seen everything there I want to see. How was the knitting store, by the way?"

Martha smiled. "Take a look in the backseat."

Sarah turned around and got her answer. The entire backseat was full of plastic, drawstring bags with the knitting store logo on them. "It looks like you bought more than will fit into your closet."

"I know," Martha said with a happy sigh. "I'll find some way to make it work, even if I have to store yarn in the potato bin."

Sarah laughed, enjoying her day in Albany. She might not have found the answer she was seeking about the mystery block, but she was one step closer to figuring it out.

Later that day, Martha dropped off Sarah in front of her house and sped away, eager to hide her new yarn purchases before Ernie came home from the auto show in Pittsfield.

Sarah walked into the house, tired from the trip but feeling energized at the same time. She and Martha had found some nice decorations for Ian's party and discussed the menu, planning to make all of his favorites.

"Hello?" Sarah called out as she walked toward the stairs. "Sasha? Are you here?"

There was no answer. She hoped that meant that Sasha and her mother were spending time together. Maybe even Mark had relented a little and the three of them were trying to work things out.

Sarah carried her bag into the sewing room, telling herself this would be a good time to work on Sasha's quilt. But first she wanted to add the information about the redbud tree to her quilting notebook.

She sat down at her desk and opened the notebook, skimming through her notes as she turned to a new page. There hadn't been one mention of a redbud tree, or any other tree for that matter, in any of the letters. There was a mountain laurel tree on the first quilt block, but that made sense as it was the state tree of Pennsylvania, the place from which the Hollander pioneers had emigrated.

So what did the redbud tree represent?

Sarah tapped her pen against the desk, sensing that the answer was close. So she decided to look in the simplest and most common place a person could find information—an encyclopedia.

Sarah booted up her computer and typed the Web address for an online encyclopedia. When the Web page appeared on the screen she typed the words *redbud tree* into the search box.

A few moments later, the information appeared, along with a picture of the dainty tree with its bright rosy pink blooms that appeared every spring.

"The redbud tree is a deciduous tree that grows to a full height of thirty to forty feet," Sarah read aloud. "It has colorful foliage with reddish brown leaves that turn yellow in the fall." The next line made her heart quicken. "The redbud tree is also known as the Judas tree, because of the belief that Judas Iscariot hung himself from the tree after his betrayal of Jesus."

She sat back in her chair. Did the quilt block symbolize betrayal? A betrayal that was somehow connected to the

Snake Trail pattern in the block? Why had the quilt maker put the two together?

The only way to way to find out was to keep reading the letters and try to find a connection. Sarah decided to put off working on Sasha's quilt until Monday during school hours. Instead, she reached for the booklet that sat on the corner of her desk.

July 30, 1849

Dear Beth,

I write to you as Emma Hollander still and it seems that shall be my name forever. I am overcome with shame and embarrassment, which seems to grow worse as each day passes. Everyone pities me, although I am sure some secretly think me a fool. And a fool I surely am to have come all this way for nothing.

Carl promises that I shall always have a place in their home, but I can hear Maude complaining about me when she thinks I cannot hear her. She does not want another woman in her new home and I must confess that I do not wish to spend the rest of my life as their burden to bear. I cannot go forward and I cannot go back, which means I only have one choice before me.

I am leaving the wagon train, Beth. I know not where my journey will take me, but I cannot bear the thought of continuing on like this. I shall leave after sundown when the others are asleep. It shall be easy enough to take one of Carl's horses, and I shall leave him the money I had set aside as my dowry.

Do not fear for me, Beth. I have come to know this country through my journey on the trail and many long talks with our trail guide. There must be a respectable place for me in this territory—perhaps I can build a refuge for women like me who are set adrift in life.

I pray that I shall write you again soon, but I can make no promises. The future is uncertain and life is perilous here, as I have seen firsthand. But I cannot hide in the schooner forever. I must go forth and make something of my life, whatever that may be.

> *Your friend,*
> *Emma Hollander*

"Oh no," Sarah breathed as she read Emma's plan, her heart breaking for the forlorn girl. Leaving the wagon train behind seemed like a horrible plan, even if she understood the young woman's reason for doing so.

She was about to read the next letter when she heard someone knocking on her front door.

CHAPTER EIGHTEEN

arah opened the door and found Mark Calhoun on the other side. He wore a gray suit and his fists were clenched beneath the long sleeves of his jacket.

"Is Tracy here?" Mark asked, not waiting for Sarah to greet him.

"No, she's not." Sarah noticed the shadows under Mark's eyes and his voice sounded rough. "I believe she's out with Sasha."

"I know," he said shortly. "I just thought she might be back by now." He raked one hand through his dark hair, leaving it standing on end. "I just wondered if..." His voice trailed off and he mumbled something unintelligible.

Sarah might not like the man, but she could see that he was in distress. "Do you want to come in?"

He hesitated and then gave a short nod.

Sarah stepped back so he could enter, then ushered him into the living room.

"May I get you something to eat or drink?" she asked.

"No, nothing." Mark began to pace back and forth in front of the fireplace. "I really didn't want to bother you like this, but I've been driving around your block for an hour."

Sarah didn't say anything for a long moment. He looked awful. "Please have a seat, Mark," she said, "I'll be back in a minute."

She left him in the living room and hurried into the kitchen to make him a ham sandwich and a glass of milk. The man looked like he had neither eaten nor slept since Sasha had left his house three days ago.

When she returned to the living room, Mark was still pacing. "I made you something to eat."

He rubbed a hand over his face and closed his eyes for a brief moment. "Thank you, but I really can't..."

"Eat," she insisted, pushing the plate and glass into his hands. "You'll feel better once you have something in your stomach."

He started to argue again, then gave up and perched himself on the end of the sofa. The sandwich disappeared in four bites and he took a long swallow of milk before getting up to set both the plate and glass on the coffee table.

"Thank you," he said hoarsely.

"You're welcome." Sarah sat down on the rocking chair, hoping he would follow her example. "Sasha's okay. She's a very sweet girl."

"A sweet girl who's throwing away the chance of a life-time," he said, pacing again. "She's spent years, almost a decade, as a matter of fact, preparing herself for this moment. And now she's ready to let it go for the sake of some scrawny teenage boy who can't even dribble a basketball much less support her."

Sarah could see that Mark was too busy focusing on Ian to look at other reasons Sasha might be ready to throw away this "chance of a lifetime." "I don't think Ian is really the problem, Mark. He would never stand in Sasha's way if she wanted to play basketball."

Mark shook his head. "No, he is definitely the problem. She's never snuck around like this before or lied to us. Everything was going fine until Ian Carper decided to mess things up."

That wasn't fair to Ian or accurate, Sarah thought to herself. She remembered Ian's remark that Sasha was used to keeping secrets from her father. The problems in this family had started before Ian ever entered the picture.

"But I'm not really here to talk about Sasha," Mark told her. "I need you to tell me if…" His voice trailed off and he swallowed hard. "Did Tracy rent your other room for herself?"

The question caught her off guard. "No. Why would she do that?"

Mark breathed a long sigh. "Last night, she threatened to move in here with Sasha and she was gone from the house before I woke up this morning, so I didn't know what to think." He shook his head. "Tracy and I aren't exactly on the same page with this whole situation."

Sarah didn't know what to say. She stood up and walked over to him. "Mark, I know this isn't really any of my business, but have you thought about counseling? I know Pastor Peabody is always available for people who need help, whether or not they're a member of his congregation."

To her surprise, Mark didn't immediately reject the idea. "Actually, I think that might help. That's what Tracy and I were talking about last night before we started arguing again. I think some counseling would help Sasha see what a huge mistake she's making with her life."

Sarah cleared her throat. "I meant counseling for all of you."

He took a step back. "All of us?"

She nodded. "This is a difficult transition time for you and Tracy, as well as Sasha. It might help to talk it out in front of a trained counselor."

He gave her a tight grimace. "I'm sorry, Sarah, I know you mean well, but there isn't that much to talk about. Our problem is simple. Sasha needs to show up for summer training at San Diego State in a few weeks or she loses her scholarship. I'm trying a little tough love to convince her to do what's right, but Tracy doesn't agree with my methods."

"I'm not sure I do, either," Sarah said softly. "Kicking your daughter out of your house seems rather extreme."

He sighed. "I didn't kick her out. I simply gave her a choice. If she wants to live with us and enjoy the comforts we give her, then she needs to abide by our rules. One of those rules has always been no boys in the house when we aren't there."

"And that's a rule I can understand. But she seems to think she can't have Ian for a boyfriend and basketball too."

"Basketball comes first. And when she talks about leaving our dreams behind for this boy, then *he* is the problem."

Our dreams. It was either a slip of the tongue or Mark really saw her college recruitment to a first-rate basketball program as their dream.

The front door opened and Sasha came inside. She froze in her tracks when she saw Mark in the living room.

"Dad?" she gasped. "What are you doing here?"

"Where's your mother?" Mark asked her.

"She's on her way home. She just dropped me off."

Mark nodded, then turned to Sarah. "Thank you for the sandwich and for letting me take up some of your time. Have a good evening."

Sarah watched as he walked past his daughter without a word and left through the front door. Sasha turned to watch him go, staring at the closed door until the roar of a car engine sounded outside, shortly followed by the squeal of tires on the pavement.

Sarah walked over to Sasha. "Are you all right?"

Sasha gave a small shrug. "Sure, I'm fine. Did you have a good time in Albany?"

Despite the girl's nonchalance, Sarah could see her lower lip trembling. "Yes, I did. Are you hungry?"

Sasha moved toward the stairs. "No, I'm still full from lunch. I think I'll go do some homework." Then she bounded up the stairs before Sarah could say anything in reply.

Sarah heard the bedroom door close above her, then the squeak of bedsprings that was only audible if someone threw herself full force upon the mattress.

"Oh, Lord," Sarah prayed aloud. "Please help this family."

If Mark's version of tough love included hurting his daughter, he was succeeding. Sarah just hoped the price he and his family had to pay wasn't too high.

On Sunday morning, Sarah enjoyed sitting with Jason and his family for the Mother's Day service at church. She sent up a special prayer for Jenna's first Mother's Day with Leah, and thanked God once again for her beautiful children and grandchildren.

To make the day even more special, she looked forward to Sunday dinner at Jason's house. She had run home right after the service to change and had received a lovely call from Jenna. After talking with her grandsons and hearing the latest reports about Leah, Sarah made her way to Jason's house.

"Come in, Gram," Audrey said, opening the door for her. She looked adorable in a pink skirt and a white sweater sprinkled with pink plaid hearts. "Dinner is almost ready."

Sarah walked inside and inhaled deeply. "It smells delicious. What are we having?"

"Amy and I made a four course meal," Audrey said as she led her to the dining room. "Dad is helping us a little, but we cooked most of it ourselves."

"That sounds wonderful."

Audrey stopped in the doorway. "We're going to start off with the soup course, so go ahead and sit down."

Sarah walked into the dining room as Audrey continued down the hallway into the kitchen. Maggie and Patty were already seated at the table, which had been set with Maggie's best china and crystal goblets.

The twins had even created elegant, printed name cards for each place setting. Sarah found her place next to the one designated for Jason and directly across from Maggie and Patty. Amy and Audrey had put their name cards at the ends of the table.

"Well, isn't this something," Sarah remarked as she took her seat. "It looks like the girls have put in a lot of work."

"They've been busy all morning," Maggie said, a twinkle in her green eyes. "I wasn't even allowed to step one foot in the kitchen."

"That goes for me too," Patty said. "The girls brought us rolls and coffee in the parlor this morning, then told us to relax until it was time to go to church."

Sarah had noticed the girls whispering to each other during the church service. Now she knew why. "I can't wait to see what we're having."

Patty smiled. "The girls assured me the meal will be fully pescetarian, so I'm certain it will be delicious."

To Sarah's delight, Patty was right. Their first course was a creamy corn chowder served in a large tureen that Jason carried to the table. Amy ladled the chowder into the soup bowls while Audrey sliced a loaf of warm bread on a platter and passed it around the table with a small crock of honey butter.

The first spoonful of chowder made Sarah look up in surprise. "This is wonderful!"

Jason laughed in the chair beside her. "You sound so surprised."

"I just had no idea that the girls could cook like this."

"I've been giving them lessons," Patty said smugly. "They're both quite talented in the kitchen, like most of the Roberts women."

"And the Hart women," Maggie said graciously.

The second course was mushrooms stuffed with crab and cream cheese, followed by the entrée course of fish tacos.

Sarah didn't think she would be able to eat another bite when Amy jumped out of her chair and announced dessert. Then she and Audrey cleared the plates and headed into the kitchen.

"I think this is the best Mother's Day meal I've ever had," Patty said, dabbing at her mouth with a white linen napkin.

Jason turned to Sarah. "How about you, Mom? Does this meal top the fried chicken and waffles that Jenna and I made for you one Mother's Day?"

A reminiscent smile tugged at her lips. The fried chicken had been slightly charred and the waffles undercooked, but just remembering the excited faces of twelve-year-old Jason and eight-year-old Jenna had warmed her heart. She had eaten every bite on her plate. "That's a meal I'll never forget," she said, reaching over to give his forearm an affectionate squeeze.

Jason laughed as he draped his arm over the back of her chair. "That's a nice way of putting it. Maybe I'll make chicken and waffles for you again sometime. I think my cooking has improved a little over the years."

"I can't wait," Sarah told him.

A few minutes later, the twins reappeared in the dining room carrying a tray with a platter of white cupcakes as well as three separate dessert plates on it. Each dessert plate contained a miniature white frosted cake shaped like a heart. When Amy set one of the dessert plates in front of Sarah, she saw that her heart-shaped cake had

G-R-A-M spelled out on the top with red hot cinnamon candies. Patty's cake read G-R-A-M-M-Y and Maggie's cake read M-O-M.

"Oh, girls, these are wonderful," Maggie said, tears gleaming in her eyes. "How did you make them into hearts? Did you buy a special cake pan?"

Amy shook her head. "We saw how to do it on YouTube. You just make a big sheet cake, then cut out the hearts. Then we made a second batter for the cupcakes."

As Sarah stared at her cake, something clicked. She had been looking at the pioneer quilt or rather, one particular quilt block, all wrong.

"I made a mistake," she blurted, then realized this probably wasn't the best time to bring it up. But she was so excited by her discovery that she couldn't hold back.

"What?" Jason asked looking confused.

Sarah smiled at the twins. "Your cakes just helped me figure out a clue to the pioneer quilt. I was wrong about the quilt maker—it wasn't Maude Hollander, it was Charlotte Hollander. She marked her initials, C.H., right in the center of the quilt."

Patty frowned. "But those initials are on a gravestone. Isn't that rather morbid?"

Sarah shook her head. "No, it tells part of the story. When Charlotte's daughter died, she wrote that she had left her heart on the prairie with the unmarked grave of her daughter. The quilt block shows both the unmarked grave and Charlotte's initials encircled by an embroidered heart."

Audrey's eyes widened. "I get it, Gram! Man, we helped you figure out a big clue!"

"You sure did," Sarah said, grinning at both girls. "But just being with you is one of the best gifts I've ever gotten for Mother's Day."

old on," Patty said, setting her fork on her dessert plate and looking over at Sarah. "So you're admitting that you made at least one mistake with the quilt?"

"Not necessarily with the quilt itself," Sarah said carefully, feeling as if Patty was ready to pounce. "I thought Maude made the quilt, but now I realize it was Josiah's wife Charlotte."

Patty turned to Maggie. "Now do you see why it's so important to get a second opinion?"

"Mother, please," Maggie said under her breath. "Not today."

Jason looked over at his wife. "What's going on here, Magpie?"

Maggie took a deep breath. "Mom thought she needed a second opinion on the quilt, so she sent a photograph of it, along with some information, to a vintage quilt expert in California."

Sarah leaned back in her chair, feeling a little sick.

Maggie turned to Sarah. "I'm so sorry. I didn't know she was doing it until afterward. I have complete faith in your judgment."

"It's all right," Sarah said softly, not wanting Maggie to feel bad for something her mother had done.

Patty turned up her hands, looking baffled. "I'm not sure why this is such a problem. Sarah is supposed to be an expert in her field—surely she sees the value of second opinions among professionals. It's nothing personal."

A muscle twitched in Jason's jaw. "I'm sure you didn't mean anything by it, Patty, but it is a little insulting."

Patty sniffed. "Well, I must say, that hurts a little, Jason. I've been trying my very best to be a good houseguest and help you two with the girls. Perhaps I've overstayed my welcome."

Nobody spoke and the tension crackled in the air. Sarah glanced at the twins, who had made them such a lovely Mother's Day dinner. Audrey was chewing on her lower lip as she looked between the four adults. Amy sat next to her sister, her head down and her gaze fixed on the hardwood floor.

"Another point of view can be helpful when there is a question about a quilt," Sarah said, injecting a cheerful note in her voice. The words came out a little strained, but she tried to soften them with a wide smile.

Patty nodded, looking vindicated. "And there seem to be several questions about the quilt that you're unable to answer. I want the presentation at the reunion to be perfect."

"Well, right now, this cake is looking pretty perfect," Sarah said, ready to change the subject. She cut into her cake, then took a bite. "*Mmm*, I was right. This is the best cake I've had in a long time."

"Maybe I'd better render a second opinion," Jason said wryly, unwrapping his cupcake.

Sarah winced at his words, knowing they had been meant for Patty and, by the expression on her face, they had hit their mark. Maggie sat beside her mother, misery swimming in her eyes.

Jason bit into his cupcake. "Girls, this is wonderful! You can make me cakes for the rest of my life and I'll be a happy man."

Amy grinned. "Really?"

"Really," he assured her. He took another bite of cake, then said, "in fact, I'm going to need some more tea, because I'll definitely be eating more cupcakes."

"Why don't you girls bring more tea for everyone," Maggie suggested.

When the girls left for the kitchen, Maggie looked over at Sarah. "I am so sorry. Please don't let this ruin your day."

"I'm fine," Sarah said, realizing she meant it. "The most important thing is that the girls don't let any of this bother them."

"Well, it sure bothers me," Jason muttered, licking a dollop of frosting off his thumb. "Patty, I just don't understand how you can invite my mother to give a presentation at your family reunion, then go behind her back to undermine her."

Patty took a dainty bite of her cake. "Oh, Jason, that was never my intention. Surely, you know better than that."

Sarah appreciated her son standing up for her, but the last thing she wanted for him was a battle with his mother-in-law. "I really am fine with Patty getting a second opinion."

In fact, the more she thought about it, that might be the perfect antidote to Patty's snide remarks. "I'm confident enough in my credentials," Sarah continued, "and a second opinion should eliminate any doubts about my work."

"Let's talk about this later," Maggie said in a hushed voice. "I hear the girls coming."

Amy and Audrey entered the dining room a moment later, carrying a full pitcher of tea. They refilled all the glasses, then sat back down at the table to eat their cupcakes.

Jason suddenly leaned over and kissed Sarah's cheek. "Thanks, Mom," he whispered. "Happy Mother's Day."

Sarah smiled at her son. She and Patty might never be friends, but she wouldn't let it ruin their Mother's Day.

On Monday afternoon, Martha came over to Sarah's house to make cream cheese mints for Ian's graduation. They had decided to make as much of the food ahead of time as possible so they could enjoy graduation day instead of spending the majority of it in the kitchen.

"I found a sale on cream cheese at Matthews' Market," Martha said, setting a grocery bag on the kitchen table so she could slip out of her jacket. She draped it over a chair, then began to remove items from the bag.

"So I've got cream cheese, powdered sugar, and peppermint extract." She snapped her fingers together. "I forgot the food coloring. I had a feeling I had forgotten something when I walked out of that store."

Sarah opened a cupboard door. "Don't worry, I've got plenty of food coloring. When you only use a drop or two at a time it can last for years."

"Oh, good, you've got blue," Martha said, taking one of the small bottles from Sarah.

"So you settled on blue and white mints?" Sarah asked her.

Martha nodded as she began unwrapping the bars of cream cheese and placing them in the mixing bowl that Sarah had set out earlier.

"I know we talked about a more creative graduation party for Ian, but I think it's better if we go the more traditional route. There's so much going on in his life right now, and I don't want to do anything that might complicate things further."

"How are Tim and Ruth handling Ian's new girlfriend?"

Martha sighed. "They seem to like Sasha just fine, although they rarely see her. She and Ian keep to themselves, as if they were still sneaking around to see each other."

"I'm trying to get used to playing chaperone again," Sarah told her. "After I came home from Jason's house last night, Ian came over. He and Sasha had the television on in the living room, but every time I passed by the room they were too busy whispering to each other to watch it."

Martha chuckled. "Do you remember when I used to send Ernie out to the living room when one of the girls had a boy over and it was getting late? He'd sit right down in his recliner and join in their conversation. The girls were mortified and the boys usually left as soon as they were able."

"I do remember," Sarah said with a smile. "And your girls ended up marrying the young men that weren't scared off. They made good choices too. You have some fine sons-in-law."

Martha nodded. "And some good daughters-in-law too, just like you. Maggie seems perfect for Jason."

"She's nothing like her mother, that's for sure."

Martha measured out the powdered sugar and added it to the bowl. "Is Patty overstaying her welcome?"

"Actually, I think it's been nice for all of them to have her here. She's spending time with the girls and exposing them to new things and ideas." Sarah scooped a cup of sugar from the bin to roll the mints in. "Unfortunately, one of her ideas is that I'm a quack when it comes to quilts."

Martha's mouth gaped. "Are you serious?"

"I am," she said softly. "She sent off photos and information about the pioneer quilt to another vintage quilt expert for a second opinion."

"You're kidding."

"I admit it hurts a bit," Sarah said, confiding in her best friend. "But I'd probably do the same if I had doubts about the authenticity of a quilt."

"You might get a second opinion," Martha said, "but you sure wouldn't insult someone in the process—especially a family member."

"I know," Sarah smiled. "Patty seems to be a bit tone-deaf in the tact department. But I can overlook it if it prevents a rift in the family."

While Martha was mixing the mint ingredients together, Sarah saw Ian walking Sasha to the back door of the house.

"Hello," Ian shouted over the noise of the mixer as they walked in. "I saw Grandma's car, so I thought I'd stop in."

Martha turned off the mixer and smiled at her grandson. "I should have known you'd show up when I was making something to eat. You'll have to wait until your graduation, though, so you're out of luck."

He plunked himself down at the table. "But don't you need someone to test them for you? I'm ready, willing, and able."

Sasha laughed as she took the chair next to Ian. "He's always eating. I gave him half my lunch."

"Only the half she didn't eat," Ian said quickly, then looked over at Sarah, "it always tastes good, Mrs. H."

"Well, I'm glad you enjoy it." She walked over to the refrigerator. "Would you two like something to drink? I have some grape juice."

"That sounds awesome," Ian said.

"No, thanks." Sasha patted her stomach. "I've been eating too much lately. I need to stay in shape."

"You don't have to train anymore," Ian pointed out as Sarah poured him a glass of grape juice. "You can eat whatever you want."

"Yeah," Sasha said, looking a little surprised, "I guess you're right."

Sarah set the juice on the table along with two glasses. "So have you two decided what you're going to do after graduation?"

"Not yet," Ian said as he and Sasha gazed into each other's eyes. "As long as we're together, it doesn't matter."

"That's right," Sasha said. "Ian makes me happy. He doesn't try to tell me what to do or tell me how I should feel. He just lets me be me."

Sarah and Martha exchanged glances, then Sarah spoke. "I'm glad you're both happy and that you're taking the time to make the right decisions for your lives. But don't wait so long that you're forced to make decisions you might not like."

Ian looked up at her. "What do you mean?"

"I mean you both have some amazing opportunities now," Sarah said gently. "Once those are gone, they may not come again. So please think long and hard about where you want to be next year and also five years from now."

Sasha looked thoughtful, her gaze on the table in front of her.

"You're both young, bright kids with promising futures," Martha added. "It is possible to be in love *and* plan for that future."

"We know," Ian said, squinting his face at Sasha and making her laugh.

"Just remember to use both your head and your heart when you make big decisions about your life, then the rest will follow." Martha smiled as she brought the mixing bowl over to the table and set it on the table between Ian and Sasha. "And since you've both got a good set of hands, you can help us with these mints."

Sasha moved her chair back a few inches. "I don't really know how to cook, Mrs. Maplethorpe."

Martha laughed. "Don't worry, hon, there's no cooking involved with this recipe. You just break off a small chunk of this dough and roll it into a ball about the size of a large marble." Martha demonstrated for them, then said, "Now you two try it."

Sarah poured some sugar into a pie dish and set it on the table, anticipating what Martha was going to show them next.

"I think mine is too small," Sasha said, holding the rolled dough in the palm of her hand.

"That's okay," Martha told her, "just add a little more dough until it's the right size. Then you roll the dough in the sugar and press it into the mold."

Ian grimaced. "Mold?"

Martha snorted with laughter and reached out to tussle his hair. "Don't worry, Ian, I'm not serving mold at your reception. Just hold on a minute and I'll show you what I mean." She looked over at Sarah. "Do you have the molds ready?"

"I sure do." Sarah retrieved them from the cupboard while Martha washed her hands at the kitchen sink. "We picked up these in Albany. There were so many fun ones to choose from."

Sarah set the clear plastic molds on the table. Each mold had room for eight to ten mints. They had chosen shapes like diplomas, mortar boards, and medallions with the current year written on them.

Sasha picked up one of the molds. "These are cool."

"And they've already been washed," Sarah told them, "so go ahead and press one of the sugared balls into the mold."

Then she walked over to the drawer and pulled out a box of wax paper. She tore off a good length and laid it across the counter.

Sasha glanced over at Ian, then picked up the marble-sized ball she had just dipped into the sugar. She pressed it into a mold shaped like a diploma. "Is that all I have to do?"

"That's all," Martha told her. "When all the spots are filled on that mold, you can pop them out and lay them on the wax paper Sarah has on the counter. They'll need to dry for about twenty-four hours so that they're firm enough to serve without losing their shape."

"And half of them will be blue," Sarah said, picking up the food coloring. "I'll make that batch while you three work on the white mints."

Sarah began putting the recipe together while Ian, Sasha, and Martha formed the mints.

"So, what do you two have planned for the summer?" Martha asked them.

"I might work for a lawn service here in town," Ian said. "I talked to the owner yesterday and he's looking for a year-round employee to mow in the summer and remove snow in the winter."

"Year-round," Martha murmured, with a slight shake of her head. "And what about you, Sasha?"

The girl didn't say anything for a long moment. "I usually coach youth basketball, but that's a volunteer job so I don't get paid or anything. Maybe I can find a job as a waitress or something."

"You should ask Liam for a job at the Spotted Dog," Ian said, rolling another dough ball in the sugar. "Or maybe your dad could use help at the furniture store." As soon as the words were out of his mouth, Ian blushed. "Sorry, Sash. Bad idea."

Sasha didn't say anything as she pressed another sugar ball into the mold. "I guess I'm not sure what I'm going to do."

"Will you stay here at Sarah's house?" Martha asked.

Sarah glanced at her friend, a little surprised at her curiosity.

"I haven't really thought that far ahead," Sasha said.

"How about you, Ian? Will you live with your folks?"

He cleared his throat. "I guess I haven't really thought about it. They always joke about turning my room into an office when I leave for college, but maybe they're serious about it."

Both Sasha and Ian suddenly grew very quiet as they rolled the mint dough and pressed each ball into a mold. Martha had made them think about their immediate future, revealing how little they had thought their plans through.

The truth was that there weren't a lot of opportunities in Maple Hill for kids fresh out of high school, not unless they were already established with a job or a trade that could carry them into the future.

Martha looked over at Sarah. "Are we about ready to start the blue mints?"

"Coming right up."

CHAPTER TWENTY

That evening, Sarah closed herself in her sewing room, determined to finish reading the letters in the Hollander family booklet. They were all leaving for the reunion in Willow Creek on Friday and she wanted to be as informed as possible, even if she hadn't resolved the discrepancies between the letters and the quilt.

She had directed Audrey and Amy to finish the letters and plot the remaining course on their map. They would have a rough draft of their presentation ready on Friday, and she had promised to go over it with them during the car ride to Willow Creek.

Sarah's fingers were still stained blue from making the blue graduation mints as she opened the booklet. She had enjoyed the time spent with Ian, Sasha, and Martha. The kids seemed to have a good time and it was nice seeing Sasha relaxed and happy for a change.

Her teenage boarder was upstairs studying, giving Sarah plenty of time to dive into the remaining letters. She settled into the chair and began to read.

August 5, 1849

Dear Beth,

I am still alive and, if you can believe it, I am now a married woman. You may think me bold to write such words after such a short courtship, but let me tell you my story before you judge me too harshly.

In my last letter, I wrote of running away and I carried out my plan. I took one of Carl's horses and rode into the night, too bereft to care which direction I went. I rode for what seemed like hours until the horse tired and I stopped to let the gelding rest and drink. I was hot and tired and almost as dirty as my poor horse.

I was also a fool. When the sun came up, I realized how little planning I had done for my escape. I had only a few provisions for myself, which I shared with my horse, and little water to keep me cool under the hot sun. With no shade of a wagon to protect me and few trees in this arid land, my skin began to burn and peel. It did not take me long before I realized my mistake and headed back in the direction of the wagon train.

You can imagine my horror, dear Beth, when I could not find the wagon train that I had so eagerly run from the night before. I circled the area for hours but could see no signs of life other than the ghastly turkey vultures that began to circle the sky above me.

I resorted to using part of a cow's skull that I found in the dirt to dig a hole on the side of small hill. I made the hole large enough to give me some relief from the hot sun and I truly thought that it would be my grave. I untethered my horse in the hope that he might be able to save himself.

I must have passed out from the heat of the sun, because the next thing I knew, it had started to rain. I awoke with sweet water pouring down on me. I opened my mouth first, letting the water quench my parched throat, and then I opened my eyes. That's when I saw that the water was not falling from the sky, but from John Grant's canteen. It was almost dusk when our trail guide found me and he claimed that it would soon be too dark for us to safely return to the wagon train.

You will be shocked, Beth, to hear that I spent the night in the wilderness with a man not my husband, but I can assure you that he was a perfect gentleman. He fed me a thick bison steak cooked over a hot fire and made me drink almost more water than I could hold. When the stars came out, he pitched a lean-to for me to sleep under while he kept guard over our camp. Truth be told, I did not sleep a wink. I was too busy thanking God for sending John to save me.

We left for the wagon train the next morning. The trail back was rocky and much steeper than I remembered. I rode on the back of his horse and was forced to hang on to him or fall off the saddle. When I questioned John about our route, he told me that he wanted to stop at an outpost to gather some supplies. It seems Harriet has depleted most of the bullets in our stock with her target practice.

Yet, it was not only bullets that John sought at the outpost but my hand in marriage. No one was more surprised than I, dear Beth, when he turned on his horse and asked me to be his wife. All my life I have dreamed of a fine gentleman proposing on bended knee or writing me pretty verses of love as Benjamin had done in his letters.

Can you picture us, Beth, atop a horse at the moment he proposed? I was dirty, sunburned, and smelled worse than the horse. My hair hung in limp locks around my face and my dress was stained and torn. John did not look much better. His dark mustache and bushy brown beard hid almost his entire face except for his gray eyes. His wavy brown hair hung to his broad shoulders and, I am sorry to say, it looked as if neither a comb nor a bar of soap had ever touched it.

Beth, I married him. I did not even hesitate and not for the reasons most people might think. I love him. I realized it the moment he splashed water on my face and told me I was the most deranged woman he had ever met. We have traveled the Oregon Trail together these past three months and have talked and argued and jested with each other more than most properly engaged couples can ever boast.

So I sign my new name with pride and love in my heart. I came to the wilderness to find love and love found me instead.

> *Your married friend,*
> *Emma Grant*

Sarah smiled to herself, surprised to find tears in her eyes. She wanted to know about Emma and John Grant's life together, but that would have to wait. She still had a mystery to solve.

Emma's letter matched perfectly with the Double Wedding Ring quilt block that was set next to the Fort Hall appliqué block. Her marriage had been chronicled on the quilt, just as Charlotte had marked her child's unmarked gravestone block with her own initials.

Sarah turned to the next letter, curious to see what happened next.

August 7, 1849

Dear Cornelia,

Greetings to you and the family. Someone has stolen my beau, John Grant, and married him, but I could not be happier. No one was more surprised than I when Emma Hollander disappeared from camp three days ago. She took one of Carl's horses and I believe Maude was more upset by the loss of the gelding than the loss of her sister-in-law. I must say, if I had been forced to endure that woman's sharp tongue and short temper for as long as Emma was, I would have run away a long time ago.

As you can well imagine, the camp was in an uproar at the discovery of Emma's disappearance. Some thought she had gone off to die from a broken heart, but anyone with half a mind could see that her Hollander pride had been wounded much more deeply than her heart.

John set off right away to find her and refused all offers of help from the other men. A few hours later, Carl's horse wandered into camp and we thought Emma might already be dead.

That night was one of the longest of my life as I waited for John and Emma to return. I could not rest and walked the night, seeing things in the darkness that were well hidden in the light of day.

The next morning, we expected John to either appear with Emma or to tell us of her demise. Some of the men grew impatient as the morning turned into the afternoon and there was still no sign of either one of them. Charles posited that they were both lost or dead and that we should continue on without them. Fortunately, no one listened to him.

We were cooking supper over the fire when one of Carl's children spotted them riding over the horizon. At first, I did not recognize the man riding the horse with Emma seated behind him. It was not until I saw his gray eyes that I realized John had lost his beard and mustache during his journey, but gained a wife. He is now more handsome than I can describe and I kick myself for not pursuing him sooner.

Yet, if I could not have him, I am glad to see him with Emma. I have never seen a bride so happy. Emma donned her wedding dress for supper, telling us of the small ceremony conducted by a traveling pastor at an outpost nearby. When John asked Emma what she wanted for a wedding present, she told him that she wanted a bath more than anything else in the world. He paid a pretty penny for a hot bath and a new set of clothes for each of them, along with a shave and a haircut for himself.

All of us made merry well into the night and Josiah blessed the marriage between them, even letting Emma and John drink from the same golden cup that Emma's parents had drunk from at their wedding in Willow Creek.

We celebrated tonight, but I fear tomorrow some hard decisions must be made. Please pray for us, Cornelia, that God gives us guidance during this difficult time and sees us through our journey until the end.

Your loving mother,
Harriet

Sarah liked reading about the pioneers' reactions to the marriage, but it was the last paragraph of the letter that really made her curious. What hard decisions had to be made? And were those decisions reflected in the Bible verse that followed the Double Wedding Ring quilt block on the quilt?

She reached for her notebook to read the quote once more. "Finally, brothers, whatever is true, whatever is noble, whatever is right, whatever is pure, whatever is lovely, whatever is admirable—if anything is excellent or praiseworthy—think about such things" (Philippians 4:8).

Then she turned to the next letter in the booklet.

August 10, 1849

Dear Pastor Simpson,

If we had known of the trials that we would face on this journey, Charlotte and I might have turned away from this mission that was given to us by our church family. I long for the peaceful meadow where we will build a new church and a new town to call home. These days on the trail have made me weary of heart and mind and soul. We have lost a daughter and now Harriet has lost a grandson. Her heart is heavy, but I know she is strong and will prevail.

Please pray for us, Pastor, as we take these final steps in our journey. I know that God is with us and my faith sustains me in the most difficult moments. Our lives may never be the same, but our faith is stronger than ever.

Yours in peace,
Josiah Hollander

Sarah slowly set down the booklet, shocked by what appeared to be news of Charles Hollander's death. Josiah had not described how he had died. He simply wrote of Harriet's loss. Had Charles finally gone off to California to seek his fortune in gold?

She looked at the quilt, seeking answers. The Judas Tree quilt block followed the Bible verse block. Betrayal? Josiah hadn't spoken of betrayal, but he had been vague enough that a person could read between the lines. Especially when the block that followed the Judas tree was an unmarked gravestone block. Did those two blocks signify a betrayal by Charles Hollander, followed by his death?

Sarah turned back to Harriet's letter, wanting to read it again. She spoke specifically of hard decisions and a difficult time. Then, in a letter dated only three days later, Josiah had written of losing Charles and the trials they had faced on the journey.

The pieces were there, Sarah thought to herself, now she just needed to figure out how to stitch them together.

The doorbell rang, breaking her reverie. As she rose from her desk, she glanced at the clock and saw that it was almost nine o'clock. With her string of visitors lately, she wondered who could be at her door now.

As she walked into the living room, she saw Sasha standing at the top of the stairs.

"I'll get it," Sarah told her, heading toward the front door.

When she opened it, Ian stood on the other side. He wore a Maple Hill High sweatshirt and a pair of jeans. A green duffel was slung over one shoulder.

"Ian?" Sarah turned on the porch light so she could see him better. "What are you doing here?"

"Hi, Mrs. H," he said, his voice tight. "I was wondering if I could rent a room."

CHAPTER TWENTY-ONE

"A re you sure you don't want me to go to Ruth's house with you?" Martha asked.

Sarah stood outside Martha's home, a full moon overhead. She had been so shocked by Ian's request that she had immediately called Martha to ask her what to do.

They had agreed that Sarah should bring Ian over to Martha and Ernie's, then one of them would talk to Ruth and Tim to get the full story. Ian insisted that he had been thrown out of the house, but neither Sarah nor Martha could believe it.

"I'm sure," Sarah told her best friend, "Ian needs you here, and I know everything that's going on with Ian and Sasha. I'll keep you posted on what happens."

Martha nodded. "I tried calling Ruth earlier, but she didn't answer. I can't stand all of this, Sarah. These kids should be planning their high school graduations and getting excited about starting their futures."

"I know," Sarah commiserated. "I think it's time for an old-fashioned, grandma-style intervention."

Martha smiled. "Does that mean we should take them all back behind the woodshed?"

Sarah laughed. "Okay, maybe not *that* old-fashioned. But these kids need some direction and nobody is communicating. I have an idea, but I'll wait to tell you about it until after I speak with Ruth and Tim."

"Good luck," Martha said, waving as Sarah headed back to her car.

Sasha hadn't seemed as shocked as Sarah by Ian's arrival at the house that night. No doubt he had warned her that he was coming via text message. Still, Sarah hadn't been able to tell if Sasha was disappointed or relieved that she had turned down his request to rent a room.

Was it possible that Sasha's feelings for Ian weren't as strong now as they had been before? Leaving home had a way of letting a person see things in a new light. If Sasha was having second thoughts about their relationship, Sarah just hoped Sasha would let Ian down easily. He was such a sensitive soul and seemed crazy about her.

Sarah drove over to Martha's daughter's house, pleased to see the lights were still on. She had no idea what to expect as she made her way to the front door.

Ruth and Tim lived in a neat, white Cape-Cod-style house with olive green siding and black shutters. The window boxes were still empty, but in the summers Ruth always planted bright red geraniums there.

Sarah knocked on the door, well aware that it was almost ten o'clock.

She was about to knock again when the front door slowly opened. Ruth stood on the other side.

"Hello, Sarah," Ruth said, "please come in." She wore a beige shift dress and a smile, but her eyes were red.

Sarah walked into the tidy living room filled with early-American-style furniture. An eleven-by-fourteen-inch portrait of Ian—his senior picture—hung on the wall by the staircase. It had been taken in the fall and he looked a lot younger than the young man who had stood on her porch that evening.

Tim joined them in the living room. He was a tall man, well over six feet, who still had the athleticism of the track athlete he had been in college.

"I just returned Mom's call," Ruth said, "so I know why you're here."

Tim waved Sarah toward the sofa. "Please have a seat, Sarah. I'm sorry that our problems have brought you over here this late in the evening."

"I don't mind," Sarah said, walking over to the sofa and sitting down. "I just wanted to make sure you knew what was going on with Ian."

Ruth sighed as she looked at her husband. "I'm afraid we don't know much, that's the problem. He's at a time in his life when he needs to make some plans and some decisions, but all he wants to do is follow Sasha around like some lovesick puppy."

"We don't blame her," Tim quickly interjected. "It's just that Ian's always talking on the phone with her but will barely say two words to us." He folded his arms across his chest. "I thought I'd try to solve that problem by taking his cell phone away from him tonight. I guess we all know how well that turned out."

"The thing is, he's not a little boy anymore," Ruth said, her voice quavering. "But he doesn't seem to realize that an education and a job and money don't just fall into your lap. I guess we should have done a better job with him."

Sarah hated the despair she heard in Ruth's voice. "You and Tim are fine parents. Anyone who's ever met Ian knows that. He's just going through a rough period right now, trying to find himself. The same thing happened to Jason."

Tim perked up. "Well, that gives me hope. Jason is a great guy."

"So is Ian." Sarah folded her hands in her lap. "Martha and I have both talked to him about the importance of making plans after graduation and I'm sure he'll make an informed decision."

"I hope you're right," Ruth breathed.

"In the meantime," Sarah continued, "I think it might be a good idea for everyone involved to meet on neutral territory and work this all out. I'll volunteer my house as a meeting place between you and the Calhouns. Sasha is already living there, so either you or Martha will have to convince Ian to show up."

"Oh, he'll be there," Tim said, "even if I have to drag him all the way."

A shadow of a smile passed over Ruth's mouth. "At least he can't run so fast since he left his tennis shoes at the Calhoun house."

Tim shook his head, his eyes narrowing. "Did you know that Mark Calhoun refuses to give us Ian's shoes back? He said he's keeping them for evidence or something ridiculous like that. No wonder Sasha is looking for someone to rescue her."

"Mark is intense," Sarah said, "but I have to believe he loves his daughter, despite his flaws. I guess we'll see what happens when we're all in the same room."

On Tuesday morning, Sasha ate breakfast and left for school before Sarah called Tracy Calhoun and told her about the meeting she wanted to have between the Calhoun and Carper families that evening. Tracy was all for it and promised that she and Mark would be there at seven o'clock sharp.

Sarah cleaned up the breakfast dishes and was about to call Ruth and let her know the meeting was set when her phone rang. She dried her hands on a dish towel, then picked up the receiver. "Hello?"

"Sarah? This is Mark Calhoun."

"Oh, hello," she said, "I just spoke to your wife."

"Yes, I know. I'm sorry, but I have a meeting tonight, so I won't be able to make it."

Sarah's hands twisted around the dish towel on the counter and, for one brief moment, she wished she could thwack him with it. "What night will work for you?"

He hesitated. "I really don't know. My schedule is pretty tight."

"How about tomorrow night?"

"I don't know," he hedged.

"Your daughter's future may depend on it, Mark."

There was a long silence over the line, then he said, "I'll try to be there, but I can't make any promises."

Sarah supposed that was better than a refusal, but she didn't hold out a lot of hope. "Does Wednesday evening work for Tracy?"

"I'm sure it will," he said. "She just left for work, but I'll let her know."

After they rang off, Sarah called Ruth and told her about the meeting.

"We'll be there," Ruth said without hesitation. "And Mom said she'd bring Ian. I know he dragged her into this mess at the beginning, so she deserves to be part of the meeting."

Sarah was glad to hear it. Between the two of them, maybe they could bring a peaceful resolution to the battle waging among these parents and their children. She thought about contacting Pastor John to help keep the peace but decided against it. Mark had already balked at the thought of seeing a counselor and might shut down completely if he saw the pastor there.

Now that the meeting was set, Sarah turned her attention to the two quilt projects that she needed to finish. The pioneer quilt was almost done. She needed to patch a few small holes and tighten some threads, but she would be done by the end of the day if she put her mind to it. Sasha's T-shirt quilt, on the other hand, would require more work than that.

The phone rang again, interrupting her thoughts. She picked up the receiver. "Hello?"

"Good morning, Sarah," Liam said in his warm Irish brogue.

She smiled, always happy to hear his voice. "Good morning, Liam. How are you?"

"Just fine. I was just thinking about our last date and the young lad who joined us for that delicious picnic dinner you made. How is Ian doing?"

She sighed. "Well, I'm afraid Ian and Sasha are still having problems with their parents." Sarah told him about the latest developments. "I just hope we can bring the kids back together with their families."

"If anyone can do it," Liam said, "you can."

She blushed. "I hope you're right.

"I know I'm right," he said confidentally, "and I also know I'd like to have dinner with you again. How does Saturday night sound?"

"Oh, I wish I could," Sarah told him, feeling a stab of disappointment, "but I'll be in Pennsylvania for a family reunion."

"We'll have to make it another time, then," Liam said, sounding as disappointed as she felt.

Then an idea occurred to her. "If you're not busy next week why don't you come to Ian's graduation party?"

"Are you sure he won't mind an uninvited guest?"

"I'm inviting you," Sarah told him. "It's at Martha's house and I'm helping her with the party. I know Ian would be glad to see you. Will you come?"

"I'd love to," Liam replied. "You have a good trip to Pennsylvania and I'll look forward to seeing you next week."

"Me too," she said, then rang off.

With a happy sigh, she turned back to Sasha's quilt. It still needed a fair amount of work. Sarah would have to sew the sashings onto the T-shirt blocks, join the blocks together, and then add the three borders to complete the top. Once that was done, she would quilt the three layers— the top, the cotton batting, and the back—together. Finally, she would attach a mitered binding to the raw edges.

Before she started sewing, Sarah decided to read the remaining letters in the booklet. There were only two left and she wanted to know the end of the pioneers' saga. She retrieved the booklet from her desk, then took it to the living room and curled up in a chair to read the final chapter of the story.

August 20, 1849

Dear Ma,

I write to you from my own farmland in the Oregon Territory. The soil here is rich and fertile. It is still a wild land, but as Josiah says, it can be tamed to sustain us for generations to come.

I plan to build a house for all of us as soon as we are done building the church. We held our first Sunday service in the meadow where the church will stand. Josiah led the service and read this verse: "Blessed is the one who perseveres under trial because, having stood the test, that person will receive the crown of life that the Lord has promised to those who love him" (James 1:12).

We have persevered these past four months and I do not regret the journey. You and my brothers and sisters must come here in the next year or two. By then, my house will be built and I shall make certain that there is room enough for all of you.

Josiah and Charlotte will be our neighbors to the west, and the Dauber family from Virginia are my neighbors to the east. They have a daughter, Bessie, who has agreed to cook and clean for me in exchange for letting her father use a pair of my oxen to plow his fields.

I shall put you in touch with John Grant so that he can recommend a good trail guide for you. He and Emma left yesterday and are on their way to his family farm in Iowa. John plans to raise horses there and Emma seems eager to help him.

I have chosen my land well, Ma, with enough land to the north and to the south for all of you to claim. We shall be together soon. God bless you all.

Your loving son,
Amos

Sarah smiled to herself, knowing from the census records that Bessie Dauber had become Amos's wife only two short years after he had written that letter. She wondered if Bessie had welcomed Amos's mother and siblings into the house or encouraged her husband to build them one of their own.

Sarah turned to the next page, surprised to find that the last letter in the booklet had been written by Charlotte Hollander.

CHAPTER TWENTY-TWO

August 30, 1849

Dear Pastor Simpson,

I write this letter to you on the day we broke ground for the Willow Bend Community Church. We held a picnic afterward and Josiah led a service to commemorate this momentous day. We have carried our faith and our traditions for over two thousand miles to start this church in the Oregon Territory. I know only too well the sacrifices that have brought us here.

We were charged with the mission to build a church in our new settlement and it will be a crowning achievement for the end of our long journey. Josiah read a verse today that seemed so fitting for this occasion. "In that day the Lord Almighty will be a glorious crown, a beautiful wreath for the remnant of his people. He will be a spirit of justice to the one who sits in judgment, a source of strength to those who turn back the battle at the gate" (Isaiah 28: 5–6).

We have battled and won, but more challenges await us. We ask for your prayers and the prayers of the parishioners in Willow Creek. We will be forever connected through God's love

*and the wondrous treasures that yoke us together in heaven and
on earth. Peace be with all of you.*

> *Your friend in faith,*
> *Charlotte Hollander*

Sarah carried the booklet into the dining room and
looked at the last block on the quilt. It was the Cross
and Crowns pattern with the words *Willow Bend* embroidered in the right-hand corner. This was further proof to her
that this quilt had been made to depict the true story of the
Hollander pioneers' journey west.

Charlotte had even quoted a Bible verse about a glorious crown when she had talked about breaking ground for
their new church. Now more than ever, Sarah believed that
Charlotte had made the quilt that now graced her table.

Yet, now that she had read all the letters, it still wasn't
clear to her why the trail in those letters differed from the
one traced on the quilt.

She hoped to find some answers when they traveled to
Willow Creek on Friday. Until then, she needed to get busy
restoring the quilt so it would be ready in time for the twins'
presentation at the reunion on Saturday and again for their
history class presentation on Monday. Sarah headed into her
sewing room and got to work.

On Wednesday evening, Ian and Martha were the first ones
to arrive at Sarah's house. Sasha sat on the living room sofa

wearing a soft blue sweater and a pair of jeans. She jumped up when Ian appeared in the front hall and hugged him.

"I'm so nervous," Sasha told him, clinging to his arm.

"Don't worry," Ian assured her as they walked into the living room. "Nothing they say can break us apart. As long as we stick together, everything will be all right."

Sarah motioned for Martha to follow her into the kitchen. "Are you ready for this?" Sarah asked when they were out of earshot of the teenagers.

"Definitely," Martha replied. "I just hope Mark doesn't make things worse."

"I know. I'm worried about that too. Tim and Ruth are already upset with the man for not returning Ian's shoes."

Martha nodded. "Ruth told me about it. I'm afraid it's going to be the Carpers versus the Calhouns with you and me as the referees."

Sarah smiled as she walked over to the refrigerator. "That's why I made some appetizers to help keep things under control. I figure the more food people have in their hands and their mouth, the less shouting and finger-pointing they'll be able to do."

Martha chuckled as she took a tray from Sarah and set it on the table. "Unless they start a food fight." She picked up a tortilla pinwheel. "At least this won't do much damage if it lands anywhere in your living room."

"But these might," Sarah said, opening the lid of her Crock-Pot to reveal the barbecued meatballs inside. She used a pair of tongs to place them on a separate platter and stuck a toothpick in each one.

The doorbell rang and the two women looked at each other. Sarah picked up the tray of barbecued meatballs. "Okay, I think we're ready."

"Let the games begin," Martha said, picking up the other tray of appetizers, along with a handful of small paper plates, and following Sarah into the living room.

The Carpers and the Calhouns arrived only minutes apart. Ian and Sasha abandoned the sofa and stood in front of the stone fireplace, both looking nervous and clinging to each other's hand.

Tim and Ruth took their place on the sofa while Tracy sat in the rocking chair and Mark stood behind her.

Sarah and Martha set the trays on the coffee table. "Everyone please help yourself," Sarah said as Martha set the paper plates next to the trays. "I made plenty."

Ian cleared his throat. "The food looks great, Mrs. H, but I don't think anyone is here to eat. They just want to tell Sasha and me why we can't be together."

"Your father and I never said that," Ruth told her son. "We don't care if you date Sasha, but that doesn't mean you have to put the rest of your life on hold."

"That's right," Tracy said, leaning forward in her chair. "College and dating aren't mutually exclusive. I met your father in college, Sasha, and we married right after we graduated. You can do both, you know."

Sarah looked over at Mark, surprised he hadn't spoken yet. He stood tight-lipped behind his wife, watching everyone but not saying a word.

"We can't do both if I'm at UMass and Sasha is in San Diego," Ian countered. "Everybody knows that long distance relationships don't really work."

Tracy looked at him. "But Sasha has a full scholarship to San Diego State, Ian. It doesn't make sense for her to stay in Massachusetts."

Sarah sensed that they were about to start going around in circles. This wouldn't work unless each person put exactly what he or she wanted on the table. Then maybe they could figure out some method to reach each other half way.

"Dad," Sasha said, looking over at her father. "You haven't said anything."

"I think he made his feelings clear when he held our son's shoes hostage," Tim said wryly, and then turned to Mark. "This whole mess might not have happened if you hadn't overreacted."

Mark stepped out from behind the chair and Sarah braced herself for the explosion.

But it didn't come. Instead, Mark said, "You're right. And I have Ian's shoes in the car. I'll make sure you get them before we leave tonight."

Sarah wasn't sure if she had ever heard him so calm before. She wondered what had changed.

Mark turned to Sasha. "Honey, if you want to stay in Maple Hill, then you can stay in Maple Hill. I'll call the basketball coach tomorrow and let her know that you won't be taking the scholarship."

Everyone in the room looked just as shocked as Sasha. She narrowed her eyes at her father. "What is this? Some kind of reverse psychology?"

Mark shook his head. "No, I'm completely serious. I didn't realize how much I had to lose until your mother made it very clear to me last night when she learned I had cancelled the meeting that Sarah had originally scheduled."

Tracy looked up at her husband but didn't say a word.

"She told me that I was at risk of losing her," he paused for a moment, taking a deep breath, "of losing both of you if I didn't let go of this obsession with basketball."

"I've told him that before," Tracy said softly, "but last night, I really meant it."

Martha looked over at Sarah and raised her eyebrows, obviously just as surprised by Mark's turnaround. "So I'm done with this tough love nonsense that was supposed to make you do something you obviously don't want to do," Mark told his daughter. "We've had a great run and I've loved watching you on the basketball court. But you're my daughter and I truly do want you to be happy. I pushed you so hard because I thought basketball made you happy."

"It did," Sasha blurted out, "it *does*. But I want to do other things too." She looked at her mother. "Do you know what I did on Monday after school? I made mints. Cream cheese mints and half of them were blue."

Tracy looked at her husband, then back at Sasha. "That sounds like fun."

"It was! I've never done anything like that before," Sasha explained. "I've been playing basketball and going to basketball camps and watching tapes of great basketball defenses and offenses for as long as I can remember. What if I want to learn how to cook and other stuff?"

"We can look into culinary school," Tracy said, "if cooking interests you."

Sasha stepped forward. "No. That's not what I want. Haven't you been listening?"

They all stared at her. Ian moved next to her. "Sasha, what's wrong?"

"I feel like everyone is deciding things for me again," Sasha cried. "What if I *want* to go to San Diego State and play basketball? My dad makes one phone call tomorrow and poof, that opportunity is gone."

Ian clasped her hand in his. "We promised each other not to let them get to us. We can figure out what we want by ourselves. We just need time."

Mark stepped toward her. "Sasha, I don't understand what you want from me."

"I want you to leave me alone," she cried, pulling her hand out of Ian's grasp and running toward the stairs. "I want all of you to just leave me alone!"

Ian started after her, but Tim stood up to block his path. "Let her go, son. You can talk to her tomorrow."

Ian stared after her as she disappeared up the stairs. A moment later, a bedroom door slammed.

"I guess the meeting is over," Martha said, reaching for her bag.

Ian slowly turned around. "Thanks for letting me stay with you, Grandma," he said, looking over at his parents, "but I think I'll go home tonight, if that's all right."

The defeat Sarah heard in his voice made her heart ache.

"Of course it's all right," Ruth said, circling her arm around his shoulders.

Mark moved toward the door. "Let me get those shoes for you."

Ian gave him a wary glance. "It's not over, you know. Sasha and I aren't over."

Mark met his gaze. "I know, Ian. Believe me, I know." Then he turned around and walked out the door.

Tracy lingered in the living room, her gaze moving to the stairs. Then she looked over at Sarah and Martha. "Should I go up? Sometimes, it seems that I just make things worse when I try to fix them."

"That's what usually happens with teenagers," Martha said walking over to the coffee table and picking up a tortilla pinwheel. "I raised four of them and never quite got the hang of it. That's why God gives us grandchildren, so we have a second chance to do things just right."

Tracy gave her a shaky smile. "Maybe I'll let Sasha be for tonight, since she said she wants to be left alone. She has my number if she needs me, and if I don't hear from her, I'll give her a call in the morning."

Sarah walked her to the door, not sure what to think about everything that had happened tonight. She certainly hadn't expected Mark to play peacemaker or to back down from his tough love stance so quickly.

After everyone had gone home, Sarah walked over to the bottom of the stairs and listened for sounds from above. At first, there was only silence, but then she heard some muffled sobs. She hovered on the first step for a moment, then made her way upstairs.

CHAPTER TWENTY-THREE

S arah tapped lightly on Sasha's door and waited for her to answer. After a long moment, she heard the girl say, "Yeah?"

"Sasha, it's Sarah. May I come in?"

There was no answer, so Sarah decided to take that as a yes. She turned the knob and slowly opened the door. Sasha had buried herself underneath the covers with only her head peeking out on her pillow. Her face was red from crying and her cheeks still wet with tears.

Sarah sat down on the bed and brushed the hair from Sasha's face. "Do you want to talk?"

Sasha gave a slight shrug of her shoulders but didn't ask her to leave. So Sarah just sat there, gently smoothing Sasha's hair back and trying to think of something to say to make her feel better.

"I have lots of food left if you're hungry," Sarah said at last.

Sasha gave her a watery smile. "You always have food. That's one of the things I like about living here."

Since the girl stood over six feet tall in her stocking feet, Sarah knew she wasn't malnourished. "I'm sure you have plenty of food at home too."

"Sure," Sasha said, making a face. "Power foods, like nuts and spinach and eggs and fruit. My dad hired a dietitian a few years ago to design the perfect endurance diet for someone who plays basketball."

"Maybe more people should eat like that," Sarah said. "You're very healthy."

"Yeah, but it gets boring too. Spaghetti with meatballs is my favorite meal, but my Dad only makes it the night before I have a game because he says it's important to load up on carbohydrates." She sighed. "Why can't we have a spaghetti dinner sometime just for fun, even when I don't have a game?"

Sarah knew the best thing for Sasha was to talk and get out everything she was feeling. "So does your dad do a lot of cooking?"

"Mostly. Mom has always worked overtime to pay for my basketball camps and stuff. Dad always took care of stuff when she wasn't there."

Sasha had a legitimate complaint about her zealous father, but much of the drama in her life was typical teenage angst and rebellion. Only in her case there was big money and prestige on the line, making the stakes for her family so much higher.

"I can't believe Dad said he was going to call my coach tomorrow." She met Sarah's gaze. "Do you think he meant it?"

"He sounded like he meant it," she said truthfully. "Do you want him to make the call?"

"I don't know." She closed her eyes. "I went to a basketball camp in New York over Christmas break. I met another girl there who had been recruited by San Diego State." Sasha opened her eyes. "She was better than me. A lot better than me. What if I don't make it? I've never sat on the bench, Sarah, not even when I was a freshman. What if I can't do it?"

"You tell me," Sarah said, feeling on more familiar ground now. Sasha's problems might seem bigger, but she had the same insecurities as anyone else. Sarah remembered a similar conversation with Jenna when it was time for her to go off to college and she had been hit with a sudden case of cold feet.

"What if I can't do it, Mom?" Jenna had asked her. "What if I can't make the grades and lose my scholarship?"

"You tell me," Sarah had said then, as she said now to Sasha. "What happens if you can't do it?"

Sasha thought for a long moment. "I'll disappoint the coach, I suppose, but she'll have a lot of good players. I won't be a star player, so other kids on the campus won't know me that well." She turned over onto her back. "I'll have to call Dad and tell him. He'll probably come out to San Diego and try to help me figure out the problem, like he did when my jump shot was off one summer."

"So you'll be an anonymous college student with an over-protective parent?" Sarah summed up for her.

Sasha smiled. "I guess maybe I'm not so special after all."

"That's where you're wrong. Every child of God is special and you've been given a wonderful talent. God wants you to use your gifts, not hide them under a bush."

"But what about Ian?"

Sarah looked at her. "Do you like him?"

"Yes," she said softly. "I like him a lot. But I like basketball too. So how do I choose?"

"If it was me, I'd pray about it."

Sasha sat up. "Will you pray with me?"

"Of course." Sarah folded her hands in prayer as Sasha did the same. Then she bowed her head and prayed, "Heavenly Father, give Sasha the guidance she needs to make the right decisions for her life. Give her strength and hope and belief in herself. Help her to use her talent to be a blessing to others. Be with her parents and the people who surround her, Lord, and give them peace of heart and mind. All this we pray, Amen."

"Amen," Sasha echoed. Then she blinked. "I think I feel a little better."

"Good." Sarah stood up and tucked the blankets around her shoulders. "Now, go to sleep and remember that to-morrow is a brand-new day. You can do whatever you want with it."

"Thank you, Sarah," Sasha said with a yawn. "Good night."

"Good night, dear." Sarah walked out of the bedroom, closing the door behind her. It sounded to her like Sasha might be going to California to college after all. She just wasn't sure how Ian would handle it.

Sasha moved back home on Thursday, although she hadn't yet made a decision about going to college in California. Now that she was living alone again, Sarah spent the entire day and evening working on both quilts.

She had stayed up later than she had planned, but she was still ready to go to Willow Creek when Jason and his family arrived to pick her up on Friday morning. He drove Maggie's red Chevy Tahoe that had room for all six of them. Jason and Maggie sat in the front, Sarah and Patty in the middle seats, and the twins in the back.

The luggage was packed in tightly around them, making it a cozy three-hour trip. Sarah held the pioneer quilt on her lap, not wanting to take a chance that it might get damaged.

"I brought snacks," Patty said as Jason headed toward the highway. "There are crackers with peanut butter and some dried fruit. I've also got plenty of bottles of fruit juice, so just let me know if you're hungry."

"Thank you, Patty." Sarah glanced over her shoulder at the girls. "Did you bring the map for your presentation?"

Amy exchanged looks with her sister, then said, "We brought two maps because we decided to do two presentations."

"It was my idea," Maggie offered. "Since there seems to be a disparity between the journey in the letters and the one depicted on the quilt, I thought the girls should each present one version."

Patty sighed. "I'm afraid that will just cause confusion, but I've already been outvoted."

"Two versions are fine with me," Sarah said, since she hadn't yet been able to actually prove that the route depicted on the quilt was the correct one. "Have you heard back from the other expert yet?"

Patty sniffed. "He didn't work out."

Jason looked at Sarah in the rearview mirror. "He wanted more money. Patty decided a second opinion wasn't worth the price of a small car."

"It wasn't *that* much money," Patty said, "but he still wanted to charge an exorbitant fee for one simple job, especially since I *told* him the letters were accurate."

"But you don't know that for sure, Mom. That's why I think both versions should be presented," Maggie said. "Then people can decide for themselves which one to believe."

Amy leaned forward, her hands curled around the back of Sarah's car seat. "You're not mad, are you, Gram? 'Cause I'm going to talk about the route in the letters and why I think it's the right one."

"Of course I'm not mad," Sarah assured her. "I'm eager to hear your presentation."

"I'm on your side, Gram," Audrey announced. "I think the quilt is right."

Patty turned around to face her. "What makes you say that, Audrey?"

"Because why would a person go to that much work only to have it be wrong? That doesn't make sense."

Sarah wanted the girl to think, not just take sides. "But why would they write letters home with false information in them?"

Audrey shrugged. "I don't know. Maybe they weren't sure where they were going."

Sarah smiled to herself, realizing that explanation worked better than most she had come up with so far.

Jason turned on the radio, filling the car with soft jazz music.

"So what's the schedule for the reunion," Sarah asked Patty.

Patty pulled a printed list from her purse. "Well, today we'll all get settled in at the hotel. Some people will want to tour the old church while others may want to tour Josiah Hollander's old farmhouse that's been renovated into a family museum."

"We have our own museum?" Amy asked.

Patty smiled back at her. "That's right, dear. Hollanders have lived in Willow Creek for centuries and many were quite prominent citizens. The museum is actually a house that looks exactly like one from the 1870s on both the inside and the outside."

Sarah turned to her. "You mentioned a church?"

"Yes, it's the same church that the pioneers attended before they made their way west."

Sarah sat up, her heart thumping. "The same church they spoke about in their letters? With Pastor Simpson?"

"That's right," Patty said nonchalantly. "The old church is quite interesting. It has several valuable artifacts on display from the early years. It's open for tourists every weekend."

They drove in silence for several minutes as Sarah thought about the letters. She had brought the booklet on the trip and decided she would go over the letters one more time to look for references to the old church.

"I can't wait to see Dad," Maggie said, breaking the silence. "When will he get there?"

"Not until Saturday morning," Patty told her. "He called me late last night and told me he plans to stop by a lake on his way down here. But he can't wait to see everyone."

Sarah's mind wandered back to the church, wondering if they had kept an archive of all the church rolls. There could be a mountain of information in those church records about the pioneers and their families.

She spent the rest of the trip reading the booklet again. This time she noticed little things that made her curious. She retrieved her notebook from her bag and jotted down short phrases and words from the letters that caught her attention and seemed to have a common theme. By the time they reached Willow Creek, Sarah was beginning to put it all together.

Jason pulled up in front of the hotel. There were several cars in the parking lot with a variety of license plates. "It looks like the Hollanders have descended," he said as they all climbed out of the vehicle.

Patty clapped her hands together. "Isn't it wonderful?" Then she urged Jason toward the back of the Tahoe. "We need to get all of this stuff inside so I can set up the conference room. Registration starts in one hour."

"Registration?" Maggie echoed. "Oh, mother, really?"

Patty nodded. "There are over one hundred Hollanders due to arrive here today and tomorrow. I think it would be nice to know all of their names and their places on the family tree, don't you?"

"I suppose that would be helpful," Maggie conceded. "What do you want me to do?"

Patty handed over a large tote bag. "I've got some games in here for the kids to keep them occupied while the adults visit. Maybe Amy and Audrey can help supervise them."

Sarah knew she should probably offer to help too, but Patty had made it clear she didn't need to participate in anything at the reunion other than the presentation. She told Jason where she was headed and hurried off to find the church, anxious to see if her hunch was right.

CHAPTER TWENTY-FOUR

The Willow Creek church was located about five blocks from the hotel. Sarah walked there after assuring Jason that she would call him if she needed a ride back. She could see the tall, white church steeple from the hotel parking lot, so she had no fear of getting lost.

Willow Creek was a town of about four thousand people, and it reminded her of Maple Hill. The streets were wide and lined with full-grown elm trees and the front yards were large and well kept.

The church itself was a simple box frame, with a gabled roof. It was painted white and three Greek-style columns adorned the front. She climbed the steps that led to the wide double doors, telling herself that Charlotte Hollander and her husband had attended this church, along with their children. So had the other pioneers who had come to mean something to her, especially Emma Hollander Grant and Harriet Hollander.

Now she hoped to learn even more about them.

She stepped through the open doors of the church and was struck by the starkness of the interior. There were two rows of pews lined up to face the pulpit and a small organ in the corner. Two square windows adorned the walls on each of the four sides of the church.

"May I help you?"

Sarah started at the sound and turned to see a frail woman standing behind her, a gray cane in her thin hand. "Oh, hello," Sarah said, "I was just taking a look around."

"That's fine," the woman said. "My name is Lois and I'll be glad to answer any questions for you if I can." She studied Sarah's face. "Are you from around here?"

"Oh no," Sarah told her. "I live in Maple Hill, Massachusetts. I'm here for the Hollander reunion."

"I'm a Hollander," the woman announced, "on my mother's side. Which branch of the family do you belong to?"

Sarah smiled. "None, I'm afraid. My daughter-in-law comes from the Hollander family, though, and I was invited here this weekend to give a presentation about a quilt."

Lois nodded. "I saw that on the agenda." She emitted a low chuckle. "That Patty is quite a firecracker, isn't she? Imagine making an agenda for a family get-together. Still, I guess it's a way to keep us all in line."

"Have you lived in Willow Creek your entire life?"

Lois nodded. "I sure have. It's a great place to grow up and raise children. My own three have moved on to bigger cities, but I like it here too much to leave."

Sarah knew exactly how she felt. She had spent nearly her entire life in Maple Hill and had enjoyed almost every moment of it. "I understand there are some artifacts here from the early days of the church."

"There sure are." Lois led her to the front of the church. "We keep them locked in a case in the anteroom. They're quite valuable and have been part of the church since it was built in 1832."

Sarah was impressed. So many old buildings and valuable artifacts had been lost to fire or a natural disaster. She wondered if the church in Willow Bend was still standing and made a mental note to ask someone at the reunion.

Lois showed her into the anteroom where a large, glass case lined one wall. Sarah walked up to it, impressed by the shining gold pieces behind the glass. There was a candlestick and a chalice, along with a gold altar cross.

"We still use the altar cross for Sunday services," Lois told her, "but we keep it locked away in there the rest of the week." She sighed. "It's a shame, isn't it? We shouldn't have to worry about someone stealing from a church, but it happens. The only way to protect these pieces of history is to keep them locked away."

"They're beautiful," Sarah said. "Do you happen to know the history behind them?"

Lois shook her head. "Not really. All I know is that they're part of a set that was given to the church when it was first built."

Sarah stared at the candlestick. Something about it seemed a little odd. Then she realized that candlesticks usually came in pairs. She turned to Lois. "Is there any chance I could see the church records from the mid-nineteenth century?"

"Of course," Lois said without hesitation. "We get requests for copies of our church records all the time, usually from genealogy buffs." She led the way out of the anteroom. "We keep the records in a vault in the basement. They go all the way back to 1832 as well."

"Really? That far?"

Lois nodded. "The Hollanders have always been sticklers about keeping meticulous records for the sake of posterity. We're very proud of our heritage." She paused at the top of the stairs to face Sarah. "So you're going to give some kind of presentation at the reunion?"

"Well, my granddaughters are," Sarah said, then she proceeded to tell her all about it.

The next day, Larry Roberts arrived just before the quilt presentation was due to begin and enveloped the twins in a big bear hug.

"There's my girls," he said, wrapping his long arms around them. He kissed the tops of their heads.

"Be careful, Larry," Patty said. "You'll mess up their hair."

Larry turned to his wife and gave her a hug. "Did you miss me?"

"Larry, not now," she said with a blush. Then she turned him around to face Maggie. "Say hello to your daughter."

"Hi, Dad," Maggie said, reaching out to give him a hug. "How was the fishing trip?"

"Hello, sweetheart. The trip was amazing. I caught almost more fish than I could eat, but not quite." He chuckled as he patted his rotund belly. "And you look even prettier than the last time I saw you."

Jason stepped forward and held out his hand. "Hi, Larry. Nice to see you again."

"Good to see you, son." He pumped Jason's hand up and down. "Were you surprised when Patty showed up at your door?"

Jason smiled. "You could say that."

Sarah approached him. "Hello, Larry."

"Why, Sarah," he said, looking startled by her presence at the reunion. "This is certainly a treat. What are you doing here?"

"She's helping us with our presentation about the pioneer quilt," Audrey told him. "We have to start in just a few minutes."

"Then we'd better go find our seats," Maggie said, reaching for her father's arm. "Come on, Dad."

"Good luck, girls," he called back to them. "I mean, break a leg!"

"A broken leg doesn't sound too bad about now," Amy said, looking a little pale. "I'm nervous."

"You'll do just fine," Sarah assured her. "Everyone in there will be fascinated by what you're about to tell them, and remember, you're family, so they have to love you no matter what. It's a rule."

Audrey grinned. "Really? A rule?"

"Well, it should be," Sarah said with a smile. "Don't you think so?"

"I guess that would be nice," Audrey agreed, then took a deep breath and looked at her sister. "Are you ready?"

Amy nodded. "Let's do this thing."

Sarah proudly watched the twins give their separate presentations about the Hollander pioneers' journey west on the Oregon Trail. Amy went first and detailed the trip according to the letters, focusing on the plight of Emma Hollander and her quest to marry a man she had never met before.

The Hollanders gathered at the reunion were enthralled, many of them having never heard that specific story before. The letters had been in the safekeeping of Patty's aunt Myrna and had not seen the light of day for decades before Patty had made the little booklets that were to be passed around later in the day.

They applauded loud and long after Amy finished her presentation. Larry even stood up and whistled, causing Amy's face to turn red as she exited the stage.

Now it was Audrey's turn. She began her presentation in the same way but focused on how the trail described in the letters differed from the trail depicted by the quilt.

Sarah was proud of the way she carefully explained the meaning behind each quilt block, although she stumbled a bit with the more difficult patterns. Sarah gave a wide smile of encouragement each time she hesitated and Audrey made it through her presentation, heaving a big sigh of relief at the end.

The crowd of relatives applauded politely, but many of them seemed confused by the conflicting tales. Even Larry was too busy questioning his wife about it to give Audrey the same standing ovation that he had given Amy.

Sarah stood up to come to the aid of her granddaughter. "Hello, everyone," she said, moving next to Audrey. "My name is Sarah Hart and I am Audrey and Amy's other grandmother. I restore vintage quilts and I had the pleasure of making some minor restorative improvements to this pioneer quilt that is a wonderful part of the Hollander heritage."

The crowd perked up when they heard her credentials, and Audrey smiled her relief that Sarah had come to her rescue.

"You've heard two different versions of the journey the Hollander pioneers took on the Oregon Trail and there's a reason for that. It's a reason I didn't fully understand until just yesterday." She smiled at Lois, who sat in the second row. "But I'll be happy to explain it to you now."

Patty shifted uncomfortably in her seat and glanced at the people around her.

"When the Hollander pioneers took off on the wagon trail, they were worried they were being followed because of the 'precious cargo' mentioned in their letters. They encountered trouble even before they reached the Missouri River, and that's when they suspected that someone might be intercepting their letters home and tracking their journey. So they decided to send false letters home so no one would know their true route until they reached their destination."

Sarah smiled at the twins, then continued. "Charlotte Hollander, in her May 30, 1849, letter to Pastor Simpson, wrote that the men on the wagon train would take turns guarding the precious cargo each night."

Sarah paused for a moment, realizing this was a lot of information for people to take in. "When I first read her letter, I thought the precious cargo she was referring to was the people on the wagon train, and perhaps they were included, but the precious cargo was actually valuable artifacts given to them by the Willow Creek church. These artifacts, which included a gold candlestick and a gold chalice, were to be used to start a sister church at their new settlement in the Oregon Territory."

She waited for that information to sink in, then saw someone in the back raise his hand. "Yes?"

"So who was following them?" a man asked.

"That's a good question," she replied. "And the answer can also be found in the letters if you look hard enough. In his May 9, 1849, letter, Josiah Hollander, who had been entrusted to start the new church, wrote that they had already encountered some trouble along the journey, but they would be more watchful so disaster did not befall them."

"But couldn't that refer to anything?" a young woman in the front row asked her. "A difficult river crossing or maybe an injury?"

"It could," Sarah agreed, "but the interesting thing is that the location mentioned in that particular letter is, for the first time, different from the location indicated on the quilt. Josiah says they will reach Nebraska City the next day and hire a guide, yet the quilt shows them using a place in Missouri as a jumping-off point."

"What other hints were there?" Larry asked, leaning forward in his chair.

Patty gave him a poke in the ribs with her elbow, but he ignored her.

"Charles Hollander wrote a letter on June 1," Sarah answered him, "in which he mentions an intruder in the camp the evening before. His grandmother, Harriet Hollander, caught a glimpse of this intruder, but no one else saw him after she fired a warning shot with her rifle."

Audrey leaned over and whispered to her. "Don't forget about the letter Amos wrote to his mom."

Sarah nodded and whispered, "Thanks." Then she consulted her notebook for the date of that letter.

"On June 10, 1849, Amos Hollander wrote to his mother and said that he felt they were traveling around in circles, which matches the Drunkard's Path block you see next on the quilt."

Audrey walked over to the quilt and pointed out the block.

"He also states that Josiah had doubled the number of men who watched the wagon train during the night." She looked down at her notebook. "Then, in his July 17 letter, Josiah writes that he will continue to fulfill their mission and settle in the Oregon Territory. He also states that the danger is still with them and they are doing their best to ward off the evil, but not everyone on the wagon train is watchful." Sarah looked around the room. "I think that is one of the clearest messages that they feel someone is following them."

Sarah stepped forward, feeling every eye in the room on her. "Which brings us to one of the most compelling blocks on the quilt. It contains two patterns. The outside of the block is a pattern called Snake Trail and represents the Snake River. The inside of the block is a Judas tree, which represents betrayal."

Patty cleared her throat and looked nervously around her. Sarah glanced over at Maggie and her son, who gave her a furtive thumbs-up sign.

Sarah took another deep breath and continued. "One of the most interesting things about these letters, and something that I didn't notice until the second time I read them, was that everyone was involved in mentioning fake locations except one person, and that was Charles Hollander. He simply never referred to where they were located. And while he talked of gold nuggets in his first letter, the letters that followed just referred to gold and how eager he was to leave the wagon train behind and make his fortune."

A man in the back row said, "Are you calling him a thief?"

Sarah tipped up her chin. "I think he and his cousin Matthew conspired to steal the precious cargo on that wagon train. The candlestick and the chalice were made of solid gold and there may have been other items as well."

A quiet buzz started among the people in the room.

"We know the pioneers had a chalice with them on the trail," Sarah continued, "because Harriet wrote that Josiah allowed Emma and her new husband to drink from the same golden cup that Emma's parents had drunk from when they were married."

"But there's no proof that Charles and Matthew tried to steal these artifacts," Patty said. "You're simply guessing from the letters."

"As a matter for fact, there is proof," Sarah replied. "I found the death of Matthew Hollander written in the church records for August of 1849. It says that he died of drowning in the Snake River while being pursued."

Sarah nodded to Audrey, who pointed out the second unmarked gravestone block on the quilt. "I believe this represents Matthew's unmarked grave on the trail. He was still a Hollander, despite his attempt to steal from them, so his death was also recorded on the quilt."

"How do you know it wasn't Charles?" someone asked. "Was he in the church record too?"

"No." Sarah smiled at Lois, who got up from her chair and came forward. "But there is someone here who can tie up the loose threads of this story."

Lois walked with her cane to the spot where Sarah had been standing and cleared her throat. "This is a letter that my great-great-aunt Agnes received from her sister. They both married Hollander boys." Then she cleared her throat and began to read.

September 2, 1849

Dear Agnes,

I never thought I would say such a thing, but I miss Emma. While she is on her way to Iowa with her handsome new husband, I am stuck in this lonely wilderness they call the Oregon Territory with only Carl and my children for company. How I long to talk to another woman who really understands me.

If you were here, I would tell you how that sassy Dauber girl flirts shamelessly with Amos. I would also tell you that we have left one of our party in chains at Fort Boise. Charles deceived us all and connived with his cousin Matthew to steal some valuable cargo on the wagon train. No one even told me that we carried such items and it seems Carl knew about it but believed I could not keep my tongue.

Their theft was discovered almost immediately and a wild chase ensued, led by John Grant. Emma was almost sick with worry for her new husband, but I had no pity for the woman who had stolen our horse. I was dismayed to learn that Carl gave her back the money she left in the wagon to pay for the gelding, but he pretends not to hear my opinions.

So now the Hollander name has a black mark upon it. It seems that Matthew and possibly some other ne'er-do-wells had been following the wagon train since we left Independence,

Missouri. Charles was sending him updates about our travels, although he had to be sly about it because Josiah read all of the correspondence before it was sent.

Harriet apologized for her grandson and I enjoyed seeing her brought down a peg. She is a headstrong woman who, just yesterday, shot her rifle so close to my feet that I plum fell over. She claims she saw a snake in the grass, but I am not sure I believe her.

I shall write again when I have a spare moment, so do not expect another letter from me soon. Oh, and all of what I have told you is to be kept a secret, so do not share it with any of the Hollanders. You know how they like to gossip.

Your sister,
Maude Hollander

The last line of the letter provoked laughter among the crowd and even Lois chuckled as she read it.

"And that," Sarah announced, "is the true story of the Hollander pioneers on the Oregon Trail."

The crowd began to applaud, all of them soon rising to their feet. Sarah motioned Amy to join her at the front of the room along with Audrey and Lois. The four of them executed a short bow and when Sarah looked up she was pleased to see that even Patty was applauding.

Audrey leaned over and whispered to Amy, "See, my version *was* the right one."

Before Amy could reply, Sarah said, "Both versions are a part of Hollander history now, so there is no right or wrong.

And now you girls are part of it too, because you helped solve the mystery."

They both beamed, then took another bow. Sarah stepped back, letting them enjoy the spotlight. She whispered a prayer of thanks that their presentation had gone so well, then thanked Lois for her part in it.

"It was my pleasure," Lois said, two rosy spots on her cheeks. "I can't remember when I've had so much fun."

Sarah had enjoyed it too, and later, she happily accepted Patty's gracious invitation to join the rest of the Hollanders at the evening banquet. The next day, they attended the worship service at the Willow Creek Church, followed by a touching memorial service for Maggie's great-aunt Myrna.

Then it was time to go home.

CHAPTER TWENTY-FIVE

One week later, Sarah stood in Martha's kitchen and added more blue and white diploma mints to a silver platter. Ian and Sasha had graduated from high school less than an hour before and were now holding their graduation receptions together.

Liam walked into the kitchen with an empty pitcher. "We need more lemonade slush. It's going fast."

"There's another pitcher in the fridge," Sarah said, then smiled up at him. "I didn't mean to put you to work when I invited you to the party, but we weren't expecting such a rush of people."

"I'm happy to help," he said, giving her a wink. "Maybe we can go out for a quiet dinner later this evening. I want to hear all about your trip to Pennsylvania."

"I'd love to," Sarah said, looking forward to it. She carried the mint tray out to Martha's living room, where one side of the room was decorated with all of Sasha's pictures and basketball trophies and the other side was decorated with Ian's pictures, art work, and high school achievement awards.

In the middle of the room was a gift table with a unique centerpiece. A pair of Sasha's basketball shoes were tied together with the laces of the tennis shoes that Ian had left at the Calhoun residence. Sasha's shoes were two inches longer, but Sarah had to admit it was a creative idea for a centerpiece.

Ernie sat in his recliner, eating one of the cupcakes that the twins had made and decorated for the occasion. Each cupcake had white frosting with the graduation year written out with blue icing.

Sarah and Martha had also made some finger foods and the lemonade slush that Tracy and Ruth took turns serving to the guests.

Jason walked up to Sarah as she set the mint tray on the food table. "Did you hear you're a local celebrity in Willow Creek?"

Sarah laughed. "Please tell me you're joking."

"I'm completely serious. You can ask Maggie. She said there was a big write-up about the Hollander family reunion and the feature story was about how you and the girls solved the mystery of the pioneer quilt."

"I can't believe it made the newspaper," Sarah said, checking the other dishes to see if they needed filling.

He grinned. "Did Lois happen to mention that her regular job is working as the editor of the *Willow Creek Tribune*? That might have something to do with it."

Sarah laughed. "I had no idea. I guess it's a good thing I didn't spill any Hart family secrets when I was talking to her."

He arched a curious brow. "I didn't know there were any Hart family secrets. Care to share them with me?"

"Not right now," she said. "I think Sasha and Ian are getting ready to open their gifts."

Sarah stepped closer to the gift table, eager to see Sasha's reaction when she saw the T-shirt quilt. Liam joined her there, exchanging greetings with several of the other guests.

Sarah's gaze moved to Mark, who leaned against a wall near the staircase. He had been unusually quiet all day, making Sarah think that his daughter leaving for college in a couple of weeks was hitting him harder than he wanted anyone to know.

She still wasn't fond of the man, but at least he had taken his intensity about Sasha's basketball career down a notch. Now he moved closer too, as Sasha began to unwrap the package with the quilt inside.

"This gift is from your Dad and me," Tracy announced, wearing an apron with the words *Senior Mom* embroidered on it with royal blue thread. The words were crooked, but Sasha had done the work herself and was quite proud of it. Ruth wore one too, although Ian had ordered it for her from the home economics club.

Sasha tore the paper off the large box, then opened it and pushed aside the tissue paper wrapped around the quilt. For a moment, she just stared, then she looked up at her parents with tears in her eyes. "You cut up all my T-shirts."

"Do you mind?" Tracy asked.

"No way!" Sasha blinked the tears away. "I love it!" She pulled the quilt out of the box so she could spread it out on the floor. "Now I can keep these memories forever."

"Sarah made it for us," Tracy told her, "so you should thank her too."

Sasha walked over and gave Sarah a hug, standing almost a good foot taller than her.

"Thank you for making my quilt," Sasha said, "and for everything else too."

"You're welcome," Sarah said, patting her back. "And you're going to do great in San Diego, I just know it."

Sasha carefully folded the quilt again, then walked over to her father. "Dad, you know what those dorm rooms can be like. I've seen the pictures of your dorm room when you were in college."

He smiled. "They can get a little messy."

She pushed the quilt into his arms. "Would you mind keeping this for me until I have a place of my own? I don't want it to get dirty or anything."

Mark cleared his throat twice before he answered her. "Sure, I can keep it safe for you. I promise I won't let anything happen to it."

"I know you won't," she said softly, then leaned over and kissed his cheek.

Ian stepped over to the gift table and picked up an envelope. "This one is for my parents," he said, carrying it over to his mother. "I know I've caused you and Dad a little stress lately."

"A little," Tim muttered, standing beside Ruth.

"Yeah," Ian grinned. "I hope this will help make up for it."

Ruth opened the envelope and pulled out the letter inside. Her mouth gaped as she read it. Then she looked up at Ian. "It's a conditional acceptance to a graphic design school in California."

He grinned. "I guess I'm going to college after all. I just have to send them my portfolio and a reference letter from my art teacher and I'm in."

"And we can still be together," Sasha said. "Well, only an hour apart, anyway. So it's all good."

Tim reached out to hug his son, relief washing over his face. "No offense, son, but you're not really cut out for a career in snow removal."

"I know, Dad. No chance of that in sunny California. Now Trina will have to shovel the driveway and sidewalks."

Martha walked up to Sarah and put an arm around her. "I guess our grandma-style intervention worked out all right. The kids are both going off to college and they're speaking to their parents again."

"I'm not sure we really did much," Sarah said as Liam smiled at them. "Sasha and Ian just finally decided to take charge of their own futures."

"We prayed and worried," Martha reminded her, "and worried and prayed. That sounds like a grandma-style intervention in my mind."

Sarah couldn't argue with that. She sent up a silent prayer, thanking God for her family and friends, the true treasures on this earth.

About the Author

Kristin Eckhardt is the author of more than thirty books, including eight books for Guideposts' Mysteries of Sparrow Island and Home to Heather Creek series. She's won two national awards for her writing, and her first book was made into a TV movie. Kristin and her husband raised three children on their farm in central Nebraska and are active in their church and community.

THE THOUSAND STORIES QUILT

BY JO ANN BROWN

 CHAPTER ONE

Sarah Hart wondered what other surprises the beautiful June day had in store for her. As she waited at a light in downtown North Adams, she smiled. Sarah often saw Carolyn Johnson at Bridge Street Church, since Carolyn and Pastor John Peabody had been dating for almost a year, but today was the first time Carolyn had sought her out before the service. When she had asked Sarah to lunch at her condo in nearby North Adams, Sarah had happily accepted. Sarah often spent Sunday afternoons with her son Jason's family, but she had already made plans to spend time with them during the upcoming week.

It would be lovely to have a chance to talk with Carolyn away from all the joyous hubbub of chatting friends and neighbors after the Sunday service. Usually those conversations were short and often interrupted as other folks attending church called a greeting or paused to talk. Today, over lunch, she and Carolyn would have a chance to get to know each other better.

Glancing at the directions she had printed out, Sarah flipped her left-turn blinker and then pulled up to a gate in front of the Mountain View Condominiums. She punched the code Carolyn had given her into the keypad, and the gates swung open.

Roses in every possible shade edged the curbs as Sarah drove into the condo complex that backed up to the base of Mount Greylock. She followed her map and pulled into an empty parking space in front of 1617 Rosebush Lane.

The front of the condo was a mix of multicolored flagstones and light gray clapboard. A wreath of dried forsythia decorated the bright green front door. The curtains on the windows had been pulled back to let sunlight inside. It looked both welcoming and elegant, exactly like Carolyn herself.

The door opened before Sarah could push the doorbell. With a smile, Carolyn said, "I hope you didn't have any trouble getting here." Her voice had warmth and serenity, which had probably been an asset in her previous occupation as a public relations expert in Boston. From what Pastor John had said, Carolyn still had a few clients, but she had come to the Berkshires to get out of the big city rat race.

Today Carolyn wore simple khaki slacks and a white shirt topped by a blue patterned scarf that accented her eyes. Her black hair was cut in a stylish bob, allowing the silver threading through it to catch the light. She stepped aside on the Oriental runner to let Sarah enter.

Sarah smiled as she walked in. "Not at all. I've driven past this neighborhood plenty of times, and now you've given me the chance to visit."

"It's lovely and quiet, which is why I decided to move in here." Carolyn put her hand on the simple newel post at the bottom of the staircase to the right of the hallway.

The condo was just as welcoming inside as from the street. The living room was decorated in a mixture of Early American antiques and art deco lighting. Sarah was amazed at how perfectly the two styles fit together. Almost as if the room had evolved through hundreds of years.

Sarah followed Carolyn through the living room and into a cozy dining room. The simple round table was topped by a white tablecloth and brightly colored dishes. A bowl in the center of the table held rose petals floating in water. The windows above an oak sideboard were open to catch the fresh June breeze.

"Can I get you something to drink while we wait for the quiche to finish baking?" When a buzzer sounded, Carolyn glanced at the kitchen that was visible through an arch. "Sounds like it's time for me to check it."

"Whatever you have is fine."

"Iced tea?"

"Perfect." Sarah placed her purse on the floor by one of the chairs and trailed into the kitchen just as Carolyn placed a pretty pie pan on a trivet. "Is there anything I can help with?"

"Thank you, but we just need to give the quiche a few minutes to set, and it will be ready. Do you want lemon and sugar with your tea?"

"Lemon, please."

"Great." She opened the compact refrigerator and took out a saucer with sliced lemons. Putting them on the counter close to where Sarah stood in the arched doorway, she smiled. "I hope you don't mind my being informal. After all those years of fancy Boston receptions, I really enjoy a chance to kick back."

"Informal is my favorite way to entertain."

Carolyn put ice in two tall glasses, poured in iced tea, and handed one glass to Sarah. "Take as many lemons as you'd like." When Sarah had selected two lemon slices, Carolyn picked up the saucer and carried it and the pitcher of iced tea to the dining room table.

They chatted about the weather and summer activities while Carolyn brought the mushroom and tomato quiche into the dining room and cut two generous pieces, placing them on the table. Sarah decided her idea of informal and Carolyn's were very different when she saw elegant linen napkins set beside the silver and bone china plates.

"What a pretty table," Sarah said as she admired the rose petals in the bowl.

"I'm not quite to paper plates and cups informal." Carolyn laughed and sat. "But, trust me, this is a huge step away from some of the meals I oversaw when I was trying to impress my clients and their clients."

"That must have been exciting."

"And exhausting." She folded her hands and asked, "Do you mind if I say grace?"

"Please." Sarah clasped her hands.

"Thank you, Lord, for bringing us together today to share this meal and to have a chance to get to know each other better." Carolyn raised her head as she said, "Amen."

Sarah repeated that, then said, "It sounds like you don't miss Boston at all."

"Oh, I do. I have friends there." Carolyn unfolded her napkin, then picked up her fork. "Several of them, after coming out to visit me, have decided to leave the pressure cooker of the corporate world and strike out on their own too."

"Leaving a regular paycheck takes a lot of courage."

Carolyn nodded. "I don't know if I would have had the courage if my grandmother hadn't left me an inheritance that gave me a cushion for my first year. But I can't tell you how happy I am that I did. If I hadn't moved here, I wouldn't have met John and the wonderful members of his congregation."

Sarah took a bite of the quiche. It was fragrant with a smoky cheese, which melted delightfully on her tongue. "This is delicious."

"Thanks."

"What kind of cheese is in it?"

"Parmesan." Carolyn sipped on her iced tea, then said, "I have it shipped from a shop in Boston's North End. I haven't found a store in the Berkshires that has anything like it."

Sarah enjoyed another bite. "I've heard good things about the deli near the Red Lion Inn in Stockbridge, but I haven't been there."

"I've got to admit I've never been there."

"Really? It's such a pretty town. There's a very nice quilt shop right around the corner from the inn."

Carolyn chuckled. "Why am I not surprised that you'd know where the quilt shops were?"

The conversation continued, convivial and pleasant, while they talked about the latest news and people they both knew. Carolyn flushed with pleasure when Sarah asked for the recipe for both the quiche and the custard that Carolyn had spooned over fresh strawberries for their dessert.

"I'd be honored," Carolyn said. "Maybe you could share your chocolate chip cookie recipe. John tells me they're about the best he's ever tasted." She put down her spoon in her empty dessert bowl. "John has also told me about what a whiz you are with old quilts."

She rose and opened a door on the sideboard. She lifted out a shopping bag by its handles, reaching in to carefully loosen the top of the bag when it caught. Setting it on the floor between their chairs, she said, "Sarah, I've got to admit that I had two reasons to ask you here for lunch today. I wanted a chance to get to know you better, but I also wanted to speak to you about a gift I'd like to give John to celebrate the anniversary of our first date." A girlish blush brightened her cheeks. "I know it sounds silly for a woman my age to want to celebrate such an anniversary—"

"I think it's absolutely lovely," Sarah said, patting Carolyn's arm. "My late husband Gerry and I believed in celebrating every occasion. One year, when the children were very young, we celebrated a day when nobody cried over a scraped knee or a quarrel."

Carolyn laughed, her disquiet vanishing. "I'm glad you understand, because I want to pick your brain about an old quilt."

Sarah's eyes widened. The words old quilt were, for her, like candy to a kid. "You want to give John a quilt for your anniversary?"

"Not exactly." Carolyn looked at the bag. "This is an old quilt that John had stored in a trunk up in his attic. He brought it downstairs when he was doing some spring cleaning last month and was considering throwing it out because it's in such poor condition. But he said he couldn't bring himself to do it because his grandmother had made it. When he said that it was a shame it couldn't be displayed, I got the idea of finding out if it could be restored."

"His grandmother's quilt?" Sarah's eyes widened. "Did he mention by any chance if this is his grandmother's Thousand Stories quilt?"

Carolyn's smile widened. "I see that John must have told you about it."

Sarah nodded as she hooked her finger in the side of the bag and opened it enough to peer in. Even without taking it out of the bag, she could see the crazy quilt was in bad shape. Some of the fabric was shredded, and seams had failed, revealing the batting.

Looking back at Carolyn, she said, "He's mentioned it a couple of times when he's talked about missionary work, because his grandparents were missionaries in China back in the thirties. From what he's said, his mother, who was born over there, gave the quilt its name. I'm not sure why."

"Me neither."

"We should ask him."

Carolyn wrinkled her nose. "I was hoping the quilt's restoration would be a surprise for him. Please don't ask him about it. He doesn't know that I 'borrowed' it instead of taking it back up to the attic. Do you think you can restore it?"

Sarah wanted to say yes, immediately, because Carolyn was being so thoughtful. However, she had to be honest. "I won't know until I have a chance to go over it and see what help it needs."

"It needs a lot."

Sarah nodded as she glanced at the bag. "I can see that. Why don't I take it home and look it over? Then I can let you know if it's possible to restore it and how much work it'll require." She hesitated, then said, "It could cost a lot to find materials to match the ones in a quilt that's more than seventy years old."

"It'll be worth every penny if you can restore it, and John can display it. The important thing is to keep this project a secret."

Sarah met Carolyn's gaze steadily. "Well, after taking one quick glimpse, I can tell you I'll need Vanessa Sawyer to order replacement fabric. She runs the Wild Goose Chase fabric shop in Maple Hill. And my family and friends are often in and out of my house, where I'll restore the quilt." When she saw Carolyn's growing concern, she smiled. "But I'll ask them to keep the secret. They've kept mum about such projects before."

Carolyn considered Sarah's words, then nodded. "I don't care if they know ... just as long as it's a surprise for John."

"It will be." Sarah brushed her hand over the bag's handles again. "I can promise you that."

Sarah was eager to get home and examine the Thousand Stories quilt, but she had one stop to make first. She had promised Martha that she would drop off a schedule of the events planned for Missions Month. The interfaith council in Maple Hill had set up many different programs and receptions during June for both adults and children. The schedules had been passed out at Sunday's services, but

Martha and Ernie hadn't been there because Martha was getting over a late spring cold.

Sarah knocked on the front door of the Maplethorpes' cozy Cape Cod house. When Martha opened it, Sarah saw her friend's nose was red, but her smile was warm.

"I look a sight, I know," Martha said in lieu of a greeting, "but I'm not contagious any more, or so the doctor said."

"I'll take the chance. A couple of other people at church were sniffling today, so you're not the only one who caught the cold."

Martha let Sarah in, then took the pamphlet Sarah held out to her. "Thanks for bringing this over. I've been looking forward to hearing the missionaries speak."

"The first one is tonight."

Martha grimaced. "I wonder if some powder will cover my bright red nose."

Sarah gave her friend's shoulders a squeeze. "Nobody will care. We'll all just be glad if you feel well enough to come."

She started to say more, but didn't as she glanced around the house in astonishment. The living room furniture had been moved back against the walls. She peered into the kitchen and saw a similar rearrangement of the table and chairs.

As if Sarah had spoken, Martha said, "We had to rearrange the furniture so Ernie could get through with his new walker."

Martha's husband had been dealing with Parkinson's for a couple of years, and the symptoms were slowly progressing. He had grown increasingly unsteady on his feet, and Sarah had noticed him holding on to furniture more and more when he walked.

"So he finally agreed to use one," she said.

Martha nodded with a weary smile. "It took his neurologist showing him pictures of walkers being used by children to convince Ernie that he wouldn't look old if he used one." She sighed. "It didn't hurt either when she pointed out that, in far too many cases, a broken hip at our age can be deadly."

"That was good advice, even if it might have been hard to hear."

"It took him several days to get the hang of it, but now he can get the walker in and out of the car on his own. Honestly, Sarah, it's a huge weight off me. I don't have to worry that he's fallen and doesn't have anyone around to help. Like now. He's down the street visiting, and I don't have to watch him all the way there and have him call me when he's leaving so I can watch him all the way back."

Sarah had known that her friend worried about her husband, but she hadn't realized that Martha was going to such extremes to make sure he didn't fall and injure himself. Martha wasn't one to complain, even when she had a legitimate reason.

"I'm glad he's finally listened to sense," Sarah said as she opened the door to leave. "For both of you."

Martha walked with her toward the car. Taking a deep breath, she said, "I don't think there's anything worse than a spring cold. I want to be outside enjoying these beautiful days instead of inside blowing my nose."

"I could stop by tonight and pick you and Ernie up for the program, if you'd like." Sarah paused by her car.

"Thanks, but I should be able to drive just fine." Martha glanced into the car at the quilt-filled bag. "New project?"

Sarah nodded, glad she had gotten Carolyn's okay to talk about the quilt with Martha. She quickly explained about the quilt, then said, "I thought I might be able to keep the secret to myself for more than half an hour. I hope Pastor John doesn't guess so quickly. That will ruin Carolyn's surprise."

"I won't tell him. Even if he does notice something's up, he's not likely to think it's a surprise for him!"

"Well, there won't be any surprise if the quilt can't be restored, and I won't know about that until I get home and examine it."

Martha made a shooing motion. "Then go. We'll see you tonight at church. I hope."

"I hope so too." So glad that her friend understood Sarah's eagerness to get started on the Thousand Stories quilt, she smiled and waved heartily as she left.

Sarah got into her car. As she started it, she glanced back to see Martha looking down the street, anxiety on her face. Old habits, especially when focused on loved ones, were difficult to break. Sarah whispered a prayer that Martha would soon find comfort that Ernie was using the walker to keep him safer.

After parking in the driveway next to her house, Sarah took her purse and the bag holding the quilt off her passenger seat. She carried them onto the porch and into the house. The enticing scent of the lemon bars she had made the night before still lingered in the foyer.

She heard rushing footsteps upstairs and smiled when Janis Wadsworth hurried down the stairs. Her latest boarder never seemed to go anywhere at less than the speed of light. Sarah wondered if Janis could sit still in the June term art class that she was taking at the Massachusetts College of Liberal Arts in North Adams. Or if Janis scurried circles around the kids she babysat as a part-time job to help with tuition costs. As busy as she was, Janis probably didn't have a chance to catch her breath. Her brick-red curls bounced as she skidded to a stop in front of Sarah. Her infectious smile lit up her freckled face, making her look far younger than her twenty years.

"Hi, Sarah!" She giggled. "Bye, Sarah!"

"Hi, Janis, and bye," Sarah said as she stepped aside so Janis could run down the front steps. When she saw a sleek white car pull up and a young man get out to open the passenger door for Janis, Sarah understood why Janis had been in an extra hurry.

As Sarah carried the bag to her sewing room at the back of the house, she couldn't help but smile. She had quite a few years on Janis, but that pulse of excitement never got old. She hadn't thought she would feel it again...and then her friendship with Liam Connolly had deepened. She wondered when Liam would ask her out again. His shop and café kept him busy, and her life was full with work and family and friends. Even so, it would be nice to have an evening for just the two of them.

Setting her purse on the desk chair, Sarah carried the bag over to the ironing board. She hesitated, then detoured to the dining room. She wanted to spread the quilt out and see what she was dealing with.

Sunlight poured through the tall windows so Sarah didn't have to turn on the overhead light. She drew out a chair and put the bag on it.

Carefully, she lifted the folded quilt out and placed it on the oak table. A green fabric had been used in several places, and it was falling apart. The rest of the fabrics seemed to be holding up better, though some of the pieces were torn. The other fabrics were bright picture patterns, flowered prints, and checks of red, blue, and yellow. None of them were green. She touched the green fabric. It was silk, which didn't surprise her because of the way it had shredded in strips. The silk must not have been able to handle the extreme temperatures in Pastor John's attic.

Bending, Sarah examined the outermost fold. The fabric there appeared to be darker than the fabric inside the fold, so she guessed the quilt had been stored like that for a long time. She must be even more cautious in handling it, because the fabric had endured uneven pressure.

"Okay, let's take this slowly," she said as if the quilt could understand her. "I know you've been in one position for a long time ... Let's see what stories you can tell me, Thousand Stories quilt."

Sarah opened the first fold, hearing the fabric and batting creak as she did. She smiled when she saw the state of the section revealed to her. It wasn't as bad as she had feared it would be. Whoever had packed the quilt away in the attic might have done the very best thing to protect it. Some slips of fabric looked as fresh as if they had just been stitched into place. Only the green silk was falling completely apart.

She continued until she had the quilt spread across her table. Several seams had ruptured, and stitches had been pulled up, puckering the cloth in a few other spots, but overall, except for the silk, that side of the quilt could be restored to its original beauty.

Folding the quilt lengthwise into three sections, she turned it over so she could look at the other side. She heard an odd crackle when she opened the folds again. On this side, the quilt was heavily worn, and the fabric was faded in half a dozen spots. Wisps of the green silk were all that remained in other places.

Sarah ran her hand along the quilt to smooth it out so she could check the seams.

"Ouch!" She pulled back her hand to see a scratch along the side. It wasn't bleeding, but her hand had brushed against something rough.

There. In the open seam between two pieces of fabric.

She frowned in concentration when she saw something poking through the quilt's top. Something hard and thin and yellowed.

What was it?

A Note from the Editors

We hope you enjoy Patchwork Mysteries, created by the Books and Inspirational Media Division of Guideposts, a nonprofit organization that touches millions of lives every day through products and services that inspire, encourage, help you grow in your faith, and celebrate God's love in every aspect of your daily life.

Thank you for making a difference with your purchase of this book, which helps fund our many outreach programs to military personnel, prisons, hospitals, nursing homes, and educational institutions. To learn more, visit GuidepostsFoundation.org.

We also maintain many useful and uplifting online resources. Visit Guideposts.org to read true stories of hope and inspiration, access OurPrayer network, sign up for free newsletters, download free e-books, join our Facebook community, and follow our stimulating blogs.

To learn about other Guideposts publications, including the best-selling devotional *Daily Guideposts*, go to ShopGuideposts.org, call (800) 932-2145, or write to Guideposts, PO Box 5815, Harlan, Iowa 51593.